DEVILS ARE HERE

Kendall Sheepman Company, Cheboygan, MI

ISBN: 978-0-9903104-3-3

Cover photo: Marta Olson (Mintaka Design, mintakadesign.com)

Printed in the United States of America

PETER MARABELL

DEVILS
ARE HERE

A MICHAEL RUSSO MYSTERY

Susan Elwood Arkles

"Hell is empty. All the devils are here."

—William Shakespeare, *The Tempest*

1

"Sorry," I said. "Meeting ran late."

"He won't be impressed," Sherry Merkel said. Merkel was assistant to Emmet County Prosecutor Donald Hendricks and keeper of his schedule. Hendricks was good at his job. We've worked together before, not always easily.

"He's waiting for you," she said, nodding at the closed door behind her desk.

I went into Hendricks' office without knocking.

"Don," I said.

"You're late." Hendricks was a rumpled, slightly overweight fifty years old with thinning brown hair brushed straight back. His tie was pulled away from an open collar, and his sleeves were pushed up to the elbows. Hendricks was twice elected by the good citizens of Emmet County. He looked tired and it was only ten o'clock in the morning.

On the side wall, underneath a huge map of Emmet County, sat Captain Martin Fleener of the Michigan State Police. Almost forty, Fleener was known as a savvy, intuitive investigator and an impeccable dresser. He tipped his chair back against the wall and took a drink of coffee.

"Morning, Michael."

"Marty," I said. "Nice threads." His two-piece suit was charcoal with a very narrow burgundy pinstripe. He wore a matching burgundy tie over a white, spread collar shirt. Classy.

Fleener smiled and raised his coffee mug in my direction.

"Sit, Russo," Hendricks said, pointing to an unappealing metal chair in front of his desk. Like the rest of his office, the chair was a washed-out shade of institutional green. I sat down.

"What can I do for you, Don?"

"I need your help, Michael," he said.

I must have looked surprised. Or annoyed.

"I'm not happy about it either," he said.

"Last time you asked for help, I damn near got killed."

Hendricks looked over at Fleener, then back at me. He leaned forward on the desk. "This won't be anything as exciting as that."

"You mean I won't even get beat up again?"

"Probably not," Hendricks said. "I want you to go to Bannister College." Bannister was a small, elite, Liberal Arts college just southeast of downtown Petoskey.

"Thanks, Don," I said. "Done my time in the ivy halls. Graduated, too."

Fleener laughed.

"Don't encourage him, Marty," Hendricks said. "Russo, will you not be a smart-ass? If only for a minute?"

I raised my hands in mock surrender. "Okay, okay," I said. "Let's have it."

Hendricks reached over, took a manila folder from the top left drawer of his desk and put it in front of him.

"I'll give you the highlights," he said. "You can take the file."

"I'm listening."

"Bannister had a robbery. Some books were stolen."

"A burglary?" I said. "You got me over here for a break-in? Isn't that why you hired a sheriff?"

He ignored my humor this time. "They were important books."

"So this isn't about the professor who got murdered last week?" I said. "What's his name?"

Hendricks shook his head. "Tomas Sandoval. Dean of Sciences. Marty's got the case."

"Any leads, Marty?" I said.

"Looking into things," Fleener said. "Some promising."

"So you don't have much to go on."

Fleener shrugged.

"Marty'll take care of the Sandoval case, Russo," Hendricks said. "The books are being ransomed."

"How much?"

"Only contact so far was a note taped to the library door." Hendricks gestured at the folder. "Copy's in here. It said, and I quote, 'Call the endowment fund. Five million or the books are gone.'"

"Five million bucks?"

Hendricks leaned back in his chair and put his feet on the corner of the desk.

"You ever heard of the Walloon Collection?"

I shook my head. "Nope."

"Me, either," he said. "Until this happened." He scratched his left ear. "Apparently Ernest Hemingway … you've heard of him, haven't you?"

"Thought I was the only smart-ass in the room," I said.

"So Hemingway spent a lot a time hereabouts. Family had a place on Walloon Lake." Hendricks dropped his feet to the floor with a thud and leaned on the desk again. "The College spent years gathering a unique collection of all Hemingway's writing. Every novel, every book of short stories and so forth. Each book is a signed first edition in perfect condition. The only collection like it in the world."

"The only one?"

Hendricks nodded. "Uh-huh," he said. "They tell me it's worth a small fortune."

"Five million according to the thief," I said.

Hendricks nodded.

"Think the thief knows about books?"

"Without evidence to the contrary," he said, "I do."

"Interesting story, Don," I said, "but why me?"

Hendricks ignored my question. "Look into the robbery, Russo. And the ransom note."

"Sure you want a private investigator for this?" I said. I get paid to look into various degrees of murder and mayhem. But stolen books?

Hendricks kept going. "What does 'gone' mean? Put them in the shredder? Sell them? Who buys special books like these anyway?"

"I like books as much as the next guy, Don, but ..." I looked over at Fleener. "The dead Dean. Any connection to the missing books?"

Fleener shook his head. "They work at the same place."

"Small town, Marty, smaller school. You gotta wonder."

Fleener nodded. "Yeah, I wonder," he said. "Books get stolen and a Dean gets killed. From the same place? But there's nothing out of the ordinary. Not right now anyway."

"The Dean was shot," I said. "Read that in the paper. Anything on the gun?"

"Russo," Hendricks said as he picked up the folder. "The Walloon Collection?"

"Right," I said, and smiled. "Got a place you want me to start?"

"Evelyn Malcolm," Hendricks said. "She's your contact."

"The President of Bannister?"

"Uh-huh. Ever met her?"

"Once or twice," I said. "Social occasions. Don't really know her."

"Very bright woman," Hendricks said. "We've served on civic committees together. Public radio, food bank. She cares about Bannister and Petoskey. She'll tell you about the Walloon Collection. The people who run it, how it functions."

"I ask again, why me? You fire all the county detectives?"

Hendricks shook his head. "It's summer," he said. "We're short on staff. Vacations. Usual hoard of tourists. We have more important things to do."

"Like find out who killed Dean Sandoval," Fleener said.

Hendricks rubbed his eyes and glanced at Fleener.

"Thing is, Russo," Hendricks said, "we're getting a lot of pressure."

"About stolen books?" I said.

Hendricks nodded.

"Who's calling, the Library of Congress?"

"You remember Wardcliff Griswold?"

"How could I forget good-ole Wardcliff?" I said. Griswold was the self-important head of Cherokee Point Resort Association, a playground for the wealthy just north of Harbor Springs. He was an arrogant man who liked to throw his weight around.

"Well, Griswold is Chairman of the Board of Regents at Bannister College," Hendricks said. "You'll be happy to know he's still a big pain in the ass. He took every opportunity to remind me about his important friends in Washington and Lansing. I think he cares more about the loss of the Walloon Collection than a dead Dean."

"Some things never change," I said. "His priorities are still screwed up. That guy did everything he could to stop me from investigating the Abbott murder out at Cherokee Point. Why would I want to get anywhere near him?"

"Oh, I don't know, Michael," Hendricks said as he handed me the file. "Thought you might like a chance to return the favor."

2

I left the County Building with the Walloon file. It wasn't very thick, but Hendricks was a thorough man. What he knew was in the folder. I walked down Lake Street towards my office. Some years ago, I renovated a two-story building in the middle of Petoskey's Gaslight District. The upstairs became the offices of "Michael Russo, Investigations." I rented the street level retail store to Fran Warren's Mackinac Sandal Company.

"Good morning, boss," Sandy said. Sandra Jeffries ran the office and kept me organized. "What'd Hendricks want?"

I dropped the file on her desk and sat down in a heavy maple captain's chair in front of the tall, skinny windows that overlooked Lake Street.

"A police file?" she said, and picked it up.

"We are now officially employed by Emmet County."

"To do what?"

"Ever heard of the Walloon Collection?"

Sandy nodded. "Of course," she said. "You read books, live around here, you know about the Walloon Collection." Jefferies was in her mid-fifties. She grew up in Emmet County and read everything she could get her hands on.

"Well, it's missing."

"What is?"

"The Walloon Collection."

"The whole thing? All the books?" Sandy didn't surprise easily. The wide-eyed look on her face told me the news caught her off guard.

I shook my head. "Very specific books," I said. "Hendricks gave me the basics."

"So this isn't about the dead Dean?"

I shook my head. "This is about giving Fleener and Hendricks more time to investigate the murder of Dean Sandoval. We're hired to find the missing books."

"And those are?"

"Hemingway's first editions," I said.

"The ones he signed specifically for the Collection?"

I nodded.

"I saw a story about missing books in the paper," Sandy said. "A week before the murder, I think." She moved her chair closer to her computer, hit a few keys, and pointed at the screen. "Here it is," she said. "Lenny Stern wrote it."

"Print it, please."

Sandy clicked the mouse three times. "Coming up, boss." She reached down next to her desk and grabbed the pages. "Here," she said. I took the pages and sat back down. I read the copy and Sandy read her screen.

"Not much here," she said. "Especially for Lenny." Leonard Stern was a savvy, veteran reporter. If it happened in Emmet County, Stern knew about it.

Sandy rested her elbows on the desk and pointed at the screen. "The story mentions the Collection," she said, "but doesn't say what was stolen. They don't even know for sure when the books were taken. Why not? I don't get that."

"Hendricks told me somebody made copies."

"Copies? What do you mean copies?"

"Somebody made 3-D copies of the Hemingway books."

"Do tell." Sandy looked surprised again.

"From a few feet away, on the shelves," I said, "nobody spotted the phonies until someone signed in to use *The Sun Also Rises*. You know it?"

Sandy nodded. "Booze, broads and bullfights," she said.

I nodded. "The guy in charge of the Collection," I opened the file, "Lewis, Dean Roger Thornhill Lewis, got a frantic call from a library staff person."

"I'll bet."

"Lewis and the staff checked every volume in the Collection, found the copies and called the Sheriff."

Sandy pushed her chair back and stretched out her legs. "A couple of things occur to me," she said. "Like, where do you get your hands on 3-D copies in northern Michigan?" She got up from her desk, walked over to the windows and leaned against the casing. "Why were the books stolen in the first place?"

"Money."

"Ransom note?"

"Five million or bad things happen to the books."

"What bad things, I wonder?"

I shrugged.

"Burn them?"

"Not if they're worth five million," I said.

"Sell them on the black market?"

"Maybe," I said. "Got to have big city connections for that."

"Lenny Stern would know where to look."

"Yes, he would," I said. "Might be a back story he didn't write about. I'll stop by the paper later."

Sandy went back to her desk. "You want to start with the Dean in charge of the Collection?"

"No. Hendricks said my connection at Bannister College is Evelyn Malcolm."

"The President?"

I nodded. "She's expecting my call."

"Then I'll give her a call," Sandy said.

3

"**T**hornton R. Bannister was a pretty interesting guy," I said.

"Is he the namesake of the College?" AJ said.

"That's him."

I sat at a window table in the City Park Grill with AJ Lester and Henri LaCroix. We'd just ordered dinner. AJ and I sipped Chardonnay and Henri drank Oberon ale. AJ was editor of *PPD Wired*, the online edition of the *Petoskey Post Dispatch* and love of my life. Henri was a businessman from Mackinac Island. His skill and experience as a former Army Ranger came in handy from time to time.

"Was he from around here?"

I nodded. "Sandy put together a bio."

Henri picked up his ale in mock salute and said, "Here's to the esteemed Mr. Bannister. What'd you find out?"

"Born and raised in Petoskey," I said. "He was a farmer until the Civil War came along. Bannister was a Major in the Michigan Brigade. Fought everywhere from Gettysburg to Appomattox. Came home disillusioned by the war."

"Imagine that," Henri said.

"Iraq and Afghanistan are not Bull Run or Antietam, Henri."

"No, but the futility is."

The waiter arrived at our table and put down a tray.

He set a plate in front of AJ. "For you, Ms. Lester."

He put down two more plates. "For the gentlemen. Bon appetit."

"The Bannisters were from Ireland," I said. "Two generations made their fortune in farming."

I ate some trout, broiled with a light lemon-dill sauce. A double baked potato kept the trout company on the plate.

"He took 350 acres from the family farm and named it Bannister College. He put up the first two buildings, one for classes and one for housing. He created an endowment with $70,000 of family money to run the place."

"Is that 1865 dollars?"

"It is," I said.

"Serious money in the Nineteenth Century," Henri said.

"It helped build the school's reputation," I said. "By the 1920s, Bannister was on its way to becoming one of the country's finest small schools. Put an elite college and Ernest Hemingway in the same town, and the Walloon Collection was born."

"Hendricks have any idea who took the books?" Henri said.

"He hadn't gotten that far with the investigation when Dean Sandoval got killed."

Our waiter stopped by and we ordered another round of drinks.

"No surprise there," Henri said. "Murder trumps robbery."

"Not for everyone," I said. "As soon as Hendricks turned his attention to the murder, Wardcliff Griswold showed up. Remember him?"

"Do I have to?" AJ said sarcastically.

Our waiter arrived with two glasses of Chardonnay and another Oberon.

"And why does Griswold care?" AJ said as she sipped her wine.

"He chairs the Board of Regents."

"I threatened to shoot that guy once," Henri said, and smiled. "Maybe I'll do it this time. Save us all a lot of trouble."

"You'll be the first one I call, Henri," I said. "When I need to shut the guy up."

The waiter cleared our plates. We ordered coffee and a slice of cheesecake for the table.

"So we go looking for literary thieves instead of murderers?" Henri said.

"Well put, Henri," I said. "You want in?"

Henri smiled. "Got nothing better to do right now."

"You still hanging around with your woman friend who works at the Perry?"

"Brenda, yes," Henri said. "Smart woman."

"And attractive," AJ said.

Henri nodded. "Very."

Our waiter put the cheesecake in the middle of the table with three forks. He served the coffee in white mugs. AJ and Henri reached for the forks. I sipped coffee first.

"Any connection between the Hemingway books and the murdered Dean?" AJ asked.

I shrugged. "Fleener said he hasn't found one. Not yet anyway."

"The man should know," Henri said.

"Where are you going to start?" AJ said. "Since you have no suspect, I mean."

"I'll start with the President of Bannister College," I said. "Sandy got me an appointment with Evelyn Malcolm. Should know more after that. At least I'll know who the players are."

"There's another player you need to find," Henri said.

"And who would that be?" I said, and drank some coffee.

"The guy who made the 3-D copies."

"Can't be too many people know how to do that around here," I said. "Or have the equipment."

"You could check out copy businesses, I suppose," AJ said.

Henri ate some cheesecake and said, "Think a small, elite Liberal Arts college might teach such a thing?"

"I know how to find out," I said.

"When do you meet with Malcolm?" AJ said.

I sat back in my chair. "Tomorrow at ten."

4

The heat of the July sun hid behind the trees. I set off on an early morning run to avoid another ninety-degree afternoon. I did some of my best thinking once I hit my stride and cleared my mind. Only a few service trucks roamed the shaded, tree lined streets of Bay View Association at this hour. There wasn't much prep I could do before meeting Evelyn Malcolm. She would set the agenda for our meeting, not me.

I slowed my pace a block from my apartment building. I clicked off my watch and walked down Howard Street. That was a good run.

I was disappointed I didn't think up an interesting question or two to ask Malcolm. At least I'd done some homework. I'd read a few articles online last night, and again this morning while I drank coffee.

Bannister is one of the best small, private colleges in the country. Each year, U.S. News ranked it in the top twenty. It had a reputation for producing graduates who later achieved success in business, education and public service. Although Bannister attracted students from all over the world, most of them lived in the upper Great Lakes region.

Evelyn Malcolm, a distinguished American Historian, came from the University of Wisconsin-La Crosse where she was Provost. She was in her third four-year term as President, elected unanimously the last two times by the Board of Regents. Bannister also hired her husband, Edward, for the History Department.

I stretched my leg muscles on the front steps of my building. I lived in a nice two-bedroom where Howard meets Rose Street. I have a decent view of Little Traverse Bay from my living room, and it's an easy walk to my office, good restaurants and AJ's house, a few blocks outside of the Gaslight District. I grabbed a bottle of water from the refrigerator and jumped in the shower.

Twenty-five minutes later, I sat at the kitchen table with an English muffin, orange juice and coffee. I'd dressed in fresh khakis, a light blue buttoned down shirt and a navy blazer. An appropriately professional outfit for meeting the Liberal Arts.

On a hunch, or maybe I'm just nosey, I opened my iPad and searched Dean Tomas Sandoval. The list for Sandoval was long and mostly academic, once I got past his murder. Lenny Stern wrote about the murder for the *Post Dispatch*. A few days later, he profiled the man for *PPD Wired*. I made a note to get hard copies. Sandoval's story was an American success story. He grew up in Southern California, the son of undocumented immigrants from Columbia. He got a B.S. in Applied Sciences from Long Beach State and a Ph.D. from UCLA in Computer Technology. Sandoval used contacts in and out of education to help secure the necessary paperwork for his parents. He'd been at Bannister for more than a decade, and had moved steadily up the administrative ladder to become Dean of Sciences in 2014. As a Dean, he was required to teach only one course. Additive Manufacturing, whatever that was.

I put my dishes in the dishwasher, took my brief bag and headed for the parking lot behind my building. I beeped the door locks, put my bag on the back seat and climbed in. I hit the start button on my BMW 3-Series and its twin-turbo motor growled to life. I smiled. I've loved performance cars ever since I grew up on the streets of Detroit. The Bannister campus is less than a ten-minute drive from downtown. Even that short drive is a treat few people understood.

I went up Bay Street, past AJ's remodeled two-story at the edge of the ravine, swung over to Mitchell Street and headed north.

Mitchell widened to four lanes at the entrance to Bannister to help with traffic flow. I turned in and followed Linton Road, which circles around the older, smaller section of campus. It was lush and green. Ivy covered brick buildings sat close to the road. A few students wearing shorts and backpacks roamed the pathways. I turned into a small lot, and parked in a spot marked for visitors. At the back of the lot sat Bannister House, the Bannister family's original two-story white farmhouse that was now the President's official residence.

I left my brief bag in the car and walked to the other side of the lot. Wexford Hall, a four-story, dusty red brick building housed the College's administrative offices. In the wall near the door, one brick twice the size of the others read, "1869." The bricks had worn down over the years and were nearly the same shade as the mortar. Only in corners of the building, where ivy and moss hung on the walls, was the original dark red color visible.

I went through the heavy wood double doors and saw a sign for the President's office off to the right of a large, square lobby. The ceilings must have been twenty feet high, and eight lamps hung down from long cords. Four-person spindle back benches sat back-to-back in the center of the room. A lone male student in shorts and sandals sat at the far end of the row with a fat textbook propped up in his lap. He was asleep.

I went through the open doorway at the President's office. It was another waiting area, much smaller than the first, and decorated pleasantly with soft gray carpet, mauve walls and a few strategically placed pieces of art. Six gray upholstered chairs with wood arms and legs sat around a coffee table. A sideboard on the wall held a coffeemaker, mugs and a large bowl filled with ice and bottles of water and juice.

"Good morning, sir," said the man at a small, tidy desk near the back of the room. He was in his twenties, with an angular face, very short hair and a neatly trimmed beard. "May I help you?"

"Good morning," I said. "Michael Russo to see President Malcolm."

He glanced at an open calendar on the desk. "A moment, please. There's coffee or juice," he said, pointing at the sideboard. The man got up and opened a door behind his desk.

I went over and poured coffee into a mug with lettering on the side. It read, "Bannister College: Educating the World."

"Mr. Russo, so good of you to come," a woman's voice said from the doorway.

I turned around.

"I'm Evelyn Malcolm." She reached out and we shook hands.

"Come in, please."

I took my coffee and followed her.

"We're going to sit over here," she said, gesturing at two sofas that faced each other in the corner of her office. It was a small room, with the same gray carpet, but the walls were linen. Several small, colorful paintings decorated the walls. Each one depicted a different building in the older section of campus. Three tall, narrow sash windows behind her desk looked out on the campus green, an area of trees, crisscrossing sidewalks and cement benches.

President Malcolm was a trim five-six, with soft gray hair, parted on the right and cut shoulder length. She wore a two-piece black suit with a white silk blouse open at the collar. I knew from the articles that Malcolm was sixty-three and a competitive tennis player, singles, at the club tournament level. Only the gray hair hinted at her age.

Malcolm picked up a bottle of water and a glass of ice from her desk and sat on the sofa across from me.

"I would like you to know, Mr. Russo," she said, "I appreciate your willingness to help us out. Bannister College has always prided itself on a quiet, professional atmosphere. We've been a proud and active member of the Petoskey community for a long time, but always off the radar screen, if you know what I mean."

I nodded.

"These last few weeks," Malcolm said, and shook her head slowly. "First the theft of one of the world's true literary treasures." She took a deep breath. "Then the unfortunate death of Dean Sandoval." Malcolm poured water in the glass and took a drink.

"The women and men of Bannister, well, let's just say it's been a difficult adjustment for all of us." She hesitated. "The glare of the public eye and all."

Difficult adjustment? Glare of the public eye? I wonder how the dead Dean's family felt.

"Don't misunderstand, Mr. Russo. Donald Hendricks means well, I'm sure. I understand why he has to focus on the unfortunate Dean Sandoval."

Unfortunate?

"Well, we don't have the luxury of choice, Mr. Russo. I must worry about the Walloon Collection, too. When you agreed to help out, I was relieved. Actually, I was encouraged. Encouraged to have you here with everything that's happened to Bannister."

Poor, poor Bannister. My coffee was cold.

"Thank you," I said. "I'm sure Don explained that my job is to get the Walloon Collection back."

Malcolm nodded. "Yes, of course," she said. "Will you and the police work together?"

"Not together," I said. "With me here, the police will have more time for the murder investigation."

Malcolm nodded and drank some water. "Certainly," she said. "I understand. Now, what would you like to know about the Walloon Collection?"

"I know about the Collection itself," I said. "How it came together, how valuable it is."

"Five million dollars, according to the thieves," she said rather dismissively.

"That's not an accurate figure?"

She shrugged. "It is if you're only talking money. The Collection's value to the prestige and stature of Bannister is impossible to quantify."

I nodded. I need hot coffee. And fresh air.

"Tell me how the Collection functions at Bannister. Who runs it? Who has access? Who says yes or no to requests for access? That sort thing would be a good place to start."

Malcolm got up, went to her desk and picked up a sheet of paper.

"Here," she said, handing it to me as she sat down. "Dean Roger Thornhill Lewis is Chair of the Walloon Collection. The Dean and two faculty members, the names are there," she said, pointing at the sheet, "control the Collection."

I glanced at the sheet. I recognized one faculty name, but not the other.

"So the Dean of Arts and Letters is also Chair of the Collection?"

"It's a small school, Mr. Russo," Malcolm said. "Overlapping responsibilities are not uncommon. He also serves on the Scholarship Committee with Dean Sandoval." Malcolm stopped and looked down. "Did serve, I mean."

They worked together? My Dean and the dead Dean?

"What is it, Mr. Russo?" Malcolm said.

I shook my head. "Nothing."

"Come now, Mr. Russo. I've been a classroom teacher all my professional life. I saw it in your face. I always know when something I've said has an impact."

"Well," I said. "Seems like an interesting coincidence, the two Deans on the same committee. That's all. Except I don't like coincidences."

Malcolm smiled. "You're right," she said. "But it's not a coincidence. Remember what I just said about a small school, Mr. Russo? We all wear more than one hat around here."

More than one hat. But small college or not, the two cases have some minimal connection. I wonder if Fleener's aware of that.

President Malcom stood up. "I've made arrangements for you to talk with Dean Lewis." She looked at her watch. "In a few minutes. The other members of the oversight committee will be there as well."

I stood up and Malcolm moved towards the door. "The Dean's conference room is upstairs. Number 301. He's expecting you."

We shook hands. "Thank you again for coming by, Mr. Russo."

"You're welcome."

Her assistant stood as we went to the outer office. "Please keep me informed of your progress."

I was about to leave when the door opened and in walked a familiar figure.

Wardcliff Griswold.

He was tall, over six feet, slender with a narrow face and thinning gray haircut short. He wore a navy V-neck sweater over a red polo shirt and tan corduroy pants with little apple-green ducks on them.

"Evelyn," he said, his arms out stretched in some grand gesture. "I hope I've arrived in time."

"Hello, Ward," Malcolm said. "You know Mr. Russo?"

"Sadly, yes," Griswold said.

"Happy to see you, too, Ward. Nice threads," I said. Malcolm's assistant, who'd been looking our way, spun his chair in the other direction, hoping to stifle a laugh.

Griswold glared at me. "Your sartorial critique is entirely unwelcome," he said. Malcolm's assistant tried hard, very hard, to make his laughing sound like sneezing.

"Gentlemen, please," Malcolm said. "Ward, wait in my office." Griswold hesitated, but Malcolm pointed and he did as he was told.

"Good-bye, Mr. Russo," Malcolm said. "Dean Lewis is waiting."

5

I saw the stairs at the far end of the main lobby and made my way to the third floor. It had not been renovated like the first floor or President Malcolm's office. The wood floors were heavily worn, and squeaked with every step. The narrow boards hadn't been sanded or varnished in years. The faded, peeling paint on the walls, bright yellow at one time, was in even worse shape.

Room 301 was half way down the hall. The door was ajar, so I walked in. It was a square room, just big enough for a round maple conference table and six wood chairs that didn't match the table or each other. A woman sat in one chair. A man stood as I walked in.

"Michael," Kelsey Sheridan said, and reached his hand out. Sheridan was an aspiring novelist who lived at Cherokee Point Resort. In his late thirties, he was a nice looking man with short dark hair and stylish glasses. He wore baggy navy shorts, a light blue oxford cloth shirt with the sleeves rolled up past the elbow and brown Birkenstocks.

"Kelsey, it's good to see you again," I said. We shook hands. "I just found out you were on this committee. Heard you were teaching, too."

"Since a year ago fall. Freshman comp. Thanks to Margo," Sheridan said, nodding at the woman.

"Like it?"

"It's a lot of work, but yes," he said. "The kids are bright and I get time to write." Sheridan smiled. "But we'll catch up another time."

Kelsey turned as the woman next to him stood. She was tall, maybe five-eight, with a fair complexion and hazel eyes. Her blonde hair was parted on one side and cut at the neck. She was in her mid-fifties but easily looked younger. She was trim like an adult woman is trim, not teenager-like skinny.

"Michael, this is Margo Harris."

"Ms. Harris," I said, and we shook hands. "Michael Russo. Nice to meet you."

She wore a light-weight navy cotton cardigan over a pink camisole with a tasteful hint of cleavage. Her navy skirt fell above the knee, showing off lean, tanned legs.

"Call me Margo, please," she said. "Kelsey's told me about you."

"Oh?"

"Only the good stuff, Michael," Kelsey said and laughed.

"Especially the excitement at Cherokee Point a few years ago," Margo said. "It would make a compelling mystery, Kelsey. I told you that."

Kelsey nodded. "Several times, Margo," he said. "Pick a chair, Michael."

"I'm supposed to meet the Dean," I said.

"He got a call on his office phone," Kelsey said. "Shouldn't be long."

I sat next to Margo, near a window at the rear of the room. "Are you in the English Department, too?"

She nodded. "It's a requirement of the Walloon Committee. Only writers of fiction are qualified to properly implement policy regarding Ernest Hemingway's work." Margo put out both hands in front of her, palms up. "Or so the theory goes."

"I know Kelsey writes mysteries," I said. "What about you?"

"Erotic romance," Margo said and smiled.

Kelsey smiled, too.

"Erotic romance?"

"Yes."

"What is that?" I said. Kelsey laughed.

"Vaginas and penises," Margo said. "Vaginas and penises. Lots of them."

"Oh."

"Why, Mr. Russo," Margo said. "I do believe you're blushing."

"They call her the 'porn lady,'" Kelsey said, and laughed again. "The students."

"Do they," I said. "That okay with you?"

"Sure," Margo said. "They're good-natured about it."

"Been teaching romance a long time?"

"Since I came to Bannister. Almost ten years now." Margo leaned forward and put her elbows on the table. "Novels like mine used to be called 'bodice rippers.' Ever heard that?"

"The guy on the cover, bare chest and long hair."

"That's the one."

"Is that considered serious fiction at a place like Bannister?"

"You bet it is," Kelsey said before Margo could answer. "All four of her books are on Amazon's list."

"True," Margo said. "More important, my classes fill up every semester."

"Hottest class on campus," Kelsey said.

I laughed. "No pun intended, I suppose?"

"Oh, yeah. A pun all the way," Kelsey said. "But money talks here just like everywhere else."

"Did I hear the word money?"

We looked up as the Dean entered the conference room.

"You must be Michael Russo," he said. "I'm Dean Roger Thornhill Lewis."

The Dean was five-seven, chubby with a soft, round face and very thin black hair. His dark brown suit jacket strained at the buttons. His white shirt was too tight at the collar. So was the paisley tie.

I stood and we shook hands.

"Have a seat, please, Mr. Russo."

I sat back down and the Dean took a chair next to Kelsey, across from me.

"I must say, Mr. Russo, I was surprised when Evelyn told me the police had moved on to more important things than the Walloon Collection."

It was the tone of his voice. He hadn't accepted the idea that a dead Dean might be more important than a dead white guy's books.

"Were you also surprised when she told you about me? That I'm here to get the Collection back?"

He nodded. "To be honest, yes," Lewis said. "Nothing personal, you understand. I assumed, incorrectly as it turned out, that Bannister Security would take over."

"Bannister Security is what?"

"Our campus police," he said. "They do much more than give out parking tickets. Unfortunately, we have real problems on campus. Illegal drugs and sexual assault."

"Sorry to hear that," I said.

Lewis nodded slowly. "Yes," he said with a sigh. "But here you are, Mr. Russo, and I, we," he said, gesturing at Kelsey and Margo, "are here to help. What would you like to know?"

"Start with the basics," I said. "Who uses the Collection? Who has access to the material? How does that system work?"

"I'm sure the police file has all that," Lewis said.

Before he could continue, I said, "I read the file, but I want to hear it from you, from people who work with the Collection every day."

Lewis thought for a minute. "Good point."

Lewis slid his chair back from the table, leaned back and crossed his legs. "The Walloon Collection is one part of Bannister's Special Collections library." He pointed vaguely out the window. "It's housed in our main library. In separate rooms on the first floor."

"Who has access?"

"Anyone in the library can walk in the door, but not everyone can use the material. You must have a legitimate reason."

"I'll want to look around," I said. "Do I qualify?"

"You do," Lewis said. "I'll call and tell them you're coming over."

"Thank you."

Lewis continued, "Material in Special Collections must stay in the reading room. Scholars sign in, specifying what they want, and sign out when they're finished."

"Who handles that task?" I inquired.

"Library staff," Lewis said. "But use of the Walloon Collection, the Hemingway material, must be approved, in advance, by one of us."

I looked at Kelsey and Margo. "Ever done that?"

Kelsey shook his head. "Never been asked."

"A few times over the years," Margo said. "I always knew the people who asked."

"Do people use the material in the main reading room?"

Lewis shook his head. "No," he said. "In a separate room, a few feet from the staff desk. There's only one door."

I sat forward, put my arms on the table and said, "Then how'd a thief cart five million bucks of Hemingway books out of there undetected?"

"That's what you're here to find out, isn't it, Mr. Russo?" Lewis said. He said it flat, without anger or annoyance. But just a touch arrogance.

We spent the next thirty minutes or so discussing the library, Ernest Hemingway and use of the Collection. I really learned very little. At least it was a start.

"If there's nothing more, Mr. Russo?" Lewis said, in that up-talking way some people use to say this conversation is over. "I have a meeting."

The four of us stood in unison.

"Thank you for your time, Dean Lewis," I said.

"You are welcome, Mr. Russo. Now get the books back, will you."

6

I walked down three flights of stairs with Kelsey and Margo. We stood on the landing outside the main entrance. The sun was high, hovering over the trees, and hot. The humidity didn't help. It was, after all, July in northern Michigan.

"Michael," Kelsey said, "nice to see you again. Let's grab a glass of wine next week and catch up."

"I'd like that."

"Join us, Margo," Kelsey said. "Russo's pretty good company."

Margo smiled. "I'm sure he is," she said. "But I'll take a rain check until you two have talked about old times." She laughed.

"Got to go," Kelsey said and went down the stairs, waving.

"Nice to meet you," I said to Margo. "I'd like to hear more about, what'd you call it, erotic?"

"Erotic romance."

"Right. Erotic romance."

"Which way are you headed?" Margo said.

"Parking lot."

"I'll go with you," she said. "I want to ask you something."

"Okay."

We took the sidewalk next to Wexford Hall. Two students, both women, walked towards us and said a friendly hello to Margo.

"Former students?"

"Last semester, yes."

We continued walking, but she didn't say anything. Thought I'd try first.

"What can I help you with?" I said.

Margo stopped and turned towards me.

"Let me see if I've got this right," she said. "As I understand it from the campus rumor mill, either the Sheriff's office sent you over or Evelyn Malcolm asked you here. Which is it?"

"The Prosecutor, Donald Hendricks …"

"I know Hendricks," Margo said. Her voice had an edge to it. Not sure why.

"Hendricks was short on help. It's the middle of the summer. Well, he asked me to find the Walloon Collection. Hendricks set it up with Malcolm."

"Did he." It wasn't question. The edge was still there.

"Uh-huh."

"So this really is about the Hemingway books? About getting the books back in one piece?"

I nodded.

"You won't have anything to do with Sandoval?" she said. "Him getting killed?"

There it was again. Two Deans. Two crimes. One conversation.

"Nothing to do with the death of Dean Sandoval," I said. "That belongs to a State Police detective named Martin Fleener. Good man. And Don Hendricks, of course."

Margo nodded slowly and resumed walking towards the parking lot. "I just wanted to make sure I got the right story," she said, her hand moving through the air for emphasis. She was still edgy.

"My car's over there," I said.

"The black BMW?"

"Yeah. How'd you know?"

"You've got company," she said, pointing at the other side of the lot.

Leaning on the driver's side of the 335 was a big guy. Dressed like a street cop. With a gun and a nightstick on his belt.

"Who's he?"

"The face of Bannister Security," Margo said. "Name's Wade Conroy."

"Think he's looking for me?"

"You'll find out soon enough," she said. "Well, I've got work in my office, so I'll leave you here. It was good to meet you."

"Thanks," I said. "Good to meet you, too."

Don't know why she asked about Sandoval or why she was edgy about Hendricks.

Margo turned to walk away, but said, "Careful with Conroy, Michael. He thinks campus is his fiefdom."

"That so?"

"It is," she said. "And he's a bully."

7

onroy was six-six, in his early fifties and well over two hundred soft pounds. He leaned on the car with his beefy arms crossed over his chest. His face was pockmarked, with two small scars over his left eye. His nose was not shaped that way by accident. He might have been a fighter once.

"Morning, Officer."

"That's Chief to you," he said as he came off the car. "Chief Wade Conroy." He didn't offer to shake hands.

"Chief of what?" I said. "I know all the cops in Emmet County. Never heard of you."

Conroy's eyes narrowed, but his voice was steady.

"Bannister Security," he said. "We take care of the campus."

"Thought the Regents did that."

Conroy just stood there. Silent. Probably didn't hear me.

"You get drunk coeds back to the dorm, tow student cars out of the faculty parking lot? That kind of thing?"

Conroy dropped his arms and put his hands on his hips.

"Heard you was a smart-ass, Russo," he said.

Wonder who told him that? And my name.

"Try my best," I said.

"That so?" he said.

"I'm a prospective student. Want to sign up for classes. Never too old to learn, you know."

Conroy took in lots of air and let it out slowly.

"Maybe a degree in English Lit," I said. "Or American History. Always thought I'd like to teach."

"What do you want on campus, smart guy?"

Had the feeling he already knew the answer.

"I was invited, Officer Conroy. Like it or not."

"That's Chief Conroy," he said.

"I just met with President Malcolm. I assume you've heard of her? She pays your salary?"

"Malcolm pays my salary," he said.

This obviously wasn't going well. I'll try being straight with him. Probably wasting my breath.

"All right, Chief Conroy," I said. "The Emmet County Prosecutor hired me to come out here. Meet with Malcolm. Try to recover books stolen from the library."

"Hendricks told you to come out here."

"Yes."

Conroy stepped away from the car. "We can take care of our own trouble," he said. "It's time to be on your way."

We? Who's we?

"I'll go," I said. "But last time I looked, this was still Emmet County and I've got a job to do."

Conroy looked down at the tarmac, then back at me and shook his head. With that he walked off, across the parking lot and out of sight.

8

"The halls of ivy sure have changed," AJ said after I described my chat with Dean Lewis, Margo Harris, Kelsey, and the Chief.

"The Campus Police at MSU were more professional than that." AJ graduated from Michigan State with a degree in Journalism. "They had a job to do, but they actually tried to help people."

We sat in the living room of AJ's two-story Victorian on Bay Street. She's been slowly and methodically renovating the house since she bought it seven years ago. She started with basic improvements like heating and cooling. Then came cosmetic changes, most recently fresh white paint with gray-blue trim. It closely resembled the original house built eighty years ago.

I'd finished some paperwork at the office and walked the five blocks to meet AJ for a glass of Chardonnay. She got home a few minutes before I arrived and fixed a plate of Horseradish cheese and crackers. She put the plate on the coffee table in front of the couch, along with two wine glasses. I poured the wine. The air conditioning hummed quietly. The fireplace a few feet from the couch would have to wait for colder weather.

AJ had changed into a baggy pair of faded red shorts and a dark green sweatshirt. It had "MSU" embroidered on the front and paint stains on both sleeves. She sat back, put her bare feet on the coffee table and sipped wine.

"I mean, State had trouble from time to time," she said.

"Like 'burn the couch?'"

AJ nodded. "Like that," she said. "But the Campus Police never hassled visitors."

I cut off a small piece of cheese and ate it with a cracker. Nice bite to the Horseradish.

"Wonder what I did to piss off the Chief?"

"Apparently you just showed up."

I put down my glass, took AJ's hand and kissed it. "Darling," I said. "With analytical skills like that you ought a be a private detective."

"One of us is enough, Russo," she said. "Cut the sarcasm and kiss me."

I leaned in, put my arm around her shoulder and pulled her to me. We kissed, slowly, lips apart.

"That was nice," she said softly.

AJ looked at me and smiled. She took my hand and said, "What did Chief what's-his-name have to be pissed about? After all, the President of the place knew you'd be there."

"Hold on a second." I took my hand out of hers. "I just kissed you and you change the subject. I was about to make a move on you, and you want to talk business? If I walked into the room naked would you still talk business?"

"Make your best moves later, darling," she said. "You won't be disappointed. I promise." AJ smiled. "But it's the reporter in me. Hendricks sent you to Bannister, President Malcolm met with you."

"What's your point?"

"Did Chief so-in-so suddenly decide all by his lonesome to follow you?"

"Good question. But I doubt it." I picked up my glass and drank some wine. "His name's Wade Conroy, by the way."

"Okay. Either Chief Wade made you his target *de jour* or someone told him to do it."

"Also told him who I was and where I'd be."

"Malcolm might have alerted Bannister Security," AJ said. "Think she told the Chief to show up?"

I thought for a minute while I ate another piece of cheese.

I shook my head. "No. I liked Malcolm right off. She's very professional, if a bit overprotective of Bannister."

"No surprise there," AJ said. "The public eye can be a cruel place sometimes. Bannister's pretty tightly wound compared to a sprawling place like MSU. It's harder to absorb the oddball hit."

"Good point."

"Who else knew about you? Besides Hendricks and Malcolm, I mean."

"The Walloon Committee," I said. "Dean Lewis, Kelsey Sheridan, Margo Harris."

"Scratch Kelsey," AJ said. "What about Harris?"

"Vaginas and Penises," I said. "That Margo Harris?"

"I forgot. Sorry." AJ pushed up the sleeves of her sweatshirt. "Well, then. That leaves?"

"Dean Roger Thornhill Lewis."

I leaned back on the couch and put my hands up, behind my head. "Okay, AJ, what would a good reporter do next?"

AJ drank the last of her wine. She raised her glass in my direction. "Want more?"

I shook my head. She got up, went to the kitchen and came back with the Chardonnay. She poured a half glass for herself and sat down.

"Add it up Michael," AJ said. "It started as a simple assignment."

"Find the Hemingway Collection."

"Right."

"Malcolm is on board," I said. "Or so it seems."

"Then it starts to go a little screwy. Margo Harris was annoyed about Hendricks or something at the committee meeting, the cop hassled you in the parking lot, and the late Dean Sandoval's name popped up twice when you never asked about him."

I moved my empty wine glass around on the table. Like that would help.

"It's time to learn more about Dean Roger Thornhill Lewis."

AJ smiled. "That's where I'd start," she said. "One more thing."

"What's that?"

"It's time to test your theory."

"What theory would that be?" I said.

"Would I pay attention if you walked through the room naked."

"Oh, that theory."

"Uh-huh. Now get going," AJ said. "Into the bedroom. I'll give you sixty seconds to get out of those clothes and stroll back in here." She lifted her right hand and made like two fingers were walking through air.

"I could wait for you in the bedroom."

"Not a chance, Russo. Time's a wasting."

9

"**Y**ou awake?"

No answer. I tried to see the clock on AJ's side of the bed, but I couldn't move. I was tangled in sheets, a blanket and two legs. Probably AJ's legs. Can't seem to move my left arm either.

"Stop moving, will you," AJ said. "I'm trying to sleep."

"What time is it? Can't see the clock."

"It's seven-ten," she said.

"Aren't you late?"

"Not if I get up in the next thirty seconds."

"I'll make the coffee."

"That would be nice."

I untangled myself as best I could, lifted the covers and got out of bed.

"What're you looking for?" AJ said.

"Boxers."

"You don't need clothes to make coffee."

"Not clothes," I said. "Boxers."

"I'd rather ogle you."

"You did plenty of that last night."

"It's never enough, darling," she said, and pulled the covers over her head.

I found my boxers near the bedroom door and put them on. Wonder how they got there?

I made my way to the kitchen, put eight scoops in the coffeemaker, filled the carafe with water and punched the button.

AJ was in the shower when I got back to the bedroom. I opened the bathroom door and went in.

"What are you doing?" she said, loudly, from behind the clear glass door.

"Ogling you, darling."

"Can't hear you," she said. But she was faking. "What was that again?"

"You heard me," I said and went back to the bedroom.

I dressed in my clothes from last night. I kept a few basic items at AJ's. Shirts, sweaters, khakis, even one dressy outfit just in case. But I'm going home after some coffee. I want to get in a short run before the afternoon heat arrives.

I was at the kitchen table, with coffee and a sliced banana, when AJ came in. She wore a long white terrycloth robe, and her hair was still shiny-wet. She poured a mug of coffee, kissed me and sat down.

"What are you up to this morning? After you run."

"You know me too well."

"It's not rocket science."

"Am I that predictable?

AJ nodded and drank some coffee.

"I'll talk to Hendricks and Fleener first," I said. "If Lewis is dirty, they'll know."

AJ shook her head. "Got a better idea."

"I'm listening," I said and ate two slices of banana.

"Start with Lenny Stern. Get his take on the Dean. He knows people, Michael. Remember?"

I remembered. Stern's contacts helped me track the men who gunned down Frank Marshall two years ago.

"I read his piece on the stolen books. It was little more than basic stuff."

I poured more coffee for both of us.

"Thanks," AJ said. "Basic was all that story needed, Michael. There's always more. I'll bet he's got interesting things to say about Bannister College itself."

"Would the same be true for his piece on Sandoval?"

"Probably," she said. "Did you read his profile?"

I shook my head. "Didn't see it."

"Read it. Good rags-to-riches story," she said. "He's got more. Count on it."

AJ looked at the clock on the stove. "Oops, I really will be late if I don't get going." She took one last drink of coffee, got up and put the mug in the sink. "See you tonight?"

"Talk to you later," I said.

AJ leaned in, kissed me and hurried out of the kitchen.

I put my dishes in the dishwasher and left AJ's mug next to the coffee-maker. She'd want more before she left for work.

I went out the back door off the kitchen and walked down Bay Street. I seldom used my car in town even in lousy weather.

Today was not lousy. The sun was already over the trees. It would be hot and sunny all day. Tourists, "fudgies" they're called colloquially, came to northern Michigan each summer hoping for days just like this. They'd flock to the beaches, restaurants, and shops in towns like Petoskey, Harbor Springs and, of course, Mackinac Island.

I looked at my watch as I opened the apartment door. Still time for a short run. Then to the office.

One thing first.

I pulled out my iPhone and tapped Lenny Stern's number.

10

The run was too short, the shower was too quick, but I was on my way to work a little after ten.

"Morning, boss," Sandy said when I walked in the office. "Banker's hours again, I see."

"I'm going to ignore your comment, thank you very much."

"You sure don't dress like a banker," she said. "I ever tell you that?"

"I'll have you know I put a razor sharp crease in these khakis."

Sandy laughed. "No, you didn't," she said. "Those things are no-irons from L.L. Bean."

"You are impossible," I said.

I put my brief bag on the floor next to my desk and went to the table by the front door for coffee.

"Did you by any chance stop at Johan's this morning?" I filled a mug with coffee.

"Silly question," Sandy said. "Better hurry. We only got raspberry Danish left. I ate the cinnamon-sugar donuts."

I took one Danish on a napkin and put it on my desk with a mug of coffee and sat down. Sandy came to the door and handed me a bottle of water.

"Thought you'd want more water after your run. It's a humid day."

"Thanks," I said. "AJ thinks I'm predictable. Do you think I'm that predictable, too?"

"AJ and I had you figured out a long time ago, boss."

I started to say something, thought better of it, and opened the water bottle for a long drink instead.

"Need me for anything right now?"

"If you're not in the middle of something, sit for a minute," I said.

"I'm good," she said.

Sandy took the straight back chair on the side wall near my desk as she always did. She was firmly convinced she did her most thoughtful brainstorming in that chair. She put a mug of coffee on the corner of the desk.

"What's up?"

I filled her in on meeting the Walloon Committee and with my unscheduled encounter with Wade Conroy.

"Who knew somebody at our prestigious little college could be so touchy?" she said. "You think there's a link between the Committee and getting hassled?"

"Can't be sure," I said. "But I don't believe in coincidences, remember?"

"How could I forget."

Sandy leaned forward and picked up her mug. "Suppose there is a link," she said. "You've ruled out the Harris woman and our pal, Kelsey. That leaves Dean Lewis."

I nodded. "So?"

"So why would Lewis pester the guy hired to retrieve five mill worth of rare books? What's the point? They're his books."

I shook my head. "I have no idea."

Sandy drank some coffee and sat back holding her mug in both hands. "We're back to coincidences, again."

"Yes, we are."

"So what happened? The Chief got up on the wrong side of the bed and decided to mess with the first PI he ran into?"

I shrugged. "Guess so," I said. "Unless …"

"Unless, what?"

I drank some water. I got out of my chair and looked out the window. I could see Little Traverse Bay over the rooftops two blocks away. No wind. The water shimmered in the heat of the sun.

"Unless someone told him to." I drank more coffee, but it didn't make events any clearer.

"But you ruled out President Malcolm, and we agree Dean Lewis makes no sense. So who?"

I sat back in my chair and bit off another hunk of Danish. I shook my head and shrugged at the same time. We were quiet for a time.

"How's the Danish?"

"Now there's a question I can answer with confidence," I said, taking another bite.

"Michael. I almost forgot. Did you call Lenny Stern this morning?"

I nodded. Too busy chewing to talk.

"He called a few minutes ago," Sandy said. "He told me you didn't answer his call back."

I tapped my phone and Lenny's call popped up on the screen.

"He leave a message?" I said.

"He's on his way over. Do you think he can help find the book-nappers?"

"Maybe, maybe not," I said. "The guy knows a lot of people, Sandy. AJ's certain he'll have something helpful to say."

11

I ended a phone conversation with a prospective client that went on too long. She wanted a divorce. Easy case. Her soon to be ex-husband took his girlfriend to Belize. Divorces are often interesting but never fun. Not sure I want to handle them anymore.

I heard someone on the stairs.

"Hey, there, Sandy," Lenny Stern said when he entered the office.

"Morning, Mr. Stern," she said.

I got up and went to the front office.

"That was nice, Sandy. The formality. But stick with 'Lenny,' okay?"

"Okay, Lenny," she said.

"Good morning," I said, and reached out my hand. I tried to sound stuffy and formal. "How is Mr. Stern today?"

Stern shook my hand and looked over at Sandy. "Has he ever played the straight man?"

"Not that I remember," Sandy said and smiled. "Can I get you coffee?"

Stern shook his head. "Get it myself. Thanks."

"Come on in," I said.

He poured a mug of coffee and went to the client chair in front of my desk.

Lenny Stern was a wiry five-four, in his late sixties. He was nearly bald except for a little scruffy gray hair hanging down around his ears. He habitually wore a black suit, narrow lapels, over a white cotton shirt, not ironed, and a skinny black silk tie. Occasionally, he wore a dark gray single-breasted. Variety is a good thing.

Stern had turned down numerous promotions to editor or features writer. At heart, he was a reporter. "Never wanted to do anything else," he told me a long time ago. Stern spent six years working on big city dailies in Chicago and Detroit. Most of the time as a crime reporter. "In those days," he said once, "if you wanted respect from the cops, you told the truth, you carried a gun." Working at the *Post-Dispatch*, he carried a digital recorder more often than a gun. "What am I going to shoot in Emmet County, a deer?"

Stern drank some coffee, and put the mug on the desk.

"You ever going to retire, Lenny?"

"What for?" he said. "I have too much fun."

"Said once you wanted to write a novel."

Stern smiled. "I've got two drafts on a flash drive at the office."

"Seriously?"

He nodded. "Finished the second draft six weeks ago."

"A crime novel?"

Stern shook his head. "Nah. Not that much exciting happens around here." He hesitated. "Well, you chased those gunmen a couple of years back." Stern laughed. "I could write about that."

"Please don't," I said. "What did you write?"

"A western," he said, and his mind went someplace else. Just for a moment. I saw it in his eyes. "Colorado territory in the 1870s, after the Civil War. A lone gunman rides into a lawless town, gets caught in the middle of a range war. Homesteaders against the cattlemen. Town fathers swear him in as sheriff, so he'll make the place safe for women and children."

"You're serious, aren't you?" I said.

"I'm always serious," Stern said. "Now why'd you want to see me?"

"Need some information," I said. "But I need more coffee first."

I went to the front office, poured more coffee, and returned to my desk.

"Now that your coffee's hot ..." Stern's voiced trailed off.

"Bannister College," I said.

"What about it?"

"Recent events," I said.

Stern nodded. "Busy place these days."

"What can you tell me?"

Stern looked over his shoulder and said, "You listening, Sandy?"

"Of course," she said. "Unless you don't want me to."

"Suit yourself," he said.

I drank some coffee. "You wrote several pieces about Bannister recently."

Stern nodded.

"The Walloon Collection. Dean Lewis. The stolen books."

"What about 'em?"

"You wrote about Sandoval, too."

"The Dean got himself shot," Stern said.

I leaned forward and dropped my elbows on the desk. "What can you tell me about Lewis? That wasn't in your stories, I mean."

"Who you working for?"

I told him about Hendricks, President Malcolm and what I got hired to do.

"You trust Hendricks?"

I nodded. "His word's always been good."

"That's been my experience," Stern said.

"How about we start with Lewis?"

Stern settled back in his chair and crossed his legs.

"Pretty dull guy," he said. "Had a nice, quiet middle-class life until a divorce caught him in 2010. Wife got the house, cottage in Cedarville, chunk of cash. Left Roger in a beat up two-bedroom south of town. On the Charlevoix Road."

"He got money in the bank?"

Stern shook his head. "Faculty salary. Some additional pay for being an administrator. He makes a few bucks in royalties from a book. That's about it."

Stern sat for a minute. He tapped the fingernails of his left hand on the arm of the chair. "You think he took the books? For the money?"

I shrugged. "Don't know," I said. "Five mill is a lot of ransom." I stared at my empty mug. "He could sell them, I suppose. Any idea who'd buy valuable books?"

"Local second hand store won't be interested," he said. "But a collector would be. For that you'd need an intermediary, a connection that fences stolen goods."

"Got a name?" I said.

Stern shook his head. "No, but I know who you should ask."

"Who?"

"Joey DeMio." Joseph DeMio ran the Baldini crime family in Chicago. They made money from drugs, prostitution, and loan sharking. Joey took over as Godfather two years ago when his father, Carmine, retired to become his son's consigliere. Father and son lived the summer months on Mackinac Island. They ran, quite legally, the Marquette Park Hotel.

I smiled. "Never need an excuse to visit Mackinac, but it never hurts to have one."

"Do you think our Dean would mess with the Mafia?"

"Don't know," I said. "Does he spend money he doesn't have?"

Stern shrugged. "Not that I can tell. Hangs out at a few bars. Tries to get laid."

"Any luck in that department?"

"Ever meet Lewis?"

I smiled. "See what you mean."

Sandy came to the door. "You guys need a refill?"

"We'll get it ourselves," Stern said.

"I know you will," she said. "That's why I don't mind asking. Give me the mugs. I just made a fresh pot."

She brought back hot coffee and handed us the mugs.

"Speaking of Dean Lewis," Sandy said.

I looked up. "What about him?"

"Roger Thornhill Lewis will never be a ladies' man. Trust me on this."

"He hit on you?" Stern said.

"Not for long," she said. "But he was on the hunt."

"When was this?" I asked.

Sandy took in a long breath and let it out slowly. "A month ago, I think. Six weeks."

"In town?" I said.

"The City Park Grill. At the bar. He was with Tomas Sandoval." Sandy laughed.

There it was again. Lewis and Sandoval.

"Those guys might as well have hung a sign around their necks. 'I want sex.' Every woman in the place knew it, too."

"That bad, huh?"

Sandy nodded. "Boss, I got a few errands. Unless you need me."

"We're fine. Take your time."

Sandy grabbed her bag. "See you later," she said, and went down the stairs.

Stern drank some coffee and muttered, "Sandoval."

"What about him?"

"Not sure, Michael."

"I read your profile," I said. "Something wrong with the rags-to-riches story?"

Stern shook his head. "No. It's the American dream come true. Undocumented parents stayed below the radar. Worked hard. The three kids started working when they were in grade school."

"What's the problem?" I said.

"He got killed."

"And you want to know why."

"You bet I do," he said, drawing out the first word.

"You on the story?"

Stern shook his head again. "Part time right now. Maury needed me to cover another story." Maury Weston was the editor and publisher of the paper and Stern's boss. AJ's, too.

"The drug bust in Oden?" I said.

"Yeah. But that'll go away soon enough," he said. "I want back on Sandoval." Stern put his left index finger next to his nose. "Something's there. I can smell it."

"Have a theory why he got shot?"

"Not good enough to write it."

"Off the record?"

Stern sat up in his chair a little straighter and folded his arms across his chest. He was being careful. Even with me.

"When I put the profile together? Talking to people. It was good stuff and it made a great story. But there were … well … what I got is rumors," he said. "Not even solid rumors, if you know what I mean?"

"Can't confirm?"

"No," he said. "Lots of pieces. That's all."

"Pretty vague, Lenny. Do they add up to anything?"

Stern put his arms down and thought for a minute.

"Sex."

Then he was quiet.

"Man's single," I said. "He and Lewis wanted to get laid. Sandy just told us that."

Stern shook his head. "It's not about that."

"What then?"

Stern hesitated. Still being careful.

"Bannister coeds," he said.

"Students?"

Stern nodded. "Students. Maybe staff, too. I don't know." His shoulders dropped. Opening the door took some pressure off.

"Jesus," I said.

"Yeah."

"You sure?"

"No. I'm not sure, damn it."

I put my hands in the air, palms out like a traffic cop. "Sorry, Lenny. Sorry. Didn't mean to push."

"I know," he said. "I know. It just pisses me off."

"Think it's true?"

Stern put that index finger next to his nose again and nodded.

"Got sources inside Bannister?"

"One or two, maybe," he said. "Trouble is, something like this? People shut up."

"They scared?"

"If it's one guy, or two, Bannister's PR boys'll label 'em bad apples and they'll go back to sleep. But if it's the institution itself? Everybody gets scared," he said. "Too many overlapping relationships. Personal and professional get all tangled up. Too much on the line."

I got up, walked around and sat on the corner of the desk. "Without someone on the record, it's all speculation."

"Dangerous speculation, Michael," Stern said. "Especially for students."

"I know a guy," I said. "Faculty. I could give you his name."

"Thanks, but it wouldn't work," he said. "Too many people know who I am."

"Maybe I could talk with him. See what he knows."

"Go ahead," Stern said. "But go easy at first. Get your guy comfortable, if you can."

I knew Kelsey Sheridan well enough to do that.

"Keep me in the loop?" he said.

"Yes."

"If there's a story, I want it first," Stern said. "Let Detroit and Chicago get on it late."

"Glad to help," I said.

Stern looked at his watch. "I'm late, Michael." He got up and we walked to the top of the stairs.

"Lenny," I said. "You know a guy named Conroy? Bannister cop."

"Rent-a-cop, you mean?"

"That's the guy."

Stern said, "He's a pain in the ass. Thinks he's a hot shit lawman."

"You have trouble with him?" I said.

"Only a little," Stern said. "He followed me while I was doing the Walloon story. He acted like I was Woodward and Bernstein out to wreck Bannister. Not that he'd ever heard of Woodward and Bernstein."

"What happened?"

Stern laughed. "Sandoval got shot, that's what happened. He lost interest in me after the *Free Press* showed up. Why are you asking?"

"Conroy hassled me the other day. That's all."

"He's not as tough as he thinks he is," Stern said. "But he's got two deputies. Their idea of fun is to throw you up in the back seat of a patrol car."

"Thanks for the heads up."

"Don't mention it," he said. "You'll call, you got something?"

"Yes."

Stern took the stairs and left the building.

I looked out the front windows, the ones above Lake Street. Every parking place was filled. People on vacation, especially families, shopped their way up and down the street. Just like every business owner wanted them to do in July.

Petoskey is a pleasant small town. Energized in the summer, peaceful in the winter. Bannister College flips that around during its leisurely summer session. That's part of why I like living here. But if I ask hard questions, I'll break the routine. People get testy when that happens.

12

Lenny Stern's comments made for a restless night. I finally got up, way too early, took a shower and made coffee. That didn't help. If Stern's hunch about Dean Sandoval was right, hunting for stolen books, no matter how unique, had suddenly become more complicated. I knew very little about what was going on. Nothing new about that.

I drank some coffee, put the mug on the side table and picked up my iPhone. I tapped a message to AJ, "you awake?" A few moments later, the phone buzzed.

"Good morning, darling," I said.

"Hello," AJ said. "Sleep well?"

"So-so. Sorry about last night, but I was worn out. Getting into bed with a good book, I just needed to do that."

"I get it, sweetheart. Which good book?"

"Well, this Hemingway thing's got me going, "A Movable Feast.""

"His memoir of Paris?"

"That's the one."

"Where he trashes Scott Fitzgerald?"

"Early and often, yeah."

"I can't even remember how long it's been since I read that," AJ said. "What are you up to?"

"Coffee," I said. "What about you?"

"Cooking oatmeal," she said. "I've actually got an apron on."

"An apron? You're not going all Martha Stewart on me, are you?"

"It ties around the waist," she said. "And I'm topless. What do you say to that, smart-ass?"

"It's hard not to laugh, you really want to know."

"You are impossible," she said. "Did you have any more thoughts about what Lenny said?"

"I've thought about little else, but I get nowhere. Nothing new since we talked about it last night. What about you?"

"Just what I told you. I'm pissed off if he's right. I hope he's wrong."

"Me, too," I said. "Only other thing, I called Henri. We'll see what he can dig up on Lewis and Sandoval."

"Lenny didn't say anything about Lewis being a dirty old man, did he?"

"No," I said. "But they hung out at the bar together, so who knows?"

"Is Henri here or on Mackinac?"

"He's here," I said. "Sent a text back. He'll come by the office this morning. Sweetheart, speaking of Mackinac… "

"My favorite island?" she said. "What about it?"

"Going up," I said. "Want to come along?"

"Love to," she said. "If I can clear my schedule here. Maury and I have to run to Grand Rapids for an overnight. We're interviewing a guy for the reporter job. When do you want to go?"

"Next day or two."

"Is this business?"

"Want to talk to Joey DeMio about stolen books."

"The Walloon Collection?"

"Yeah."

"Think he's involved?"

"No," I said. "But he'd know who would fence valuable books. By the way, how's the oatmeal?"

"Waiting for it to cool. I'm ready with milk and brown sugar."

"I'm proud of your culinary talents," I said.

"Thank you, darling. You know, this kitchen's pretty hot. I'd better leave my top off."

I looked at my iPhone. She ended the call.

"And she thinks I'm impossible?" I said to an empty living room.

13

I didn't have any appointments today, unless I counted Henri. Only Sandy would care if I dressed more casually than usual. I took black jeans, a burgundy polo shirt and Chaco sandals from the closet. I opened the second drawer in the dresser next to my bed and grabbed a pair of boxers.

I walked up Howard Street and across the parking lot behind my building. It was muggy, but heavy gray clouds kept it from as being as hot as last week. The clouds promised rain. Maybe cooler air would follow the storm through town.

I went in the back door of McLean & Eakin Booksellers and up the stairs to the main floor.

"Here you go, Mr. Russo," said the woman at the desk as she handed me the *New York Times*.

"Thanks." I left by the front entrance and walked to my office four doors away on Lake Street.

"Jeans?" Sandy said when I walked in. "As if your khakis weren't casual enough." She noticed my sandals and shook her head. "You won't impress clients in that outfit."

"Don't have any clients to impress," I said.

"You can always impress me," said a familiar voice from my office.

"Thank you, very much, Henri," I said louder than usual and with a nice touch of sarcasm.

"Anytime."

"Sandy, call the Marquette Park Hotel. See when I can get a few minutes with Joey DeMio. Then come sit down."

"Will do."

I stopped at the table and filled a mug with coffee.

Henri sat behind my desk with his feet on the left corner. He wore baggy denim shorts, a yellow t-shirt and dingy Brooks running shoes. Despite the heat, he wore a thin black nylon jacket. It was zipped half way to cover the "Gen 4" Glock in a holster on his right hip.

"Morning, Russo," Henri said, and dropped his feet to the floor. "Want your chair?"

I shook my head. "This is fine," I said and sat in a client chair.

Sandy took her usual spot at the side of the desk. "I talked to DeMio's secretary."

"Carlo something?"

Sandy nodded. "Vollini. The guy with the two-pack a day voice," she said. "Call when you plan to go up. He'll get you in."

"Thanks."

"For what reason are we assembled here this morning?" Henri said.

I drank some coffee and answered, "Got a job for you."

"Do I get paid?"

I looked at Sandy. "Does he get paid?"

"Same as last time," she said.

"That much," Henri said. "In that case, I'm in."

I gave him the condensed version of the Walloon investigation so far. "That it?"

I shrugged. "This is where you come in."

"Of course it is."

"Start with Dean Roger Thornhill Lewis. Dig into his background, tail him. Everything you can find out."

Henri nodded.

"Next, Tomas Sandoval. Same thing."

"Hard to tail a dead Dean," he said.

I rolled my eyes. "Please," I said.

Henri leaned back and put his hands up behind his head. "Really think Sandoval was chasing students?"

"Don't know," I said. "But Lenny Stern's right more often than not."

"Think Lewis is in on it, too?" Henri said. "The girls?"

"Don't know that either," I said. "Let's find out."

"There's a lot you don't know, Russo." Henri came forward in the chair and his hands landed with a thud on the desk. "But that's why you called me."

"Need all the help I can get."

"Speaking of help," Henri said, and looked over at Sandy. "You go to Johan's this morning? I'm hungry."

Sandy shook her head. "Sorry. Cooked eggs at home."

For a quick moment, the image of AJ in an apron cooking oatmeal popped into my head. Not now. Need to focus.

"One more thing," I said. "You know a cop named Conroy? Wade Conroy? Works at Bannister."

Henri laughed. "The Chief?"

"Do I take that as a 'yes?'"

Henri nodded. "You meet him on campus?"

"Uh-huh," I said. "He magically showed up at my car, tried the whole intimidation routine."

"Sounds like the Chief," he said.

"How do you know him?"

"Took a run at Fran two years ago," Henri said. "Had to have a chat with the man." Fran Warren, my tenant in the retail store, was Henri's half-sister.

"What do you mean, 'a run?'"

"She teaches retailing at Bannister," Henri said. "Evening college." Henri drank some coffee and put the mug back on the desk. "Conroy stopped her one night. Said she was speeding. It was a roust. Got her out of the car. Patted her down."

"That's bullshit," Sandy said.

"No ticket. Made some nasty comments about how she was dressed. She ignored him, of course. She was back in class the next night."

"That when you had your chat?"

Henri nodded. "Told him he's not deputized by Emmet County. Told him he ever went after Fran again, I'd be back." Henri looked over at Sandy. "He never bothered her again."

"What do you know about Conroy?" I said.

"Enough. Good ole' boy from Arkansas, Louisiana. Bounced from one job to the next. Lumber, oil fields, that kind of thing. Graduated from a community college, a police academy. Deputy jobs here and there. Got hired at Bannister seven, eight years ago. Promoted to Chief of Bannister Security when the other guy retired."

"Who promoted him?"

Henri shrugged. "Regents, be my guess. I can find out."

"Do," I said.

Henri stood and looked out the window. A steady rain had started. A light wind pushed it against the glass. It wouldn't be long before tourists driven from the beaches by rain packed the sidewalks of Lake and Howard, to the delight of businesses in the Gaslight District.

"Can I go earn my salary now?"

"Yes, you can," I said. "The sooner the better."

He came around the desk, zipped up his jacket and said good-bye.

14

Clouds and fog hung so low over Little Traverse Bay that I couldn't see the end of the breakwater. I moved my chair and put my feet on the window sill. It didn't help. A light, misty rain dotted the glass. The weather people on TV and the internet were all wrong. The promise of cooler, dryer air seemed as distant as the Wisconsin side of Lake Michigan.

The office was quiet. Sandy was out. The phone, office or cell, didn't ring. No text messages.

AJ was delayed in Grand Rapids to hold another round of interviews. I hadn't heard from Henri. Not sure if he went back to Mackinac or was still in town. Lenny Stern hadn't called either, but I didn't expect him to since I was the one trying to confirm his suspicions about the late Dean Sandoval.

Peace and quiet is comfortable for only so long. I was getting nowhere. It would be a fine time to get an email or text with a surprising piece of information. Better yet, a mysterious woman with a shady past could walk through the door and toss clues on my desk.

I heard someone on the stairs.

"Hello, boss," Sandy said, stopping at my door.

"Oh, it's you. Hi," I said. "Must have been daydreaming. Sorry."

"Who'd you expect, Miss Wonderly?"

I stared at Sandy for a moment. "Dashiell Hammett, right? *The Maltese Falcon?*"

"Right," she said. "Unless I'm Brigid O'Shaughnessy."

"Very funny," I said. "How was the dentist?"

Sandy gently shook her umbrella and put it next to the coat rack. "I won't even dignify that with an answer," she said. "Glad you made coffee. Back in a second."

Sandy came back with a mug and sat in her usual chair. She drank some coffee. "Tastes good," she said. "You actually made it strong enough."

"Thanks a lot."

"So, boss, what's up?"

I explained my wandering mind as best I could.

"Well, we could get hold of Henri," she said. "But he doesn't have what you want or he'd have called."

"Yeah, I know."

"Lenny Stern's waiting to hear from you, isn't he?"

I nodded.

"What about Marty Fleener?" Sandy said. "You could tell him what you've learned."

"What have I learned, Sandy? What do I tell him? That I've got suspicions about a respected, and dead, member of the community? I'm sure the grieving family would welcome that news. Besides, what I got from Lenny's off the record."

Sandy picked up her mug and held it like a hand warmer.

"We need confirmation of Lenny's suspicions," Sandy said. "One way or the other."

"That'll be tough without somebody going on the record," I said.

Sandy nodded. She put her mug down and leaned forward. I'd seen that look in her eyes before. She was focused.

"We need someone who shares the same suspicions. You know, who's seen things, heard things. Someone familiar with Bannister."

"Not confirmation?"

"No, no," Sandy said. "But someone you could talk to. Someone to give you a reason to keep looking."

"Kelsey Sheridan?"

"You can trust him."

"Yes, I can," I said. I thought for a moment. "I got a couple of calls to make. See if you can find Kelsey. Text first. Probably be faster."

Sandy got up and left my office. I opened a folder and found the phone number I needed.

I'd just hung up when Sandy came to the door.

"All done?"

"Yeah."

She moved to the front of my desk and opened a small spiral notebook.

"Kelsey's stuck in his office the next two days. He said give him a time and he'll pencil you in, pretend you're a student appointment."

I put my hands up over my head, fingers spread out. "Sis, boom, bah."

Sandy rolled her eyes. "Don't do that in his office, boss."

"No?"

Sandy shook her head. "It's not funny," she said. "Just dumb."

She tore a sheet out of her notebook and handed it to me. "Directions to his office."

"Thanks," I said, and took the sheet. "Kelsey's a pretty sharp guy."

"No argument from me, boss," Sandy said. "One thing to keep in mind, though."

"What?"

She down sat in the client chair instead of the side chair.

"Well, he's still a man, if you get what I mean?" She put her notebook and pen on the desk, sat back and folded her arms. "If the atmosphere at Bannister is really ugly for women, talking to a man about it may not be the best option."

"I get your point, Sandy, but Lenny said this was students getting messed with. Can't imagine Kelsey'd miss that."

"Me, either," she said. "It's just, well, guess I'd be more confident if you talked to a woman."

"Don't know any woman out there well enough," I said. "At least Kelsey and I have history." When Carleton Abbott was murdered at Cherokee

Point Resort a few years back, it was Kelsey Sheridan who willingly talked to me about that cloistered community. He helped crack the case.

"Okay," Sandy said. "I hope you're right. Let me know in the morning."

"You got plans for tonight?"

"Nothing exciting," she said. "Sit on the porch after dinner, read for a while. Watch the sunset if the clouds go away." Sandy lived on Crooked Lake, just north of town. The front porch of the two-story house she shared with her elderly father faced west, across the widest expanse of the lake.

"See you in the morning," I said.

15

A long, thin line of traffic edged its way east on Mitchell. It took two lights to cross Division. Luckily most people turned to head down the hill, so I had a clear road to Bannister. Good thing I got three hundred horses under the hood for the two minutes it'll take to get to campus. Need every damn one of them, too.

Kelsey's directions told me to follow Linton Road as it circled around the old section of campus. His office was in Morrell Hall on the far side of the circle. I turned in when a small sign pointed to parking behind the building.

Morrell Hall was a tired old two-story with a huge arched entrance in the middle of the structure and large sash windows spreading out each way from the door. Like the other original buildings around the circle, its bright red brick had long since faded into a dusty, dull shade of pink.

The building's rear façade matched the one on the street side. I parked near a large, carved wooden sign that announced faculty offices for History and English. I went through the arched door and found a directory. Kelsey was on the second floor.

I went up the stairs, pushed through the door into the corridor and ran into Margo Harris.

"Third door on the left," she said, going right past me and down the stairs. "He's waiting for you."

I had no chance to say hello. She was in a hurry, but the tone of her voice conveyed more.

The hallway was lined with faculty offices. The heavy wood moldings around each door stood in stark contrast with the peeling light green paint on the walls. The old wood floor was covered in squares of 1940s asphalt tile, a dirty, dark brown with colored speckles.

I counted three doors on my left and stopped. On the other side of the corridor, one door down, about ten students sat on the floor. Backpacks littered the area. A few read books, the rest stared at phones, their fingers dancing on the keypads.

Kelsey's door was open. I tapped on the door and went in.

"Kelsey," I said. "Hello."

"Michael," he said, and came around his desk. The office was ten-by-ten with one big sash window that overlooked the parking lot. Only a desk, a small, dented two-drawer file cabinet and two chairs filled the space. Each piece was metal and a shade of mushy green. No one could claim that Bannister overspent on interior decorating.

We shook hands.

"Good to see you, Michael. Sit down."

I took one of the chairs.

Kelsey wore a wrinkled pair of khakis, penny loafers without socks and a pale blue and white striped short-sleeved shirt.

An eight-inch stack of student papers sat on one corner of the desk, a Mac laptop on the other. A large coffee mug that read "Stratford Festival" on its side was jammed with pens, pencils and markers.

"Sorry I have nothing to offer, Michael," he said. Kelsey picked up an insulated travel mug and tipped it in my direction. "Brought this from home. Only coffee here's in the department office." He gestured vaguely at the hallway. "They don't like to share."

"Bannister doesn't seem to spend student fees on maintenance and repair." I glanced around the room. "Got to be in the Big Ten for that," I said sarcastically.

Kelsey laughed. "You have a lot to learn about the halls of ivy, my friend. If we were in Ann Arbor or East Lansing, my office would still look like this."

"Maybe when you become an important novelist, Bannister'll pop for an office makeover."

"If I become an important novelist, I'd still pay for my own upgrades, thank you very much."

"Getting any inspiration from being on the Hemingway committee?"

"I hope so," he said. "I'll take all the help I can get."

"You finished your novel, right?"

Kelsey smiled. "Yeah, almost two months ago. I'm trying to get it published."

"If we were at City Park Grill, I'd offer a toast to your first publication."

Kelsey raised his travel mug in the air and said, "Here, here."

"Any luck with a publisher?"

"You're gonna love this," he said, and laughed. "A publisher says, 'have your agent call me,' and an agent says, 'what have you published?'"

"Sounds annoying."

"Certainly is. But I'll keep at it," he said. "Something'll click."

"Weren't you going to write about Cherokee Point?"

"I gave up," he said. "Who'd believe me? If I tell the truth, readers would think it was too over the top."

"The place is over the top," I said. "Especially the people."

"I rest my case," Kelsey said, and thumped his fist on the desk like a gavel.

We talked for a while before the conversation turned to Bannister College. Kelsey asked how I was doing on the Walloon Collection.

"Wish I knew more," I said, also wishing I had coffee.

Kelsey leaned forward and put his elbows on the desk. "Anything I can do, Michael?"

"As a matter of fact," I said. "Tell me about security for the Collection. Is it as tight as Lewis said?"

"No," he said, shaking his head. "Special Collections doesn't get much traffic. It's easy to know who comes and goes. It really depends on who's at the desk. Some staff members pay attention, some don't. A lot of time is spent getting coffee, in the restroom. That kind of thing."

"What can you tell me about Dean Lewis?"

"Lewis? Is he a suspect?" Kelsey said, his eyes widening.

I shrugged. "I keep asking questions, see what adds up."

"Why are you asking?"

I explained what Lenny Stern told me without mentioning students. "That the Lewis you know?"

"Pretty much." Kelsey drank some coffee. "Looking for women in the bar. Imagine that. Almost makes him sound exciting."

"Does he hit on women?" I asked. "In the office?"

"Our colleagues?" He sounded surprised.

I nodded. "Faculty, staff?"

Kelsey stared at the stack of student papers for a moment.

"Not that I've ever seen," he said. "The Dean's a pretty boring guy. Quiet. He tries to be charming sometimes."

"Meaning what?"

"Harmless stuff, mostly. He pretends to be interested in a woman's kids. Tries to be funny. That kind of thing."

"Does it work? Are women charmed by him?"

Kelsey shrugged. "I've seen some of the clerical staff smile politely. But he's their boss, remember. I've never seen him try that with faculty women."

"What about students?"

"Students?" Kelsey straightened up and stared at me. "Students?"

"I told you," I said. "I ask questions, see what I get."

Kelsey thought for a minute. "You're talking a whole different ballgame, Michael. Hitting on students? That's a helluva long way from stolen books."

"Yes, it is."

"No more questions," Kelsey said and waved his index finger in the air, side to side. "Not until you tell me where you're going with this."

I ignored him.

"Tomas Sandoval," I said. "Ever see him hit on students?"

"Enough, Michael. You can't just toss out names and ask if they hit on students. One of those guys is dead, after all. Now, tell me."

I folded my arms over my chest and took a deep breath.

"I am looking for the Hemingway books, Kelsey, but things I wasn't looking for keep popping up. All I have are unsubstantiated rumors. Don't know if they're linked to the stolen books or not. But if evidence of ugly stuff surfaces, I keep it quiet until I have enough to go to the cops."

I leaned forward on the desk. "That's where you come in."

"Let me guess, Michael," Kelsey said. "You want what I know. Rumor, fact, whatever, and you want this conversation kept quiet. Is that it?"

I nodded. "For the time being, yes. I trust you, Kelsey. If I'm on the right track, help me out. If not, tell me. What do you say?" I sat back.

"I wish I had a stiff drink." He looked right at me. "Okay."

"All right, then," I said. "Start with Lewis."

Kelsey glanced at his laptop like he wanted to check his email. He reached out and closed the lid. Almost absentmindedly.

"If he went after students, I never saw it."

"Any reason to think he has?"

"No," he said. "Nothing."

"What's your gut reaction?"

Kelsey shrugged. "It doesn't fit, that's all."

"Tomas Sandoval?"

"Why those two men? Why not two other guys?"

"When I ask people about Roger Thornhill Lewis, Sandoval's name comes up. I don't put them together, others do. That's why."

"Together at work? Like that?" he said. "They served together on the Scholarship Committee."

There it was again. Kelsey just put them together.

"Not at necessarily at work," I said.

"What do you mean, 'together' then?"

"A solid source saw them together at a local bar," I said. "Trying to get laid."

Kelsey nodded slowly. He was quiet. I didn't push. He put his hand on the travel mug but didn't pick it up.

"Wish they had hot coffee in this place," he said, but not to me. "It's … I wonder now … about …"

"About Sandoval?"

Kelsey didn't say anything.

"Did Sandoval go after students?"

"No," Kelsey said. "I mean, not that I saw."

"What then?"

"I never thought much about it," he said. "Until now." He drank coffee this time. A long swallow.

"Kelsey?"

"We hear students talk all the time," he said. "About lots of stuff. You know, twenty-year old stuff, dating, music, sex, *Facebook*. Before class starts, at the next table in a coffee shop. We don't really listen, but you hear things."

"About Sandoval?"

"More than once," he said. "Girls. Female students, eighteen, twenty. Never gave it much thought."

"Now you do?"

Kelsey nodded. "Yeah, now I do. It sounded like girls gossiping about professors. You know, 'he's a hunk' or 'he's gay.' Stuff like that."

"They talk about Lewis or Sandoval?"

"Not Lewis," he said. "As far as I know. But Sandoval ..."

Kelsey leaned on the desk again and clasped his fingers together.

"What about Sandoval?" I said.

"Kept hearing, 'he creeps me out.' More than once."

"Anything more specific than that?"

He nodded. "I'm getting there, Michael."

Kelsey rubbed his eyes.

"Sandoval'd stand over a desk and try to look at girls with cleavage. You know, down their shirt or tank top. He did a lot of touching from what I heard. The girls didn't like it."

"Is it ever appropriate to touch students?" I said.

He shook his head. "Only in professional ways," he said. "Shaking hands, like that."

Kelsey was quiet again. We sat for a time. Kelsey got up and looked out the window. Hard to tell what it was about the parking lot that held his interest.

There wasn't much more to say. I stood up and he turned around.

"I'll be going," I said. "Thanks for taking time to see me."

We shook hands.

"Are we suspects, Michael? Margo and me? The Hemingway books, I mean."

The question came out of nowhere. Like it just occurred to him.

I shook my head. "I know you pretty well, Kelsey. You're not a suspect."

"What about Margo?"

"I don't know her at all," I said. "But it seems unlikely. Can't say more than that."

"She's a good woman," Kelsey said. "Smart, appealing, ambitious."

"Attractive."

He nodded. "Attractive. I like her. We've had some candid talks. You know, the late night, extra wine kind of talks." He hesitated. "Funny thing, though, she's pissed at you."

"Me?"

"Uh-huh."

"I don't even know her," I said. "Only saw her that morning at the meeting. And just now on the way here."

"The Walloon Committee," he said slowly, remembering. "She asked me questions about you. Who you worked for. What you were doing here. That sort of thing."

So I wasn't imagining things.

"Sorry to hear that," I said. "Can't imagine what I did. Maybe I'll ask."

Kelsey shrugged.

"All right," I said. "I really do have to go."

We shook hands and I left his office.

16

I walked down the stairs and out the back door. Kelsey backed up Lenny Stern well enough that I needed to ask more questions. It was still suspicion and rumor, but it was unlikely they were both wrong.

I crossed the parking lot and went for my car. That's when I saw Chief Conroy.

This time he wasn't alone. Two deputies stood with him. They didn't look happy. The Chief leaned on a dark blue SUV with a LED light bar across the roof. Large script letters on the door proclaimed, "Bannister Security." Smaller letters below it said, "On Guard."

I wasn't happy either. It was going to be a long summer if these guys kept showing up. How'd they know I was here? They tailing me? Somebody tell the Chief?

Conroy gestured in my direction and said something to the deputies. Conroy folded his arms as the deputies started towards me. I got to my car and waited. Not much point trying to leave, since the SUV blocked the only exit.

The deputies moved apart when they got to me. Not a good sign. They'd done this before.

"Gentlemen," I said. "What can I do for you?"

"You can leave," said the older cop. His voice sounded like a rake on a gravel road. He was white, in his mid-forties, and overweight. He'd spent too much time in the bar. He didn't get puffy cheeks and a blotchy red nose lounging on the beach at Petoskey State Park.

"Easy for you to say." I looked at his name badge. It read, "Floyd Jordan." I gestured at the patrol car. "But you got the exit blocked, Floyd."

"That's Officer Jordan to you," he said.

The other cop was taller, over six feet, black, and younger. Probably in his twenties. He was all spit and polish, creased pants and shirt and very shiny shoes. This guy spent way too much time at the gym. His badge read, "John Ribble."

"Thanks for pointing that out," I said. "But the road's still blocked." I pointed at the SUV, leaned against the 335, and folded my arms. Seemed to work for the Chief. "So unless you move that thing …"

'What you doing here anyway?" Officer chubby said.

"Flunked a History exam," I said. "Had to see my prof."

"The Chief said you had a smart mouth."

"That was nice of him," I said, and smiled.

"Maybe we ought to teach this asshole a lesson," Officer chubby said.

I came off the car and put my hands on my hips. "Why don't you just move that truck of yours and I'll get out of here."

"Might haul you to the station instead," Jordan said.

I shook my head. "No," I said. "You can't do that."

"You won't have any choice."

"Am I under arrest? What's the charge?"

We had attracted attention. Three students, two men and a woman stood nearby. They'd put their backpacks on the ground to watch the show.

Conroy noticed the students, too. He adjusted his hat and started towards us.

"What's the matter, boys?" the Chief said. "Mr. Russo giving you a hard time?"

"Said he ain't going with us, Chief," Officer chubby said. "Asked 'is he under arrest.'"

"That so?" Conroy said.

I glared at Conroy. "If you arrest me, Chief, I want to know why. What law, what ordinance I've violated. Got that?"

"How 'bout this asshole, Chief," Officer chubby said, and laughed. "Thinks he's a goddamn lawyer."

"I am a goddamn lawyer," I said. "You gonna roust me, do your homework. Now move the truck."

"You tell 'em, dude," one of the students said, and they all laughed.

Conroy glared at the students. He looked at Jordan and said, "Floyd."

Officer Jordan moved close to me. His hands were behind his back and he leaned in, a few inches from my face. He glared at me for a few moments, then turned and walked to the SUV. He climbed in and drove it over near us. Without another word, the Chief and Officer Ribble got in and they pulled away.

"You are awesome," one of the students said, emphasizing each word. He came over and the others followed. He wore long black shorts, a faded red t-shirt that read "Traverse City" on the front and flip-flops.

He reached out and we shook hands. "You da man," he said. "It's 'bout time they the ones got told off."

"You had trouble with Conroy before?"

All three nodded. "Those guys think they real cops. Big and tough with us."

"Us?" I said. "You three, you mean?"

He shook his head. "Nah. Us, man. The student body are us."

"Why do they do that?"

"Because they can," said the woman. She was twenty, about five-one, and wore a soft pink cotton dress that fell to the knee. "They got nothing else to do," she said. "The fat one … he even tried grab-and-tickle on me."

I shook my head. "Sorry to hear that."

"We call 'em 'BS,' my man, 'BS.'"

"That's for 'Bullshit Security,'" the woman said.

I chuckled. "Shouldn't have missed that one," I said and smiled.

"Hey, man, you really a lawyer?"

"Yes," I said. "But I got rousted anyway."

He smiled. "Yeah, but you told them off."

I beeped the door locks.

"Take care," I said and got behind the wheel.

The students said good-bye and went on with their day, talking and laughing as they walked away. Whatever the deputies had in mind changed once we had an audience. The students had fun at Conroy's expense because I told them off. Question is, why did I have to?

17

When the traffic cleared, I pulled onto Mitchell and headed back downtown. I kept an eye on the mirrors more than usual. Don't know what I expected. A big, blue SUV tailing me?

I parked in the lot behind my office rather than at home. I went up the stairs to Roast & Toast and ordered a small Latte. A single malt scotch sounded better, but it was too early in the day for that. I picked up my drink and took it to the office.

"Too bad you didn't call me," Sandy said, pointing at my Latte. "I woulda had you get me one, too."

"Next time," I said, and sat across from Sandy's desk.

"Deal," she said. "You have a few messages. Only two call backs. They're on your desk."

"Thanks."

I caught Sandy up on my trip to the land of the ivy tower.

"I don't know, boss," she said. "That's a pretty strange place."

"Certainly seems that way," I said. I removed the lid from my coffee and took a drink. I swiped the whipped cream off my upper lip. "Hmm. Good."

"Think about the people for a minute," Sandy said. "The President has an agenda, the campus cops sound like they belong in a "B" movie, an English prof's pissed off at you. See what I mean?"

"Doesn't seem like a happy bunch, that's for sure."

"Is that really what their lives are like?

"Don't know, Sandy," I said. "But a murder on campus has got to mess with your sense of safety. The stolen Hemingway books can't help either."

"I know, but they act like Bannister is the sun and the world revolves around them. They must think people pay attention to every little thing that happens out there."

"Sure a lot different than Michigan State," I said. "Unless it affected the football team, most folks in the Lansing area couldn't care less what happened on campus."

"Bannister's always seemed like an ideal place to work," Sandy said.

"You're on the outside looking in."

"Sure, the grass is greener," she said. "But it has to be interesting. Lots of smart people and all those kids with tons of energy."

"Kelsey Sheridan likes it pretty well," I said.

"Yeah, and we know his head was screwed on straight before he started teaching there."

"That we did," I said.

I finished the last of my Latte and tossed the cup, free throw style, in the wastebasket next to Sandy's desk. "All net."

The office phone rang and Sandy answered.

"Yeah, AJ, he's here. Hold on." She pointed the receiver at me and punched the hold button. "Says you didn't answer your cell."

I stood up and took my iPhone out.

I went to my desk, sat down and picked up.

"Sorry, sweetheart," I said. "Cell was on vibrate."

"At least you weren't ignoring me, darling," AJ said.

"Not a chance. What can I do for a defender of the printed word?"

"Buy more newspapers?"

"Very funny," I said. "I'm the only guy I know who still reads dead trees newspapers."

"Part of your charm, dear," she said. "Listen, I saw Lenny Stern this morning. He asked me if you'd learned anything about Sandoval."

"And you said?"

"I was diplomatically vague."

"Thank you."

"I had nothing to tell him anyway."

"I'll give him a call," I said.

I told AJ about my latest adventure.

"Bullshit Security," she said. "Got to love that. It's comforting to know the next generation is on top of things."

"Not to mention funny."

"I'd like to be more encouraging, Michael, but all you have are rumors about Sandoval. If that's where you stand, it ain't much."

"Sheridan backed up Lenny's information," I said.

"If I'm writing this for *PPD Wired*," AJ said, "you don't have it. No evidence, no one on the record. I don't write a piece like that."

"I know, I know. I get the point." I slid my chair back and put my feet on the corner of the desk.

"Anything new on the Walloon books?"

"Like clues, you mean?"

"That's your real case, Michael. The rest is rumor."

"I get that AJ," I said. "Rumors like this are hard to ignore though."

"Shift your focus," she said. "Find the books. Let the other story come to you."

"Would you do that? You had a hot lead?"

"You don't have a hot lead, darling."

"Would you ignore a story?"

"I'd write the story I got, Michael. I'd chase the rumors later."

I dropped my feet to the floor, stood up and went to the window. The air was clear, the water on Little Traverse Bay shimmered in the hot sun. Be nice to be out there right now, sitting on the breakwater watching the small sail boats maneuver around each other.

"Michael?" AJ said. "Still there?"

"Yeah," I said. "By the way, why'd you call?"

"Mackinac. When are you going up?"

"Haven't decided," I said. "Today, tomorrow. Can you get away from work?"

"The rest of this week is nuts," she said. "I'm stuck at my desk."

"Sorry to hear that," I said.

"Me, too, babe. Maybe next week. We could get a room at the Cloghaun." The Cloghaun was a quiet Victorian B&B on Market Street and our first choice for overnights on the island.

"I like the sound of that," I said. "Remember the one with the big-enough-for-two-people claw foot bathtub?"

"You bet I do, darling."

"Got an idea," I said. "I'll run up and talk to DeMio this afternoon. See what he knows about stolen books."

"Okay."

"Meet me when I get back. We'll get something to eat."

"How about a burger at the Side Door?"

"Side Door it is," I said. "Call you when I get on the ferry."

I put down the phone and went out to Sandy's desk.

"Call Carlo Vollini. See if Joey's got some time."

"Should I cue music from *The Godfather* first?"

"You should pick up the phone, is what you should do first," I said. "I'll be in my office."

"Hey, boss," Sandy said.

I stopped and turned around.

"Remember, Joey DeMio's a dangerous man."

"Hard to forget," I said.

18

I grabbed a navy blazer off a hanger on the back of the door. Always best to be very business-like when I deal with the Mafia. Not sure my khakis, green polo shirt and the blazer are a match for Joey DeMio's tailored suits from Chicago, but it's what I got.

I said good-bye to Sandy and went downstairs and found a parking ticket tucked under the windshield wiper of the 335. Knew I should have parked at my apartment building.

I drove out of the lot, over to Howard and stopped at the light at Lake Street. The sun was high in the sky and hot. The heart of the Gaslight District was crowded with tourists wandering aimlessly, laughing and pointing at store windows. Hard to believe even more people show up whenever a warm, easy rain forces people off the beaches.

When the light changed I edged up to Mitchell, turned left and headed out of town. Traffic was thick but it moved along. I went down the hill on Division and north on U.S. 31. On a busy summer day, the ride to Mackinaw City took fifty minutes even with traffic. I put the radio on Interlochen news, settled comfortably in my seat and motored on. No chance to play boy-racer today. Have to wait until October for that.

Mackinaw City was as busy as Petoskey. I drove straight down Central Avenue and into the Shepler's parking lot. In the middle of the season, ferries left every half hour. Just enough time. I found a spot and hurried to the ramp. I took a seat in the back row just as the horn sounded. *Miss Margy*, Shepler's newest and largest boat, backed away from the dock and we were off.

/ The Straits of Mackinac. I've made this trip many times over the years and I'm never bored. The ferry ride itself is, well, fun. I felt that way as a kid. I still feel that way. Most of the travelers portside looked left, gaping at the Mackinac Bridge. Me, too. It was impossible not to look at the marvelous structure that connects Michigan's two peninsulas as it gleamed in the summer sun.

Fifteen minutes later, the *Miss Margy* slowed as we pulled into the harbor at Mackinac Island. I always took a moment to glance at the expanse of the island, the bluff houses, Fort Mackinac, Grand Hotel. While we waited for the crew to tie up the boat, I noticed a familiar figure leaning next to a railing on the dock. Santino Cicci, one of Joey DeMio's two gunmen.

Cicci was a trim six feet tall with a chiseled face and a small, neat goatee. He wore jeans, lime green running shoes and a black cotton shirt. The shirt was loose and baggy to cover the holster on his right hip.

Locals did not like Cicci or his pal, Gino Rosato, who usually moved about together. They were trouble. They pushed people around and dared anyone to challenge them. Few did.

After the crew moved four luggage carts off the boat, all of us departed. Cicci came over as I got to the top of the ramp. I didn't see Rosato, but that didn't mean he wasn't close by.

"Santino," I said, and smiled. "You my welcoming committee? Pretty thoughtful, if you ask me." I looked around, in an overacting kind of way. "Hey, where's your buddy? The boss ship him back to Sicily?"

"Keep it up, smart guy," Cicci said. "You'll cross the line one day and I'll shut that big mouth of yours once and for all."

"No, you won't," I said. "You don't take a piss the boss doesn't say so." Geez, I sounded too much like them. "Are you my escort or do you trust me to find the hotel all by myself?"

"On your way, Russo," Cicci said. "Mr. DeMio's waiting."

"Well, let's go, Santino," I said with a grand wave of my arm. "We wouldn't want to keep the boss waiting."

I walked up the dock to Main Street. The top of the dock was a mass of tourists and dock porters, luggage and taxis, horses and bicycles. Just another July day on Mackinac Island.

I turned right and headed towards Marquette Park. I had some extra time, so I cut up Astor Street to the Mackinac Sandal Company in the middle of the block. Fran Warren came down the front steps just as I got there. She was in her early fifties, about five seven with soft blonde hair pulled back into a pony tail. She wore a brick red sleeveless top over charcoal shorts.

"Michael," she said as I stopped. "What a nice surprise to see you here."

"Hello, Fran," I said, and we hugged. "Came to collect your rent."

"No, you didn't, Russo," she said. "You don't even notice when the rent's late."

"Sure I do, Fran. Just don't worry about it, that's all. Haven't seen you at the Petoskey store in awhile."

She shook her head. "Way too busy here."

"That's good to hear."

"Come on," she said. "Walk with me. I'm going to get the mail." Fran put her arm through mine and we were off to Market Street.

"What are you doing here, anyway?"

"Meeting Joey DeMio in a few minutes."

"And how is Mackinac's favorite Mafia Don?"

We stopped in front of the Island's post office, a one story, clapboard sided building with a white picket fence along the sidewalk. Mail is not delivered on Mackinac Island. Everyone has a box, so the post office is a hub of activity. People come and go all day long, chatting with friends outside at the bike rack or inside standing in line for window service.

I shrugged. "Have no idea how he is," I said. "You probably see him more than I do."

"I saw him last night, in fact," Fran said. "Henri and I had dinner at the Woods. Joey was there with a gorgeous woman. Didn't recognize her."

"See Rosato or Cicci?"

Fran nodded. "Cicci watched from the bar, not the dining room."

"That was polite of him."

"Uh-huh," Fran said. "Henri tells me he's working on a case for you. He didn't say what, so I didn't ask."

"Spy versus spy," I said. "Very hush-hush."

Fran laughed. "You guys are too much. My brother's bad enough, but hook him up with you? Spy versus spy, my ass."

"Fran," I said, trying to fake shock. "Such language from my favorite tenant."

"Your only tenant, you mean. On your way, Michael. Got to pick up my mail and get back to work."

"Nice to see you, Fran," I said, and started down Market Street for Marquette

Park. Back Street, as Market Street is also called, was usually less congested than Main Street, especially in the summer. I got to Fort Street and walked across the grass. The park was filled with people, young and old, tourist and local, soaking up the sun, having a quick lunch, or sitting in front of Father Marquette's statue for a vacation picture.

Santino Cicci walked along the sidewalk on Main Street and kept an eye on me.

At the east edge of the park stood the Marquette Park Hotel, an elegant four-story building built before the Civil War as a private home. It sat closed and badly in need of repair when Carmine DeMio, Joey's father, bought it in 1998. He bought a historic cottage on the East Bluff at the same time and restored both of them. How much money DeMio spent was the subject of speculation and much gossip for months.

I walked up the curved drive and went in the front door. The air conditioning was a welcome treat. The lobby was small and quiet with two long, upholstered couches near a fireplace on one side of the room and the reservation desk at the back. Gino Rosato sat on one of the couches with his back to the wall. He was a big, chubby man with a round, puffy face and a red nose.

"Hello, sir. May I help you?" said a woman with a Jamaican accent behind the desk. She was in her twenties, with her hair pulled back tight. She wore a blazer with a crest of the hotel on the left breast pocket.

"Michael Russo to see Joey DeMio."

"Of course, sir," she said. "One moment." She picked up the phone and punched two buttons. "Mr. Russo, sir." She put the phone down.

"Down the hall, sir," she said to me and pointed to the side of the desk. "Knock first."

"Thank you," I said.

The door was open when I got there. Guess I didn't need to knock. Carlo Vollini held the door and quietly closed it after I went in. The title "secretary" was misleading when it came to Vollini. Forget about a curvy blonde with a steno pad. He was a big man, about six-six and two-thirty. He wore dark wool slacks and tan sweater over a blue button-down shirt.

The office was a big, square room with high ceilings and tall bookcases on three walls. To one side was a small fireplace and two love seats with a coffee table. A large mahogany desk sat in front of a wall of windows that looked out on the swimming pool.

Joey DeMio sat behind the desk. He stood but didn't reach out to shake hands, not that I expected him to. Joey was in his early fifties, with short black hair brushed straight back. He worked out at the hotel spa every morning, as he told me once, and it showed. He wore a charcoal suit and a white spread-collar shirt with a black tie.

"Take a chair, counselor," he said in a deep, clear voice.

I sat in one of two mahogany captain's chairs in from the desk. Vollini sat near the fireplace.

"Thanks for taking time," I said.

"You got five minutes." Never let it be said that the mob wasn't gracious.

"You know anything about valuable books stolen from Bannister College?"

"Where do you get off? Come here accuse me of stealing?"

I shook my head. "Cut the crap, Joey. Never said that, and you know it."

"I paid my debt," he said. "That's over."

I nodded. "We're even, Joey."

"Then what do you come to me for?"

"Because you're the only guy who's got what I need." I leaned forward. "Have you heard about the Walloon Collection, or do I got to fill you in before I ask a question?"

Joey looked over at Carlo. Vollini got up and put a manila folder on the desk with the cover open. Joey moved a sheet of paper or two.

"So?"

"Collection's worth a lot of money," I said. "I'm hired to get it back and not pay five million ransom. You know who took it?"

Joey shook his head slowly. "Next question."

"You know a fence who'd take the books?"

Joey shook his head again. I'm getting nowhere. Maybe I should get out of here.

I was about to get up when he said, "Jesus, counselor, you got a lot to learn."

"Why don't you enlighten me."

"Nobody ordered a robbery like that. No professional anyway."

"No?"

"If the books were stolen on order, they'd be out of the country by now. Europe. Asia, probably. Into a private collection."

"You think the books are already gone?"

He shook his head. "You miss the point, counselor."

Joey pushed his chair back, put his feet on the desk and clasped his hands behind his head. The pro was about to pontificate to the naïve.

"No professional did this," he said. "With or without orders."

"Who then?"

"This is an inside job, Russo. The 3-D books are a clever touch, but it takes the right person to make the dummies, get into the library, make the switch and carry out the real books. Not an easy or fast thing to do."

"Think the books are still in the country?"

Joey laughed. "In the country? They're still in the neighborhood."

"How 'bout the ransom?" I said.

"The ransom is fucking amateur hour, counselor," he said. "A ransom is how you get caught. The books are too unique, too easy to spot. A pro moves the merchandise as far away as possible as fast as possible." Joey put his feet on the floor.

"You want to find the books?" he said. "Stick close to home. The closer the better."

Joey stood up and put his hands on his hips. Carlo stood, too. My appointment was over.

"Anything else, counselor?"

I shook my head and stood up. "You told me what I needed to know, Joey. Thanks."

"Don't make a habit out of it," he said. A gentleman to the end.

I heard the door open behind me and Carlo waited patiently for me to go. I said good-bye and went out. The door closed softly behind me.

Rosato wasn't in the lobby. Guess I was no longer a threat to the boss.

The air hit me like a wall of humidity when I walked out to the front porch. The view of the harbor, of ferries arriving or leaving, of boats in the marina was a marvelous sight.

"Michael," a voice said as I was about to go down the steps to the driveway. I turned around.

"Michael," Carmine DeMio said. "Come sit with me." He was ten feet from the front door, sitting in one of many white Adirondack chairs arranged on the porch. Five chairs down from Carmine sat Santino Cicci.

I went over and sat next to Carmine. He was in his mid-seventies, on the heavy side with thinning gray-black hair combed back, just like his son's. He wore faded jeans and a black silk shirt, casual clothes befitting a retired Mafia Don. Carmine handed over control of the Baldini family to Joey two years ago.

We shook hands.

"Good to see you, Michael," he said. "I trust Joseph was able to accommodate your needs."

"Yes, he was."

Carmine smiled. "I encouraged him to meet with you," he said. "To help you."

"I appreciate that, thanks."

"To help you as long as your interests do not conflict with our interests."

Wonder what happens then? I get thrown off the end of the coal dock?

"I assure you, there was no conflict, Carmine. Just needed to be pointed in the right direction. That's all."

Carmine nodded as if he was pleased that it all worked out. Now he wouldn't order Cicci to shoot me.

"You know, Michael, you did a service for the family a few years ago." He put his hand on my arm. "That nasty business at Cherokee Point. Remember?"

"Yes," I said. Hard to forget murder. But you'd think he was reminiscing about another Thanksgiving dinner ruined by good ole Uncle Charlie ranting uncontrollably about politics.

"I remember a kindness, Michael," he said. "I encouraged my son to remember it also."

"Well, thank you, again, Carmine."

Carmine nodded at Cicci, who quickly got out of his chair and came over to us.

"Santino, I'm going home now."

"Would you like a taxi, sir?" Cicci said. Carmine's house was above the hotel on the East Bluff. It was a long walk up stairs or a steep hill.

Carmine shook his head. "I'd like to walk."

"Good day, Michael," he said, and the two of them left the porch.

I looked at my watch. Just enough time to make the five-thirty Shelper's to Mack City. I went down the driveway and headed to the boat dock.

The sidewalks were still crowded with people who were now shopping for dinner. They gathered around menus taped in restaurant windows or read cardboard copies given out by eager staff.

I got in line on the Shepler's dock, pulled out my iPhone and sent a message to AJ that I'd be at the Side Door by seven.

"All aboard for Mackinaw City, folks," the deck hand said, and we inched our way down the ramp to the *Wyandot*. I found a seat by the window and sat down.

Joey DeMio was convinced the Walloon theft was an inside job done by amateurs. That's the kind of thing a Mafia Don would know. He gave me a place to start, and it narrowed the field of suspects. Dean Lewis was the obvious choice. He knew everything there was to know about the books themselves, about the security procedures. Was Sandoval part of the Walloon theft? Was his murder? Many questions, few answers.

"Clear," the deck handed shouted, and the *Wyandot* eased away from the dock.

The captain of the *Wyandot* would find his way to the mainland. Be nice if I found a few clues.

19

Fifteen minutes later, I walked off the *Wyandot* and found my car. I beeped the locks and got in. I tapped another note to AJ, "leaving MC."

I went up Central Avenue, under the freeway and looped around to pick up I-75 south. A few minutes later, I exited at U.S. 31 and got in line with all the traffic going to Petoskey. The trip home through Pellston and Alanson didn't promise to be quick.

At six-fifty, I pulled in at the Side Door and parked the 335.

The lot was only about half full of cars and trucks. The Side Door Saloon was a popular hangout anytime of the year. The after-work crowd, mostly locals, already occupied many of the seats at the long bar and a few of the tables. In July, tourists arrived later, after they'd had their fill of sun, sand and shopping.

I found two barstools at the far end of the bar and sat down.

I saw AJ come through the door. I always felt a thrill at the first sight of her, dropping in at my office, when she got home or meeting me at the Side Door. I hope I never lose that feeling. AJ stopped and looked around but didn't see me. I waved my arm vigorously. She finally saw me, waved, and made her way to the empty stool next to me.

"Hello, darling," she said and leaned in to kiss me. I kissed her back. Never want to lose that feeling either.

"You look quite sexy this evening," I said, and smiled. She wore a navy linen jacket over a white camisole with a dark khaki skirt that fell below the knee.

"You always say that, Michael," she said. "I love you for it. Don't ever stop."

"Is that all you love me for?"

"Of course not, darling, but I'd think more clearly with a glass of wine."

"Hard day?"

"Longer than I planned," she said. "But not particularly difficult."

"Mr. Russo, Ms. Lester," the bartender said as she put two small napkins on the bar. "What can I get you?"

"Hi, Allison," AJ said. "Chardonnay, please."

"Me, too."

"You guys are way too easy," Allison said, shaking her head. "Back in a minute."

"Why was your day difficult?"

AJ was looking off to the side, over my shoulder.

"What, dear? I'm sorry. What did you say?" She glanced away again, just for a second.

"I asked about your day," I said. "It was difficult?"

"Yeah ..." She looked away again, in the same direction.

"What are you looking at?"

"Sorry, darling," she said. "A woman over there." She gestured with a nod. "Sort of behind you."

"What about her?"

"She keeps staring and pointing. At us, I think. Or you. Do you know her?"

I turned slowly, pretending to be subtle. I recognized the woman at first glance. I waved. Margo Harris raised her glass in my direction. But she didn't smile.

Allison arrived with two glasses of wine. AJ took a sip and held the glass in her right hand.

"It's Margo Harris," I said.

"The writer from Bannister?"

I nodded.

"Is she ... what do they call her?"

"The porn lady," I said. "She's a serious writer, but it's called erotic romance."

"She's the one on the Walloon committee?"

I nodded again. "That's her."

"Quite attractive if you like tall blondes in their late forties, Michael."

Margo wore a French blue tank top over a white skirt and black sandals.

"I do like tall blonds, but Margo's in her late fifties."

"Seriously?"

"Uh-huh," I said, and drank some wine.

"How do you know that?"

"She told me."

"A woman told her age? Out loud?"

"Yep."

AJ smiled. "Hope I look that good when I'm almost sixty."

"You will, darling, you …"

"Michael, she's coming our way. Over here. She doesn't look happy."

I turned on the barstool as Margo got to us. AJ was right. She looked annoyed. Again.

"Margo," I said. "How are you tonight?"

"A little drunk," she said. "No, more drunk."

"Margo, this is AJ Lester."

AJ reached out to shake hands. "Ms. Harris. Happy to meet you."

Margo shook AJ's hand and said, "Well, you won't be happy for long."

"And why is that?" AJ wasn't taking the bait. I've heard that sarcastic voice before. She was pushing back.

"I'm pissed at him," Margo said, nodding at me. "Pissed as hell, if you really want to know."

"Why, yes, Ms. Harris, I would like to know why you're so pissed at Michael." The sarcasm just got deeper.

"Easy, AJ."

"I've drunk too much wine, Russo," Margo said sharply. "But I don't need help from you. I know when I'm being set up."

Two women sitting next to AJ overheard us and were trying hard not to look.

"Margo," I said. "You've been annoyed about something since the first time we met."

"Damn right," she said. "But now I'm angry. Very angry."

"I have no idea what you're talking about," I said.

"Well, it's time you got schooled," she said. "Get your ass to the parking lot."

Margo stretched out her arm and pointed at the door. "Now."

"The parking lot?" I said. "We gonna have a fight?"

"You're goddamn right we're gonna have a fight."

"Guns or knives?"

"Don't fuck with me, Russo," Margo said. "I'm not in the mood."

She looked at AJ, "Excuse us." Then back at me, "You. Let's go," she said and went for the door.

The two women could resist no longer. They turned and watched the unfolding drama.

I got off the stool. "I'll be in the parking lot, darling, in case you need me."

"Text if you need back up, dear," AJ said and smiled. More sarcasm.

"Very funny."

I went out the door and looked for Margo. She was on the other side of the parking lot.

"That's an Audi A-7 you're leaning on," I said as I walked up. "Don't think the owner would appreciate it."

"I don't give a shit," she said, and moved away from the car. "I'll kick his ass after I kick yours."

I took a step back, put my hands on my hips, and looked right at her.

"Margo, what did I do to piss you off so badly?"

"It's what you didn't do, Russo," she said. "What you didn't do."

"Is this about the Hemingway books? The ransom? What?"

"You're a stupid jerk, you know that?"

"So I've been told," I said.

"The books?" she said. "Seriously?"

"They're worth a lot of money."

Margo flung her arms up in the air, like she tried to swat flies. "I don't care about the goddamn books."

"Margo, tell me what's going on or I'm going back inside."

Margo leaned back on the Audi again. She folded her arms across her chest and was quiet for a minute.

She came off the car and turned towards me. Her face had lost some of its hard edge.

"You really don't know what I'm talking about?"

I shook my head. "No."

Margo looked away, out at U.S. 31 like she'd developed a sudden interest in July traffic.

I waited.

She turned back and said, "How much do you know about Roger Thornhill Lewis?"

"Not a lot," I said. "English professor, runs the Walloon Collection."

Margo nodded. "Do you know about the Scholarship Committee?"

"Think I heard of that," I said. "I guess."

"With Tomas Sandoval, now dead, and Caleb Reed, not dead. They give scholarships to students who need money."

"Who's Caleb Reed?"

"College of Ed. Dean."

"Okay," I said. "What's your point?"

"They're predators."

I started to say something, but thought better of it.

"Lewis is the worst. He goes after women, especially pretty, young students in desperate need of money. Occasionally, he picks on somebody his own size."

"He hit on you?"

"Only once."

I waited.

"I told him if his dick was that long, he could stick it in his own mouth."

"Good for you."

"Fuck good for me," she said. "We're talking about eighteen-year-olds here. Or twenty. They're vulnerable, they want school, they need money. They're targets for those guys." She hesitated. "They're just girls, Russo. Kids."

"Sandoval, Lewis and the other guy?"

"Reed. Predators. All of 'em."

"My god," I said. "Hard to believe."

"Not hard from where I sit," Margo said.

"Why?"

"It's organized," she said. "It's all planned."

"Planned? Like a scheme?"

Margo nodded. "Lewis'd know which girls needed money because they applied for scholarships. To his committee."

"A ready-made list every semester?"

Margo nodded. "You got it."

"Anyone go to the cops?"

"Sure. A few of us." Margo shrugged. "Didn't stop Lewis or his buddies."

"Cops didn't believe you?"

"Who knows," she said. "No evidence. Students too scared to talk. The cops were all men, of course. I even talked with Don Hendricks. Once."

"Hendricks is a good guy."

"You say. He listened patiently, but …" She shrugged.

"No evidence," I said.

Margo nodded. "Regents don't care either. They think we're trouble-makers."

"How 'bout Griswold?"

Margo shook her head. "Griswold's an arrogant prick. His only saving grace, he detests everybody. He likes to throw his weight around, but not to help us."

"So where do I fit in?"

"We heard the Prosecutor sent you to Bannister. We thought, we hoped, you were there to get Lewis and his buddies. You know, the Hemingway books were just a cover."

I shook my head. "No," I said. "It started with the books."

We were quiet.

"I have to go," Margo said, and turned away.

"Margo?"

She stopped just for a moment, but didn't look back. Then she went inside.

20

"Michael?" AJ said as she walked up to me. I was still in the parking lot, standing next to the A-7 with my hands in my pockets.

"You okay?"

"No," I said, shaking my head. "I mean, I'm all right. It's just …"

AJ put her hand on my arm.

"I saw her come in," AJ said. "She picked up her purse and left with her

friend. I waited for a few minutes. But you didn't come in."

"Sorry," I said.

"No, no. It's okay," AJ said. "You want to go back inside?"

I shook my head. "I'd rather not. Just don't feel like, you know, being in a bar."

"My house then," she said without missing a beat. "Get your car. I'll see at

home."

She walked away and I went to the 335, beeped the locks and got in.

AJ pulled into traffic on 31 just ahead me. We turned at Division and again at Mitchell. My window was open and I was suddenly aware of the hot night air. Just past Kalamazoo, we took Ottawa to AJ's house over on Bay.

"Let me get out of these work clothes," AJ said. "There's wine in the fridge or scotch in the pantry."

I got two glasses from the cupboard, a wine glass for AJ, a tall glass for me. I took a pitcher of iced tea and the Chardonnay from the fridge and filled our glasses.

I was on the couch in the living room when AJ came back downstairs. She wore long navy shorts and a faded red T-shirt that said "49740" in large numbers on the front. She dropped her Chaco sandals on the floor next to the couch, sat down and picked up her glass.

"You hungry?" she said. "We didn't eat. Want a sandwich?"

I shook my head. "Not hungry. Maybe later?"

"Sure." AJ put her glass on the coffee table. "So what happened with the porn lady?"

I drank iced tea and reprised my chat, if you want to call it that, with Margo Harris. It didn't take long. But my tale of what she told me in the parking lot was more involved than I thought. I hit the highlights. AJ's a reporter, she'd know what to ask.

"That's an ugly story," AJ said.

"Certainly is."

"Not much to go on. We really only have Margo's word."

"You don't believe her?"

"I do believe her, Michael," she said. "But what story do I write? Where's the evidence? It's the reporter in me."

"Margo backs up Lenny Stern," I said.

"So what? A rumor supported, and I use the word, 'supported,' loosely, by an unsubstantiated allegation. No wonder the cops didn't follow up."

AJ drank some wine and put her glass back on the table.

"I'm surprised that Don didn't take her more seriously. Didn't listen to her."

"Hendricks listened to her. Don took her seriously," I said. "You know that. But he's still the Prosecutor. He's got a job to do. I suppose Margo might have confused inaction with not paying attention."

"She doesn't strike me as a woman who confuses easily," AJ said. "Besides, she's angry, Michael. She's scared for those girls."

"So she gets angry at me?"

"Sort of angry," AJ said.

I nodded. "Sort of angry 'cuz the private eye who showed up talked about stolen books."

"When Margo really wanted 'Spenser for Hire' to get the bad guys."

AJ got up and went to the kitchen. She came back with the bottle of Chardonnay and poured some in her glass.

"Hungry yet?" she said, and sat down.

I shook my head.

"Speaking of bad guys, Michael…"

"Yeah?"

"Do you think the Sandoval murder's part of this?"

"You mean the stolen books or blackmailing girls for sex?"

"Well, I didn't think about it," she said. "But …" AJ settled back on the couch and put her feet up on the coffee table.

"But what?"

"I'm not sure," she said. "It's seat-of-the-pants time. Maybe I asked the wrong question. Follow me here for a minute."

"Have at it, reporter lady."

"When I asked about Sandoval, I meant blackmailing girls. I never thought about the Walloon books. So I must have assumed they're separate things. Separate crimes, so to speak."

"Okay."

"What if we assume the opposite," she said.

"Which is?"

"They're not separate crimes. The stolen books and the murder are connected, related in some way."

"How?"

"Hell if I know," AJ said. "You're the detective, you figure it out."

"You're the reporter, AJ. What's your nose-for-news tell you?"

AJ dropped her feet on the floor and reached for her glass. She drank some wine. "Instinct only, Michael. Nothing hard to go on."

"You got experience to go on, AJ."

She nodded. "True."

"Well?"

"Assume the murder and the stolen books are connected. They're either part of something bigger or two parts of the same thing. Hell, I don't know. Maybe one happened because of the other. It makes more sense Sandoval got killed because of the books rather than the other way around."

We were quiet for a minute. I drank the last of my iced tea and AJ sipped more wine.

"There are two different committees, right?"

I nodded. "Uh-huh.

"How many people? Both committees?"

"Well, Dean Lewis runs the Walloon Committee with Kelsey Sheridan and Margo Harris."

"Throw out Sheridan and the porn lady," she said. "That's one."

"Three guys on the other committee," I said. "Lewis, Sandoval and the Education Dean, Reed."

"One's dead, so that leaves us with two. What do we know about Reed?"

"Zip."

"That's a big help."

"Lewis is the common denominator," I said.

"Then he's our link between the stolen books and the murder."

"Whoa. Pretty big leap there, Lois Lane."

"Got a better idea?"

I shook my head.

"What would Sam Spade do?"

"Light another cigarette."

AJ rolled her eyes, but kept her composure. "After the cigarette," she said. "And don't say pour a drink."

"Don't know about Lois or Sam," I said. "I'd go with what we know."

"It's time to push Lewis, then," AJ said.

"Henri's checking on him."

"Good," she said. "If there's something there, Henri'll find it. What about Reed?"

"Just heard about him," I said.

"Put Henri on him. See what turns up."

I nodded. "First thing in the morning."

AJ picked up my hand and kissed it. "Want a sandwich yet? Got some fresh chicken salad in the fridge. Made it with my very own hands. Multigrain bread, sliced tomato, a few chips. What do you say?"

"You have one, too?"

She nodded, got up and took the empty glasses to the kitchen. I followed her with the wine bottle.

"Get plates while I make the sandwiches," she said.

I put two plates on the kitchen counter, and took napkins and our glasses to the small table on the sidewall. The window overlooked the ravine behind her house. I got more iced tea and poured Chardonnay for AJ. She put down our sandwiches and a bowl of chips.

"Tastes good," I said. "Guess I was hungrier than I thought."

"You were pretty shaken in the parking lot, Michael," she said. "You don't usually get that rattled."

"Yeah," I said. "I know. I was shocked by Margo's story. I guess part of me doesn't want to believe that could happen. Here, anywhere, to our children."

AJ smiled. "You've got a good heart, Michael. Something else I love about you."

"But she's right, AJ, they're just kids with dirty old men after them."

"It's worse than that. Those guys got all the power," AJ said. "The students have no power. To make matters worse, they need money for school. They can't go to the cops or they're out of school. The administration? Same thing. The girls're screwed no matter what they do. It's brutal."

I finished chewing a bite of sandwich. "Right now, Lewis is all we got."

AJ dropped a napkin on her plate and finished the last of the wine. I took my plate and AJ's to the sink.

"I'll clean up, dear, if you want to get going. I have an early meeting anyway."

"It's a deal," I said. "I'll get hold of Henri in the morning."

"What about Lewis?"

"Get to him as soon as I can."

"You going to hit hard?"

"Count on it."

21

I took a shower and shaved while the coffee brewed. I put on khakis, the no-iron kind, a light blue cotton shirt and deck shoes.

I poured coffee into a mug that read "Made in Detroit" on the side, and sat down at the kitchen table. I checked messages, but nothing from Henri. The rest didn't matter. Neither did most of the emails.

After I rinsed the pot and put my mug in the sink, I grabbed my bag and a nylon rain jacket. The sun was gone, but not the heat, not yet anyway. Dark gray clouds hung low over the bay. Rain would be here by late afternoon.

My iPhone buzzed and I pulled it out. "Waiting," the message said. It was Henri.

I walked up Howard to Bay, then across the parking lot behind my building. I cut through McLean & Eakin and picked up my *New York Times* at the desk.

"Morning, boss," Sandy said when I walked through the door.

"Morning, boss," Henri said from my office.

"Good morning both of you," I said. "Anyone hit Johan's this morning?"

"Of course," Sandy said, "but you're too late."

Henri appeared at the door. He wore loose black shorts and a baggy green shirt to cover the holster on his hip.

"Still got lots of coffee," Sandy said. A carafe of coffee sat quietly next to an empty Johan's box on the side table.

"You get my text?" I said to Henri.

"Last night, yeah," he said and refilled his mug. "I was busy."

"Brenda Fuller?" Sandy said.

"A nice evening," Henri said, and smiled. He took his coffee and went back to my office. I hung my jacket on the hall tree, got coffee and joined him.

"Come on in, Sandy." She carried coffee, too, and sat in her usual chair.

"Got any news?" I said.

"Plenty," Henri said. "Should I start with Hillary and Bill?"

"Later," I said. "How about Roger Thornhill Lewis?"

"Been a busy boy," Henri said.

"That so."

Henri nodded. "Sandoval, too."

"Skip the academic bio, tell me something I don't know."

"That'll be easy," he said, and drank some coffee. "Most of what I found out you don't know."

"I'm waiting."

"Lewis got himself a two-bedroom condo at Bay Harbor."

"The old cement plant?" Sandy said.

I shot her a look. "Don't start."

"Yes, boss."

"Thought he lived in a low rent apartment? Just out of town," I said.

"Didn't say he lived at the condo in Bay Harbor."

"Expensive place," Sandy said. "Especially if you don't live there."

Henri smiled and said, "Makes for a few interesting questions, doesn't it?"

"How much does he make as a Dean?" Sandy said.

"Not that much," I said.

"Paid cash," Henri said. "No mortgage."

"Paid cash?" Sandy said. "Why the hell would you live in a dump if you owned a snazzy condo at Bay Harbor?"

"He doesn't own the condo."

"But you just said ..."

Henri shook his head. "Didn't say he owned it."

"For crissake, Henri," I said.

Henri smiled and raised his hands in mock surrender.

"Okay," he said. "Just having some fun."

"Henri."

"The condo's owned by the Hadley Company, which is owned by OMATS Corporation," he said. "All caps."

I looked at Henri, then at Sandy. "Never heard of them. Local businesses?"

Henri nodded. "Parent company is an L.L.C. licensed right here in the Great Lakes State."

"Sandy," I said. "Check it out, would you, please."

Before she could get out of her chair, Henri said, "Don't bother. They're dummies. Both of 'em. Hadley. OMATS. Get it?"

I shook my head.

"Me either," Sandy said.

"OMATS," Henri said. "*The Old Man and the Sea.*"

"The Hemingway novel?" Sandy said.

"Got him the Nobel Prize. Hadley Richardson was Hemingway's first wife."

"You're enjoying this, aren't you, Henri," Sandy said.

"You betcha," he answered, smiling.

"Bizarre, that's all," I said, and shook my head.

"It gets better, Michael."

Sandy slumped down in her chair and waited. I just stared at Henri because, well, I didn't know what else to do.

"The officers?" Henri said. "Listed on the OMATS incorporation papers. Three names."

"Lewis must be one of them," I said.

Henri nodded. "Chief cook and bottle washer."

"The other two?"

"Tomas Sandoval and Caleb Reed."

"Are you fucking kidding me?" I said.

"Perish the thought."

"Aren't those papers public records?" Sandy said.

Henri nodded. "Indeed, they are."

"For smart guys, that's pretty damn dumb," Sandy said.

"They're academics," Henri said. "Since when does intelligence get in the way of stupidity?"

"So what's the apartment for?" I asked. "Why the phony corporation?"

"They want to hide that they own it," Sandy said. "Somebody might wonder about the cash."

"Money's got to come from someplace," I said. "You know where?"

Henri shook his head. "Not yet."

"Back to Michael's question," Sandy said. "Do they drink beer and watch football on Sunday afternoons?"

"No," I said. "It's where they take the girls, the scholarship students."

"I don't want to hear this," Sandy said, and stared at her coffee mug.

Henri nodded. "Tailed Lewis," he said. "Two afternoons, two different girls. They were young."

"You know who the students are?"

Henri shook his head. "But I'll find out who the next one is."

"Will there be a next one?" Sandy said. Before either of us could say anything, she said, "Never mind. Of course there will."

We sat quietly for a minute. My coffee was cold, but I didn't want more.

"Lewis the only one you saw out there?" I said.

"Never saw Caleb Reed, if that's what ..."

Henri was interrupted by the office phone.

"I'll get it," Sandy said, and went to the outer office.

She came back to the door and said, "It's Margo Harris. For you."

I picked up the landline. "Ms. Harris? Good morning." After a quick chat, I put the phone down.

"Going to meet her at Julienne Tomatoes in a little while."

"Is she feeling guilty about last night?" Sandy said.

"How'd you know?"

"It's a woman thing, boss. Did she offer to buy lunch?"

"Uh-huh." I looked at my watch. "You got anything else, Henri?"

"Couple of things," he said. "Won't take long."

I settled back in my chair. Seemed like I'd been there a long time.

"The late Dean Sandoval," Henri said.

"The man with a terrific life story," Sandy said.

"You said he'd been busy, too?"

"Yep."

"The corporate papers alone don't mean much," I said. "He could have been an investor looking to make a buck. Can we tie him to Lewis?"

"I believe we can, Michael." Henri got out of his chair and came around my desk to the window. "It's starting to rain," he said, and tapped on the glass. "Jacket's in the car."

"You won't melt," Sandy said.

"No, I won't melt." Henri reached for his mug. It was empty. He put it back down on the desk.

"Remember you told me Sandoval only taught one course?"

"Uh-huh."

"Remember what it was?"

"Adaptive something or other," I said. "Don't remember."

"Additive manufacturing, actually." He looked at both of us. "Any guesses?"

Sandy shrugged. I shook my head.

"It is, and I quote, 'extrusion sintering-based processes.' Otherwise known as 3-D printing."

"Bullshit," Sandy said. "You made that up."

Henri picked up my newspaper. "Read all about it in the *New York Times*. Several articles the last few years." He dropped the paper on the desk. "My guess? The dead Dean made 3-D copies of Hemingway's missing books."

"Hard to bet against that."

"Might be a good time to search the guy's computer," Sandy said.

"Legally?" Henri said.

I nodded. "If files exist for those book jackets, I want them as evidence. Fleener could get a warrant."

"On our say-so?"

"We have more than that," I said. "OMATS, the apartment, Lewis and the students, even Conroy's sticking his nose …"

"Michael," Henri said. "Conroy. I almost forgot."

"What about him?"

"He got the chief job through a nationwide search. Regular screening, hiring committee for interviews. That kind of thing." Henri went back to the chair in front of my desk.

"Search committee was chaired by Wardcliff Griswold. Lewis was on that committee, so Lewis knew about Conroy ahead of time."

"Another piece," I said.

Henri nodded. "I know a guy. A county deputy. They all hate Conroy. Hate to deal with him. Word is Conroy gets money under the table. Booze, too."

"From Griswold?" Sandy said.

"Don't think he'd get involved in that," I said. "A pain in the ass, yes." I shook my head. "But that?"

"Lewis on the other hand," Henri said. "Lewis is a better bet."

"Anything on the deputies?"

Henri sat back in the chair and crossed his legs. He pulled a small spiral notebook out of a cargo pocket in his shorts. He flipped a few pages.

"Floyd Jordan." Henri looked up. "He's the older, white guy. Flabby around the middle." He went back to the notebook.

"He's bounced from job to job. Career's passed him by. Conroy hired him. They worked together in some rural nowhere town in Arkansas."

"The other deputy?" I said.

"John Ribble. Young, black, career's just getting started. Not like the other two. Likely Ribble's an Affirmative Action hire."

"Conroy must love that," Sandy said.

"Not much, according to my contact. Apparently pressure came from several quarters to have at least one minority at Bannister Security. They got Ribble. He seems like a straight shooter overmatched by a couple of bullies."

I looked at my watch again. "Got to meet Margo Harris. You done, Henri?"

He nodded.

22

said good-bye to Sandy and Henri, put on my rain jacket for the five-minute walk to Julienne Tomatoes. The rain came down. I pulled up the hood and stayed close to the storefronts. I walked up Howard, crossed Mitchell against the light, and went into the restaurant. Julienne Tomatoes is a long rectangle of a building with high ceilings, wood floors and easy chairs in the front window.

Margo sat at a two-top on the sidewall. She wore a sleeveless lavender top over a black linen skirt. She stood and waved. I smiled and went over.

"Hello, Margo," I said, reaching out my hand.

"Michael," she said, and we shook hands. "Thanks for coming. Want to order first?"

"Yes," I said. "I'm hungry." We went to the back counter and ordered. Quiche of the day for me, a small tossed salad for Margo. She paid.

When we sat down, Margo said, "Michael, I need to get this out of the way. I apologize for last night."

She stopped when our food arrived. I ate a bite of quiche. Tasty and warm as always.

"I accept your apology, Margo."

"But I haven't finished yet," she said.

"Okay." Maybe I should let her talk, I'm hungrier than I thought.

"I apologize for being, well, for too much wine. I was rude to you and Ms. Lester."

"Thank you. We'll survive just fine."

"I meant what I said, you know." Margo leaned in and her voice got softer. "About Lewis and the girls."

"I know you did."

She looked around. No one heard us.

"I'm getting coffee, want some?" I said.

"Yes, I'd like some."

I filled two mugs with hot coffee and took them to the table.

"Thanks," she said. "I'm not drunk anymore, but I'm still pissed off."

Margo needed to talk and I was content to listen. I sat quietly and ate my quiche.

"It took a while to figure those bastards out," she said. "I didn't believe it. Not at first anyway." She stopped and ate some salad followed by coffee. "Then things started to happen."

"What kind of things?"

"Most of the students in my classes are women. I get a few guys, but they're usually too embarrassed to sign up for a chick-lit class."

"You'd think they'd love the sex."

Margo smiled. "Erotic romance, Michael, erotic romance. Oh, they read my stuff, you know, the hot parts, but taking a class is different."

I drank coffee. "So what kind of things?"

"My classes are small, eight or ten a semester's about it. Most classes at Bannister are small, after all." She sat back and wiped the corner of her mouth with a napkin. "One day, a student just stopped showing up."

"Students cut class," I said.

Margo nodded. "All the time," she said. "But I'd get formal notice of withdrawal from school. That does not happen all the time."

She ate some salad. "I didn't think about it at first. When I lost three students in two years, well, that was odd. I asked around. Admissions office. Student affairs."

I'd finished my quiche and was thoughtfully considering another piece.

"Were they any help?"

Margo shook her head. "Students withdraw from school for lots of reasons. The file usually says, 'personal reasons' and that's the end of it."

Margo finished her salad, pushed the bowl to the side and moved her coffee mug.

"One day, a year or so ago, I met a colleague for lunch. The City Park Grill, I think it was." Margo drank some coffee. "She teaches American History. She told me that two of her students dropped out of school. Same class, same semester. She wondered why."

"Personal reasons?" I said.

Margo nodded. "Then I lost another one. Only this time the kid stopped at my office to say good-bye."

"You had a chance to talk to her?"

"A little," she said. "She was pretty shaken. I asked her why. Lost her scholarship, had to go home. Saginaw. That's all she said."

A staff member stopped at the table. "How was lunch today?" We told her the food was fine. She smiled and took away our dishes.

"I got together with my History friend and we compared notes. Five of our students, all female, quit school around the same time. You know where this is going, don't you?"

"They all had scholarships."

"Had scholarships, lost scholarships, couldn't afford school."

"And dropped out."

Margo nodded. "And dropped out."

"How'd you get to Lewis?"

"The girl from Saginaw? I called her home. Her mother answered the phone. She was downright rude when I said I was from Bannister. She wouldn't let me talk to her daughter. But the mother eased up when I told her my name. I heard it in her voice. When my student came on, I asked what happened. She beat around the bush, but finally said, 'I wouldn't put out,' that's what she said, Michael. Long as I live, I'll never forget that. 'I wouldn't put out.'"

"Was it Lewis?"

"Sandoval. When she said no, Lewis had a go at her."

"Jesus," I said.

"Yeah," Margo said. "She said no again and lost her money." Margo moved her empty mug on the table. "I can't prove this, but the girls knew the score. They talked. They knew what they were up against."

Margo sat quietly.

"I had a talk with Lewis, told him about the students who quit. He tried to blow me off with confidential this and confidential that."

"You tell him what your student said?"

Margo leaned in. "Every goddamn word. Want to know what he said?" I nodded.

"Prove it. That's what he said. Prove it. He threatened to ruin my career if I pushed the matter."

"What did you do?"

"I pushed the matter," she said. "Right into the Provost's office, the President's office."

"What did they have to say?"

"Never got to either one," she said. "It was an associate something-or-other or a chief-of-staff."

"You never talked with Malcolm?"

Margo shook her head. "I even tried that idiot who runs the campus cops."

"Conroy."

"Him, yeah."

Margo shook her head. "Nothing happened. Sandoval's dead. Lewis is still here."

"Know anything about Sandoval's murder?"

She shook her head. "Only that I didn't shoot him."

"Did Lewis try to get you fired?"

"Not that I'm aware of," she said. "I'm still here, too."

"The cops?"

"I talked with a Sheriff's deputy first. I finally ended up at the Prosecutor's office. All men. They listened patiently."

"Hendricks is a good man," I said. "A professional."

Margo nodded. "So you said last night. But I'm sober today. I charge a prominent member of a prestigious institution with blackmail and rape. I can't prove it, so what's a Prosecutor going to do?"

"Would it surprise you to know that Lewis has a condo at Bay Harbor?"

"He moved to Bay Harbor?"

I shook my head. "Doesn't live there," I said.

Margo's shoulder's sagged. Her face looked sad, drawn. She added it up fast.

"Is that where?"

"Where they'd take the girls," I said. "Yeah."

"How did you find that out, Michael?"

"Thought I'd nose around, see what popped up."

"Weren't you supposed to recover the Walloon books? Didn't you tell me that?"

I nodded. "I can do two things at the same time. Besides, it's the same guys, Margo."

"It could be a coincidence."

I shook my head. "No, it's not."

Margo leaned in again. She said quietly, "You think Sandoval's murder had something to do with the scholarships? With the girls?"

"Maybe," I said. "Can't put the puzzle together. Not yet. But a lot of pieces are out there."

Margo stared at me. "You're going to stay on this, aren't you?"

"Yes."

"Why?"

"It's got to stop, Margo," I said. "Cops'll get Sandoval's killer. But black-mailing students for sex? Money for sex? It's got to stop."

"Let's hope it has stopped," she said.

I shook my head. "Two more girls," I said. "At least."

Margo sat straight up. She wasn't quiet this time. "Two more? How do you know?"

"A friend's been watching the condo. Saw Lewis with two different young women."

"Do you know who they are?"

I shook my head. "Can you help with that?"

"Maybe," she said. "There might be a way. Let me think about it."

Margo looked at her watch. "I'm late," she said. "Got to teach in an hour. Thanks for coming."

"Thanks for the lunch," I said. "And the talk."

She smiled. "You're welcome."

Margo picked up her shoulder bag and we left.

Outside the restaurant, Margo turned to me and said, "Are you going after Lewis?"

"Yes."

"He won't like that."

"Glad to hear it."

23

The rain had eased into a light mist and the sun started breaking up the
clouds. Steam came off the tarmac and people were back on the streets, moving about.

If little else was clear, it was time to see Lewis. I couldn't see the whole picture. It was all guesses. Good guesses, but still guesses. Time to push Lewis and see if anything changed.

Sandy was gone when I got back to the office. Running errands, her note said. I spent the afternoon catching up on the activities of two clients, one of whom was scheduled for Probate Court at the end of the week. I was happy not to think about Lewis, Bannister or Hemingway's books. At least for awhile.

I picked up the desk phone and called AJ's number at the *Post Dispatch*. She answered on the first ring.

"I don't feel like going out for dinner, Michael," she said. "Why don't you come to the house when you're done. We'll eat at home."

"You got anything in mind for food?"

"Not off the top of my head, no." That means there's little worth eating at the house.

"What's in the fridge?"

"Um, not sure." That means we'd both be happier if I figured out dinner.

"I'll stop at the store and get something," I said.

"Good idea," she said.

Three hours later, I finished work, stopped for food and pulled into AJ's driveway. I went in the kitchen door and put two grocery bags on the counter.

"Is that you, darling?" AJ said from the living room.

"Who'd you expect, Mario Batali?"

"One could only hope."

"Thanks a lot," I said. I went into the living room, leaned over and kissed her. She'd already changed into denim shorts and a faded gray T-shirt.

"That felt good," she said. "Another one, please."

I sat down on the couch, put my arms around her and kissed her. Hard. She kissed back.

"That's better."

"What're you reading?" AJ held a hardcover book in her lap. A glass of wine was on the coffee table.

She held the book up. "It's called *For the Love of Lola*."

"Never heard of it."

"Guess who wrote it?"

"I haven't a clue," I said.

"Margo Harris."

"No kidding." The cover featured a man with a torn shirt, ripped abs and long blond hair. "Is that Lola's lover?" I said, pointing to the guy on the cover.

"One of many, I've found out." AJ flipped through the pages and stopped. "Here. Listen to this, dear. It's Lola talking. 'I like my Chardonnay thick and buttery, just like my men. But not thick in the cranium, mind you.'" AJ put the book down. "I've never quite thought of Chardonnay in those terms."

"Probably just as well."

"Sex sells a lot of books," AJ said.

"It's called erotic romance."

"Of course it is," she said, and put the book on the coffee table. "But right now I'd rather hear about about your lunch with Margo Harris. And whatever Henri had to say, too."

"Okay, but let me get some wine." I went to the kitchen, put the groceries away, poured a glass and returned to the couch.

"I'll start with Henri," I said, and recapped my day with Henri and Margo. AJ listened quietly and sipped her wine.

"Well?"

"One thing," she said. "I agree with Sandy. For smart guys they're pretty dumb, signing those papers."

"Arrogant?"

"Sure, it's arrogant," AJ said. "But *The Old Man and The Sea*? Give me a break. I'll bet they had a good laugh at being so clever."

AJ put her glass down and leaned forward with her elbows on her knees.

"If Margo and her friend lost students? The kids who dropped out? How many more girls are screwing those guys just to stay in school?"

"Two for sure," I said. "I'd like to think that was it."

"So would I," AJ said, "but I'm afraid they'll be more."

"You that sure?"

AJ nodded. "Does this look fly-by-night operation to you? Just a couple of dirty old men?"

I shook my head.

"Or a well thought out scheme?"

"How does a scheme like that survive? Scholarship money, the condo, students dropping out. Hard to hide all that. Do you think the administration is covering its ass or got its head in the sand?"

"It's both, Michael," she said. "Bureaucracies, even small ones, play CYA all the time. You know that. It's systemic."

"Seems tough to ignore something like that at a small school like Bannister. It would be easy to get lost in a cavernous institution like Michigan State."

"But Bannister has this image," she said. "This Pollyanna-like view of itself. Sparty has no such illusions."

I nodded. Sad but true.

"Bannister has a track record for ignoring reality. In East Lansing, every piece of dirty linen is washed eventually."

"Think the administration'd cover up for Lewis?" I said.

"I sure hope not," she said. "If the story breaks, they won't keep a lid on it."

"The cops are already on campus with the Sandoval murder."

"Because they couldn't overlook a body, Michael," she said. "But it'll blow up if blackmail, sex, money for condos in Bay Harbor are thrown in."

"Sandoval taught a 3-D printing class."

"Does Martin Fleener know that?" AJ said. "That his body and the Walloon heist are tied together?"

"We think they're tied together, AJ. Don't know for sure."

AJ stared at me. "Want to bet against it?"

I shook my head. "Not a chance."

"If you were my reporter, Mr. Russo, I'd send you to talk with Dean Lewis, then Captain Fleener."

'Cuz you're sure Lewis is the link between the crimes."

AJ nodded. "And a predator."

"Wonder if Fleener's put the same pieces together."

"He hasn't," she said.

"No," I said. "Or we'd know about it."

AJ smiled. "You're starting to think like a reporter, Michael."

"All the news that fits."

"Not exactly."

24

"**D**ean Lewis'll meet you in his office at eleven," Sandy said, and handed me a sticky note. "So you don't forget."

The July heat had finally broken overnight. A hard northwest wind blew off Lake Michigan and took the humidity out of town.

"How can I forget?" I said. "It's the only thing on my schedule this morning."

"Except for the banana," Sandy said, pointing at my breakfast. "And the *New York Times*. Is Maureen Dowd on Hillary's case again?"

"Certainly is," I said.

I finished the last bite, the rest of the op-ed page and most of my coffee. It was time for Roger Thornhill Lewis.

I took a navy blazer off the hall tree and walked back to my apartment to get the car. It was seventy-two, but the air almost felt chilly after so many days of heat and humidity. It'd be nice to run in the afternoon and not worry about the heat.

I put my brief bag on the back seat, climbed in and hit the start button. I went over to Mitchell and pointed the 335 north to Bannister College. I circled around Linton Road on campus and parked in a visitors spot behind Morrell Hall. Lewis' private office was one floor up from Margo Harris and Kelsey Sheridan.

I went in the back door and up the stairs to the third floor. A small sign with an arrow said "Office of the Dean." Bannister hadn't spent any more money decorating floor three than it had on Kelsey's shabby floor. Peeling paint must be an architectural feature.

I put on my blazer and walked through an open door into a small waiting room painted the same, dull institutional green as the rest of the building. Four blond wood straight back chairs lined one wall, and a long overstuffed and over used three-person couch filled the other side of the room. A door at the back of the room was ajar.

"Hello?" I said. "Anybody home?" In a moment Dean Lewis came through the door.

"Michael," he said. "So nice to see you again." Lewis still looked stuffed into his clothes. The white button down strained at the collar, and the navy and green striped tie only made the impression worse. His herringbone jacket was unbuttoned but it didn't fit well either.

We shook hands. "Thank you, Dean Lewis, for making time on such short notice."

"Happy to oblige," he said. "Come in and sit down, won't you?"

Don't mind if I do, Dean. We'll see how long it takes before you toss me out.

"Please call me Roger," he said. "No need for formality here."

"All right," I said and sat down. The Dean's office stood in stark contrast to the rest of the building. No peeling paint here. No leftover furniture either. Three walls were lined with oak bookcases, the fourth with tall sash windows. A square area rug in the middle of the room picked up the color of the burgundy walls.

Lewis gestured at two chairs in front of his large oak desk. They matched. I took a chair and Lewis sat down behind the desk.

"Nice office, Roger," I said, still looking around the room. "A stark contrast to the rest of the building."

"I paid for it myself, that's why," he said. "Five minutes after I moved in I could see that it needed a makeover. The administration wouldn't shell out ten bucks, so I did it myself."

"Well, you did a nice job."

"Thank you, Michael," he said. "But I suspect you didn't come out here to lavish praise on my office."

"No."

"Have you any word on the Walloon Collection? Have the thieves contacted you?"

"No," I said. He asked the questions with the same level of enthusiasm he used talking about office décor.

"Have you made any progress?"

"Some progress," I said.

"Do tell," Lewis said, but before I could answer, "Any more on the ransom? Do you know who the thieves are?"

I shook my head. "Nothing like that, no."

"What then, Michael?" He sounded annoyed. That's something. Let's try this.

"It's an inside job," I said.

No obvious reaction. If Lewis was our man, I didn't catch him off guard. The guy's got a tough poker face.

"How do you know?" he said. "If you don't know who stole the Collection, I mean."

"It's not about the thieves," I said.

"What then?" Annoyed again.

I adjusted my blazer and crossed my legs. For effect.

"It's what happened after the Walloon Collection was taken from the library," I said.

"We received the ransom demand."

I nodded. "That's an amateur play," I said.

"If you think five million is 'amateur play,' you certainly have more money in the bank than I do."

I shook my head. "No," I said. "It's not how much. Only amateurs would demand a ransom in the first place. It this was a professional job, that would have been it. We'd have heard nothing. The Collection would have vanished."

"Vanished?" Lewis said. "Vanished?"

"Into a private collection, most likely. The books would have been stolen because someone wanted Hemingway's books, not money."

Lewis leaned back in his chair. He thought for a minute. He came forward and put his elbows on the desk.

"That makes no sense. Even thieves want money," he said. "That's why they steal things."

"Sure," I said. The Dean was almost funny. "But in this case, amateurs demanded five million bucks. Professionals would have been paid to plan the robbery, do it themselves or hire other pros to do it. To steal the books."

"You seem quite certain about that, Michael," Lewis said. "Have you much experience with this sort of thing?"

"Not much at all." I anticipated his next question, so I said, "But I know people who do."

"The police, you mean?"

I shook my head. "Professionals on the other side of the law." He didn't expect that. "Professionals who would plan the crime and carry it out." I caught him off guard.

This seems like a good time. Here goes.

"I do have a few questions, if you don't mind."

Lewis shrugged. "Of course not."

"Where'd you get the money for the two-bedroom at Bay Harbor?"

"Beg pardon?"

"The condo at Bay Harbor," I said. "You paid cash."

I really caught him. I saw it in his eyes.

"I'm afraid I don't understand."

"Sure you do, Roger," I said. "You and your pals bought a really nice place. For cash."

"You must have me confused with someone else. I live in a very inelegant apartment. A consequence of my divorce, I'm …"

"Ah, come on Rog," I said, and smiled. "The papers are public record in Michigan. Surprised you didn't know that."

Lewis started to say something but moved his hands up to cover his mouth. I'd got to him and he knew it.

"OMATS Corporation," I said. "Thought you were pretty clever with that one, didn't you? *The Old Man and the Sea*. Since we're talking clever, the Hadley Company?"

"What gives you the right to meddle in my affairs, Mr. Russo?"

So we're back to Mr. Russo.

"You did, Rog, old boy. You and the Prosecutor and Bannister College gave me a hall pass. That condo cost a lot of dough, Rog. Didn't you think people'd wonder? How you paid for it, I mean."

Lewis came out of his chair.

"Get out," he said. "You have no right to accuse me. Get out or I'll call Security and have you thrown out."

"Ah, Chief Conroy," I said. "I wouldn't want to tangle with that good' ole boy, now would I?"

"You would not, sir," Lewis said. Then louder, "For the last time, get out."

I eased myself out of my chair. "Whatever you say, Rog. But I shall return."

"No you won't, Mr. Russo. Chief Conroy will see to that, I assure you."

"Give my regards to the Chief, will you?" I said.

"Get out."

I left Lewis' office and went for the stairs. When I got outside, I scanned the parking lot for Conroy or his deputies. Nothing. Just cars and students and a pleasantly warm summer day in northern Michigan. Perfect day for an afternoon run.

25

I don't understand," Sandy said. "Why didn't you tell Lewis you know about the girls?"

It was a little after ten. I sat with Sandy in the outer office and sipped coffee. I ran longer and faster than I had in quite a while yesterday afternoon. Beautiful day and too much adrenalin after playing with the Dean. I treated myself to extra protein this morning, eating Eggs Monaco at Twisted Olive on my way to work.

"Caught him off guard," I said. "He thinks I like him for the Walloon robbery. That's okay. Let him think that." I sipped some coffee and put my mug on the corner of Sandy's desk. "He's a smart guy."

"Evidence to the contrary," Sandy said.

"Yeah, yeah, I hear you," I said. "But I don't want to tip him off about the girls. Besides, we can't prove Lewis is trading money for sex."

"You can't even prove he stole the books," Sandy said.

"No, but I'd rather have him worry about that," I said. "There's time to build a case for blackmail."

"Not if you're one of the kids who needs a scholarship, there isn't."

"I didn't mean … I know how that sounded."

"It's okay, boss," Sandy said. "I know what you meant."

I stood and looked down on Lake Street. Tourists were out early this morning. The sidewalks were crowded with shoppers who'd decided against another day at the beach. Wonder how many were too sunburned?

"If we get Lewis for the Walloon heist, he can't target the girls anymore," I said. "But we're not sure who else is involved."

"Sandoval's dead," Sandy said. "That leaves Caleb Reed, right?"

"Most likely," I said, and shook my head. "I'd like to be sure, that's all."

We heard someone on the stairs. Sandy and I turned towards the door.

"Good morning, Sandy. Good morning, Michael," Martin Fleener said.

"How is our Captain of the State Police this morning?" I said. "Tailing suspects? Ready for a car chase? You and Helen need my services?"

"You finished?" Fleener said.

I nodded.

"Want some coffee?" Sandy said.

"Thought you'd never ask."

Sandy started out of her chair. "I'll get it, Sandy," Fleener said. He went to the side table, filled a mug and sat down. Fleener wore a dark gray single-breasted suit with a black and white striped tie over a white spread collar shirt. The man's a stylish dresser, who never disappoints.

He drank some coffee. "Ah, that tasted good. Out early this morning," he said. "Missed breakfast. Either of you stop at Johan's?"

We shook our heads. "Sorry," Sandy said.

"You working a big case?" I said.

"You ought to know."

"Uh-oh," Sandy said. "Not sure I like the sound of that."

"I ought to know?"

Fleener nodded. "Bannister College. Ever heard of the place?"

"Uh-huh." Seen this act before. Fleener liked to smart-ass his way to the real point. His way of tempering annoyance. Or anger.

"We sent you out there find some goddamn books."

"The Walloon Collection, yeah."

"Find 'em yet?"

I shook my head.

"How 'bout the bad guys? You know, who stole the books?

"Not yet, no."

"You messing with anything else out there?"

I shook my head, again. "No."

"Then what the hell's Henri LaCroix doing at Bannister College?"

"Taking classes?"

"Wrong answer."

"You can say that again," Sandy said.

"Maybe Henri wants …"

"Be careful, Russo."

"Think I'll run to the bookstore," Sandy said. "Back real soon."

"You're not going anywhere," I said.

"Russo," Fleener said. "I need to refill my mug here." He took the mug in both hands and held it out in front of him. "Then how about we try again?"

"Say 'yes,' Michael," Sandy said.

I nodded. "Yes."

Fleener got up and walked slowly, ambled you might say, across the room to get coffee. He sat down, drank some coffee and said, "Now, what's Henri LaCroix doing at Bannister?"

"He's giving me a hand," I said.

"Looking for the Walloon Books?"

I nodded.

"LaCroix?"

"Yes."

"You got an Army Ranger, a trained killer who did tours in Iraq and Afghanistan searching for stolen books?"

"Yes."

"That's a little over the top, don't you think? A huge dose of overkill. And, Michael, watch your answer."

"A question first?" I said. "Serious question."

Fleener nodded.

"How you coming with the Sandoval case?"

Fleener adjusted the crease in his pants. "We're making progress."

"Any solid leads?"

"A few."

"But you haven't put it together?"

Fleener shook his head. "No, we have not."

"Okay if I take a stab at your problem?"

"Have at it," Fleener said with a wave of his hand.

"You got a body, a shot dead college professor. You got no gun, no motive. You don't even have a theory of the crime. You don't know if the murder's connected to Bannister or Petoskey or drugs, gambling, whatever. All you got's a body and pressure to solve the case."

I sat back in my chair. "How'd I do?"

Fleener took a deep breath and let it out slowly. "Closer than I'd like to admit."

"You remember what class Sandoval taught?"

"This has to do with the Hemingway books, does it?"

"Humor me."

"Science. Some kind of science, I think it was. Why?"

"Additive manufacturing," I said. "That's what he taught. Additive manufacturing."

Fleener said nothing.

"Know what that is?"

Fleener shook his head.

"3-D printing, Marty. The dead guy taught 3-D printing."

Fleener slowly moved his head to one side. Like he'd just remembered an important errand. I could almost hear the wheels turning.

"We didn't check," he said. "We missed that." Fleener reached for his mug and drank some coffee. "How'd you catch it, Russo?"

"Henri caught it," I said. "He was digging."

"No shit," Fleener said. "But that's not enough to link the murder and the robbery. If that's where you're going with this."

"Big coincidence, don't you think?"

"Small town, Michael. Smaller college. But we'll take a look."

"Did you know Lewis chaired two College committees?"

Fleener shrugged. "I'd have to check my notes, but, yeah, I think so."

"The Walloon Collection Committee and the Scholarship Committee."

"So?"

"Three people on each committee."

Fleener stared at me like he was waiting for the punch line.

I nodded. "One committee with the dead Dean Sandoval and Dean Caleb Reed from Education."

"Which committee?"

"Scholarship Committee, Marty. The three of them. The Scholarship Committee doles out money to deserving students who need help with tuition, books, that kind of thing."

"I'm listening," he said. The wheels turned a little faster.

"Did you know those same three guys own an expensive condo at Bay Harbor?"

Fleener shook his head.

"It's shielded behind two dummy companies, but they own it."

"Henri find that, too?"

"Uh-huh."

"You think they stole scholarship money to buy a condo? Then tried to hide it?"

"Maybe."

"Maybe?"

I looked over at Sandy, but I already knew what she'd say.

"Your call, boss," she said. "I say go for it. Tell him."

"The three Deans of the Scholarship Committee decided which applicants got money. Some female students were offered a deal. Say 'no,' they don't get money and are forced to drop out of school. Say 'yes' and the Deans take them to the condo."

Fleener was staring. At me.

"What are you saying, Russo? Be clear."

"It's blackmail, Marty. If you're female and need money to stay in school, you got to fuck a Dean. Money for sex."

"You can prove this?"

"Not yet. Don't have enough. Yet."

"What do you have?"

"Henri saw Lewis go into the condo with two different women on different days."

"Have you told anyone about this? Outside the office?"

"Asked Lewis about the condo," I said.

"Stop," Fleener said. "Hold on."

He pulled out his phone, tapped it several times and waited. He looked at me, started to talk, then said into the phone, "It's me. Put Don on." He listened. "I don't care if it's the fucking King of England. Get him."

Back to me. "This is nuts, Russo. We don't ..."

"Yeah, Don. Sorry to break in on your meeting." Fleener talked with Hendricks, quietly and to the point. "We're on our way."

He tapped his phone and put it in a coat pocket.

"She's a Queen, Marty," I said. "The Queen of England."

He ignored me.

"Let's go. He's waiting."

26

"All of it, Russo," Don Hendricks said. "Understand?"

We sat in the Prosecutor's office, me in front of his desk, Fleener on the sidewall with his chair tipped back against the wall. Two stacks of manila folders sat next to an old-fashioned telephone with lighted buttons. A keyboard and monitor sat on the other side. Hendricks had barely enough space for his elbows and a yellow pad. He took up all of it.

"From the top," he said.

I told him. Every detail. He made a few notes, but mostly he listened.

"Let me get this straight," he said. "You asked Lewis about the condo?"

I nodded.

"You never mentioned the girls, taking students to the apartment."

"No."

"You all but accused him of stealing the books."

"Not in so many words, but close enough."

Hendricks sat back. He thought for a minute.

"Nothing about blackmail? Or taking money from a College fund?"

"No."

"Then Lewis probably assumes you like him for stealing the books."

"Be my guess," I said. "Especially since I was sent out there to find the Collection."

Hendricks looked over at Fleener. "You got anything to add, Marty?"

Fleener let his chair come down to the floor quietly. "Not really, Don," he said. "But I've talked to Lewis a few times about the Sandoval case. He's no dummy."

"Meaning what?" Hendricks said.

"I think we have to assume Lewis is paying attention because Michael knows about the condo."

"What about that, Russo?" Hendricks said.

I shrugged. "Sure, why not? But he's got no reason to think I know more."

Hendricks pulled his tie loose and unbuttoned his shirt collar. He leaned forward on the desk.

"This isn't the first time you've heard about blackmailing the students, Don."

"Are you talking about the Harris woman?"

I nodded. "She's the one put me on this. She wasn't particularly happy with you."

"I knew that," he said. "But the woman came here with serious charges against prominent people ..."

"And no evidence," I said.

He nodded. "No evidence, nobody on the record, nothing. These are eighteen or twenty-year-olds. I can't push them around to file charges. I tried to explain that, but she wasn't having any of it."

"Well, she convinced me, Don."

"I can see that."

Hendricks flipped to a new page on his yellow pad.

"All right, gentlemen," he said. "Bannister started with robbery and ransom, then Sandoval's murder, now we might have blackmail for sex."

"It's stronger than 'might have,' Don," I said.

"I'm not arguing with you, Michael. But we need more. The question is where do we go from here?"

"We?" I said.

Hendricks smiled. He seldom did that. A mild grin's all you ever saw. He pointed at me and said, "Michael, you put us in this spot. You're going to help us get out of it."

"I don't want out," I said. "Can't get those kids out of my mind. A college scholarship's their ticket to a good job, a better life." I shook my head. "I remember when all you had to do was get good grades."

Hendricks picked up the desk phone and punched a button.

"Give me thirty minutes," he said into the phone. "No interruptions." He put the receiver down.

"Let's get to it."

27

"I thought we'd be done faster than that," Fleener said.

Our thirty uninterrupted minutes took ninety minutes. Luckily, Hendricks only got buzzed once, and we had the semblance of plan.

"You always think that, Marty," Hendricks said.

"Ever the optimist, Don."

"You first, optimist."

Fleener tilted his chair back on the wall. "Finding Sandoval's killer is my first job," he said. "Of course, it always was. When I talk to people now, I keep the students in mind."

"Be careful especially with Lewis and Reed," Hendricks said. "We don't want to tip them off."

"I graduated the academy, Mr. Prosecutor. I can handle these guys."

"Yeah, yeah. Be careful anyway."

"I'll get the lab people moving on Sandoval's computer."

"Can't imagine he'd be dumb enough to leave a Hemingway file on the hard drive," I said. "Be too easy to tie him to the robbery."

"It might not have to do with dumb, Michael," Hendricks said. "He might have gotten himself shot before he wiped the file."

"Either way," Fleener said. "I'll get it checked."

"See what you can come up with on Caleb Reed," Hendricks said. "His file's pretty thin."

Fleener nodded. "Okay."

"We assume Reed's involved until proven otherwise," Hendricks said.

"Henri's checking Reed out, Marty," I said. "I'll let you know what he gets."

"I don't want LaCroix working this," Hendricks said.

"He's already on it."

"Then tell him he's done," Hendricks said.

"Why?" I said. "I'll take all the help I can get."

"I told you before, Russo, trouble follows LaCroix. People have a way of ending up dead when he's around."

"You got somebody dead now." I leaned forward. "Besides, Don, he's dug up good information. He'll get more."

Hendricks looked over at Fleener.

"I don't like the guy any more than you do," Fleener said. "But Michael's right. He gave us some good intel."

"Okay," Hendricks said. "But here's the deal. Keep LaCroix on a tight leash. He's your responsibility, understand? He screws up just once, that's it. Any half-assed excuse, I'll throw him in jail. You too, if I feel like it."

"You're overreacting," I said. "This isn't two years ago, Don. No guns this time. It's a simple investigation."

"After the stunt you two pulled in Levering. Going after hired killers in my county. That was bullshit, Russo."

"Gentlemen," Fleener said. "Let's keep our eye on the ball, shall we. Look Michael, Don's right. Keep LaCroix in line. That or he's out. Agreed?"

"Agreed," I said.

"Can you live with that, Don?" Fleener said.

Hendricks moved his pen around a few times. "Yeah."

"Good," Fleener said. "Now where were we?"

Hendricks coughed. Twice. He looked over at Fleener. "You're all set then?"

Fleener nodded. "I am."

"Russo," Hendricks said. "You stay on the Walloon robbery. It may not be top of the list from here on, but it's your cover."

"Will do," I said.

"It's a good bet the robbery and the murder are linked in some way. If that turns out to be the case, we need to know who took the Collection."

"It would be nice to know why," Fleener said.

"Find out who, we'll know why," I said.

"You still think Margo Harris will cooperate?" Hendricks asked.

I nodded. "As soon as she finds out you're taking this seriously, she'll jump at the chance."

"The students?"

"I'll talk to Margo," I said. "She's got the best shot getting one of them on the record. No scared kid will talk to you guys. Probably not to me either."

"Bring me something I can use, and I'll go after these guys."

"Do my best," I said.

"Well, that's leaves me," Hendricks said. "I'll talk to Evelyn Malcolm. Carefully, of course. If she's as worried about Bannister's reputation as you think she is, I'll play on that."

Hendricks put the cap on his pen. "Is that it?" he said. "Can I get back to my day job now?"

He looked at Fleener.

"Done."

"Michael?"

"One last thing," I said. "What about Conroy?"

Hendricks shook his head. "That guy's a pain in the ass."

"Funny. That's what he says about you. Says he doesn't take orders from you."

"Makes you wonder who gives him orders."

"Word is he gets money and booze under the table."

"That from LaCroix?" Hendricks said.

I nodded. "Nothing on who's paying him off. I bet on Lewis."

Hendricks shook his head and sighed. "I've tried more than once to get that guy to act like a professional. You'd think he'd catch on."

"He might if he really was a cop," Fleener said.

"He's got a snazzy uniform, Marty," I said. "Big gun, too."

"Sheriff's deputies don't like him," Hendricks said. "Or the city cops."

Fleener laughed. "Yeah. They call him 'Wyatt Earp.'"

"What do I do if he quits hassling me and starts pushing?"

"If that happens," Hendricks said, "do what you need to do. I'd prefer you called a cop, Michael, but you might not have a choice."

28

Fleener dropped me at the office on his way out of town. I went upstairs and sat at my desk. Sandy was gone. Her note said, "Back soon. Lenny Stern called." Stern could wait. I pulled out my iPhone and tapped, "Can you talk?" to AJ.

The phone chimed faster than I expected given it was the middle of the work day. I looked at the screen and saw a small thumbs-up icon. I punched AJ's name.

"Hey, Michael."

"Hey, back. Glad I reached you."

"Is everything okay?" she said. "You're all right, aren't you?"

"I'm fine, AJ. Sorry. Didn't mean to sound like something's wrong."

"I always worry when the guy I love works a case with a body."

"That's very sweet."

"It goes with the territory," AJ said. "What up?"

"Haven't been to Chandler's in awhile," I said. "Want to go?"

"For dinner?"

"Uh-huh. What time works?"

AJ told me, and we agreed to meet. I swung my chair around and propped my feet on the window sill. As hard as it was, I'd accepted the idea that Lewis, Sandoval and maybe Reed were trading sex for scholarship money.

Two things bothered me.

For an arrest, let alone prosecution, we needed proof. That's where Margo Harris comes in. She's our best chance to get a student on the record. Maybe I'll think of something else. Maybe she will. Maybe it'll come out of thin air.

Sandoval is dead. His murder is likely tied to the Walloon robbery, Dean Lewis and blackmail. Need evidence for that too. The inescapable conclusion is that someone we've already talked to is a killer. Not a comforting thought.

I reached down and pulled open the bottom left drawer of the desk. Next to the tape dispenser was a Smith & Wesson .38 in a worn brown leather holster. In perfect working order. I'm a member in good standing at the Sportsman's Gun Club just south of Alanson. Practiced last week, in fact. AJ insisted I stay sharp.

I was going over a Probate Court file when the office phone rang.

I used my officious voice since Sandy was still out: "Michael Russo, Investigations."

"Good afternoon," a woman's voice said. "This is Camille Simmons, Secretary to the Board of Regents at Bannister College. I'd like to schedule an appointment with Mr. Russo."

"What would you like to see him about?" I said.

A moment's silence. "No, the appointment's not for me," she said, in a voice that signaled discovery of my unredeemable stupidity.

"For who then?" I said, refusing to use "whom."

"Oh, yes," she said, and chuckled. "Well, the appointment's for our Chair of the Board."

Uh-oh, I knew where this was going.

"Mr. Wardcliff Griswold. He'll be at your office tomorrow at ten."

"Let me see if I can pencil Ward in," I said.

"That's Wardcliff, sir," she said.

"Yes'um. Wardcliff tomorrow at ten. Tell him not to be late, will you? The boss is very busy."

"Aren't we all," she said, and hung up.

I put the receiver back and looked at my watch. Oops, I'm late. And I needed a drink.

walked up the block to Howard, crossed against the light and went into Chandler's. It was busier than usual. Crowded, in fact.

"Michael."

I turned to see AJ's smiling face at a four-top near the front window. She wore a navy two-piece suit with an ecru cotton shirt open at the collar. Business-like and attractive.

I leaned over and kissed her.

"Hello, darling," she said.

"Hello, back," I said and sat down. "They're busy tonight."

"Jack said it was a fundraiser for some group or other."

I looked over at the bar and waved at Jack. In his fifties, Jack was a fixture behind the bar. He smiled and pointed. I nodded.

"How was your day?"

"Good. Maury and I got lots done."

"The holiday issue?"

"Yeah," she said. "It's coming along."

Our waiter stopped at the table. "Good evening, Ms. Lester, Mr. Russo."

"Andrew," I said. "How are you?"

"Fine. Thank you for asking."

He put down a Chardonnay for AJ and Dewer's and rocks for me. "Jack caught your signal," he said. "No specials tonight because of the fundraiser."

"Is the kitchen backed up?" AJ said.

He shook his head. "Just don't order hors d'oeuvres, you'll be okay. Back in a few."

AJ reached across the table and took my hand. "What's new at the Prosecutor's office?"

I raised my glass. "Here's to the Prosecutor's office."

AJ tapped my glass. "Why are we toasting the Prosecutor?"

"We need some good luck," I said.

"Because?" she said.

While we sipped our drinks, ordered dinner and enjoyed being together, I outlined my earlier discussion with Hendricks and Fleener.

"You three are that certain it's an inside job."

"With Joey DeMio's help," I said.

"No better man to know these things," AJ said. "Anyway, you guys seem convinced that Sandoval's murder has got to be part of … of whatever the real crime is."

I sat back and looked at AJ.

"What?" she said with a wry smile.

"You're thinking like a reporter again."

"It's second nature, you know that."

"I thought being an insatiable lover was second nature?"

"That, too," AJ said. "Be serious, Michael."

Andrew arrived with a tray. "Rack of lamb for Ms. Lester," he said, and put a plate down. "Beef tenderloin, Mr. Russo. Enjoy."

AJ glanced at her dinner. "Which crime is the real crime, Michael?"

I cut into my tenderloin and ate a bite. Delicious and cooked to a perfect medium-rare. "Let's go backwards," I said. "Makes no sense to kill first and steal second. Does it?"

"The only way that works is if the two crimes are not related at all." AJ picked up a lamb chop and nibbled a bite.

"But we're sure they are related," I said. "The Walloon caper had to be first."

AJ nodded. "Did something go terribly wrong with the robbery and Sandoval got killed?"

"Or did something go bad between Sandoval and his fellow thieves after the robbery? We assume the thieves to be Lewis and maybe Caleb Reed."

"People kill for money, sex or revenge," AJ said.

I shrugged. "Five million bucks is a lot of money."

"If the ransom's ever paid."

"People who write ransom notes always think it'll get paid," I said.

"True."

"We don't know enough about sex and revenge," I said.

AJ pushed her plate aside and drank some wine. "Speaking of sex, darling."

"We were speaking of murder and ransom, I thought?"

"I changed the subject."

"Yes, you did."

"I remember when you always had sex on your mind," AJ said.

"Still do when I'm around you."

Before AJ could say a word, Andrew stopped to clear our table. We asked for the check.

"A quick question," AJ said. "Then we can go back to murder and mayhem."

"Shoot," I said. "No pun intended."

"Bullshit," she said, and smiled. "Your puns are always intended."

I raised my hands in mock surprise. "*Moi?*"

She let that go. "Will you spend the night with me?"

"Yes."

AJ nodded. "Good," she said. "Now finish your thought."

"It's Bannister College."

"What about it?"

"Lots of stuff bothers me," I said. I glanced around. The fundraiser folks were crowded around the bar and two large tables at the back of the room. No one cared what I had to say.

"Bannister has a terrific reputation," I said. "One of the best small colleges in the nation. It's a steady, dependable employer in Emmet County, its people are involved in the community." I looked up in the direction of the bar. Jack saw me and pointed. I shook my head and waved a thank you.

"But what, Michael?"

"It's hard to pin down," I said. "Bannister is a world unto itself."

"The 'ivory tower' cliché, you mean?"

I shook my head. "More than that," I said. "The people. I don't know, professors, staff, even polar opposites like the President and the Chief of Bannister Security."

"Pretty broad range of people you got there, Russo."

"I know, I know, AJ. But their perspective is always the best perspective. Life outside Bannister doesn't seem to measure up."

"Does this have anything to do with Lewis and Sandoval?"

"Yes and no," I said. "If I'm right about that, what I just said, the murder and robbery only made me more aware of that arrogant attitude. It wouldn't surprise me to hear Lewis rationalize trading sex for scholarship money."

"I hope you're wrong about that," AJ said.

"Me, too," I said. "Me, too. But not so sure I'm wrong."

AJ leaned on the table. "Do you remember," she said. "It was right after I moved to Petoskey, 2000 or 2001, I got a call from the Dean of Students. Remember that?"

I shook my head. "No. I was only ogling you back then, sweetheart."

"I was asked to join a taskforce to write a sexual assault policy on campus."

"Bannister didn't have one?" I said. "In 2001?"

AJ shook her head. "Eleven people," she said. "Two of us from off campus. It broke down into two factions, those in favor of a vigorous, clear statement …"

"Which included you."

"Of course," she said. "But we were a minority. The other group wanted a policy filled with generalities and platitudes."

"They had a reason, I'm assuming."

"Uh-huh. A policy of specifics would scare parents who'd see Bannister as a dangerous place and not send their daughters. They wanted to hide and hope rape would go away."

"Pretty screwed up, don't you think?" I said.

"I do think," she said. "Fortunately we prevailed and convinced one extra vote. We got the policy written and sent to the Regents for approval. That was almost twenty years ago, Michael. Has so little changed?"

I shrugged. "Can't answer that."

We sat quietly for a minute, comfortable with each other in the busy restaurant. "Let's go," she said. "It's time for me to play with your body."

"Something special in mind?"

"Kisses," she said. "Lots of them."

AJ paid the bill and we said good-bye to Andrew.

Outside, AJ said, "Did you walk?"

"Yep," I said. "Car's at home."

"Well, then, cute buns," she said, and smacked me on the fanny. "My car's right there."

30

"It's six-thirty," I said. "Don't you have to get moving?"

We were awake. The sun came through the blinds and put fine lines of light on the wall. AJ was cuddled up against my back, her right arm draped over my waist.

"In a minute," AJ said. "You?"

"Nothing 'till ten."

"Is that Griswold?"

"None other."

"Lucky you."

"Nah. Lucky was last night. Dinner and love making with a gorgeous woman. To think, it all started with good old-fashioned kissing."

"Like making-out in the back seat," she said, and giggled. "Did you ever do that, Michael?"

"No."

"Never?"

"I had an old Austin-Healey 3000. Two seat sports car. Be tough to … ouch! Why'd slap my stomach?"

AJ threw back the sheet and sat up. "You are impossible. You know that?"

"What'd I do?"

She got out of bed and stood there with her hands on her hips. "I swear I line up five sexy women as bare-assed as I am right now, you'd look at the sports car."

I need to think fast here.

"I only have eyes for you, dear," I said.

AJ picked up a pillow and hit me over the head. "Make the coffee, smart-ass. I don't want to be late."

I found my boxers in a mound of clothes near the bed and went to the kitchen.

I put my clothes from last night on, sat at the kitchen table and looked out on the ravine. Rain drops dotted the window. I set my iPad to the *New York Times*.

I'd finished my second mug of coffee when AJ walked in, filled a mug and sat down. She was dressed in a green and white silk dress. Her black hair glistened in the soft light.

"Just have to put some make-up on," she said. "Do you want a ride home?"

"Sure, thanks," I said. "It's already stared to rain."

"Wouldn't want you to melt, darling," she said. "You have to be all strong and rah-rah for Griswold this morning."

"Don't remind me."

She drank some coffee. "So you don't know why the arrogant ass's dropping by?"

I shook my head. "Not sure, I'll bet Lewis complained."

"Wow," AJ said, and got up. "You must be a private eye."

I looked up. "Don't you have to finish in the bathroom?"

"I'll be ready in a minute," she said and put her mug in the sink.

AJ dropped me at my apartment building. I took a shower, dressed in a fresh pair of khakis, a black polo shirt and scruffy deck shoes. Wanted to look all country clubby for my first appointment.

The warm rain was steady but light. I hung my jacket on the hall tree by the door. Sandy was at the courthouse this morning, so I made coffee and waited.

When I heard footsteps on the stairs, I went to the door. I opened it just as Griswold got there. I expected him to dress the part. He did not disappoint. The blazer was black with brass buttons, the polo shirt was white, the dark khaki slacks were perfectly creased. In a time of uncertainty, it's reassuring to know that some things never change. Wonder if that included Griswold's attitude?

"Mr. Griswold," I said. "Please come in."

"Thank you, Mr. Russo," he said.

"My office," I said, pointing to the open door behind us. Griswold went by and handed me his raincoat as if I were the cloakroom attendant. He took the client chair in front of my desk, pulled up his slacks to preserve the crease and sat down.

"What can I do for you, Mr. Griswold?" I said as I sat behind the desk. Wonder if I'll be surprised by his answer? Do I really care?

"Mr. Russo," Griswold said. "We got off on the wrong foot, you and I. Four years ago, the other day in President Malcolm's office ... it would behoove us to begin anew."

He hasn't changed the way he talked either.

"It would?"

"Most certainly it would, sir," he said. "I propose we cease with formalities and return to the familiar. Ward and Michael. But only if you approve, sir?"

"Return to the familiar?" I said.

"Yes," he said. "What do you say? Shall we be good chaps?"

Good chaps. He wants us to be good chaps.

"Certainly, Ward," I said. "Let's be good chaps. Call me Michael."

"I do hope, Michael, that I did not detect a hint of sarcasm in your voice. That would be an inauspicious beginning, to be sure."

A hint of sarcasm? Maybe he's brighter than I thought.

"No offense, Ward," I said and smiled. "Now what brings you here today?"

"I wanted to speak to you about Dean Roger Thornhill Lewis."

Uh-oh. I'm shocked. There must be gambling in the back room.

"What about him?" I said.

"You've had several conversations with him, have you not?"

I nodded. "Yes."

"For what purpose?"

I shrugged. "It's no secret that I'm investigating the theft of the Walloon Collection."

"Why Dean Lewis?"

"He chairs the committee responsible for the Collection," I said. "Knows the security procedures, people who staff the office. Seemed like a good man to talk to."

Griswold seemed fidgety.

"I also talked with the faculty members from the committee," I said. "But you already know that, Ward."

He sat up straighter in the chair, pulled the crease in his slacks again.

"Dean Lewis believes that you've been, well, unkind to him in your time together."

"Does he now?"

"Yes," Griswold said. "His very word, 'unkind.'"

I leaned forward and put my elbows on the desk. I'll look more serious that way. I know why Lewis wants me off his back. Wonder if Griswold knows why? Somehow, I doubt it.

"Ward, I'm trying to recover a very valuable collection of books. And not pay five million bucks in the process. I need information, answers, so I ask hard questions. If some people are annoyed, well, so be it. I was hired to do a job."

Griswold rearranged himself, again, in the chair. "Roger Thornhill Lewis is not 'some people,' as you put it. He's a respected member of America's literary community."

"Good for him," I said. "Good for Bannister. Still got a job to do, Ward."

His slacks got pulled again.

"Actually, Michael, Dean Lewis believes you've all but accused him of involvement in the theft of the Hemingway books."

"That's because Lewis helped steal the books."

"Your accusations are most certainly baseless," Griswold said. "Or charges would have been filed."

"Haven't got enough evidence for an arrest," I said. "But I'll get it, and Lewis will be charged."

"Do you have any idea what your unsavory snooping around campus is doing to Bannister College?"

"Basketball ticket sales dropping off, Ward?"

"It would help Bannister College if you took this situation seriously, Michael. Can't you see that?"

"What I see, Ward, is that you want me to go easier on Dean Lewis."

"Are you not capable, Michael, of seeing the larger picture? Seeing what's truly important?"

"Ward, this isn't the first time you've tried, unsuccessfully I might add, to obstruct an investigation. You did it four years ago after the Abbott murder, you tried it again last year."

Griswold shook his head. "This is more important than two men sitting in a shabby office," he said.

Shabby office? I resisted the temptation to give my room the once-over.

"Reputation is more important than any one man, Mr. Russo," he said.

It's back to "Mr. Russo." Not a good sign.

"We're just people, Mr. Russo. But Bannister College is …"

Griswold's voice faded off, like he'd been transported to some distant land far from Petoskey, Michigan.

"… is life itself, Mr. Russo," he said. "Are you incapable of understanding that?"

"Did it ever occur to you, Ward, that another attempt to obstruct an investigation will discredit the very institution you so desperately want to protect?"

"The only discrediting done here, sir, will be to your career."

"Is that a threat, Griswold?" Two can play this game.

"I don't threaten, sir," he said. "I do."

I stood up. "If you want a fight, Griswold, call for back-up, 'cuz you're going to need it. The last time you tried a bullshit stunt like this, you got your hat handed to you."

Griswold stood. He straightened the collar on his shirt, then the blazer.

"You have not heard the last of this, I assure you," he said. "Do you know what a restraining order is, sir?"

"I'm a lawyer, in case you forgot."

Wardcliff Griswold shook his head in that disdainful way I saw him use on servants in that big, beautiful Victorian house at Cherokee Point Resort.

"I plan to push the good Dean as much as I need to," I said. "Just so you know."

"The courts will have something to say about that."

"You better start with the Prosecutor."

"Why should I bother with a public servant like him?"

"Because he sent me to get the stolen books back," I said. "And that's what I intend to do." I came around from behind the desk.

"Get out of here, Griswold, before I throw you out."

He turned, took his raincoat and went down the stairs. Sandy came in the office a moment later. She carried a familiar paper bag.

"Hey, boss," she said. "Was that Griswold? Only saw the guy once a couple of years ago."

"What did you get at the bakery?" I said. "Missed breakfast."

"Tell me about Griswold first."

"Not a chance," I said. "I'll get us coffee. Bring the bag."

Two cinnamon sugar donuts and one almond Danish later, I'd given Sandy both substance and feel of my time with good ole Wardcliff.

"Where does he get off threatening you?" she said. "What was he trying to do?"

"Get me off the Walloon case."

"Or leave Roger Thornhill Lewis alone." Sandy drank some coffee.

"He's tried that before," I said.

"And you never listened," she said. "What's different this time? You think he knows about the scholarship fund?"

I thought for a minute. "No, Sandy. I don't think he knows. Griswold's a lot of things I don't like ..."

"Arrogant, condescending."

"For sure," I said. "But I don't believe even Griswold would condone blackmailing students for sex."

"Not even to protect dear old Bannister?"

"This isn't going away. Too many people know."

"I'd love to see a front page story in the *Post-Dispatch*."

I sat forward. "Hey," I said. "That gives me an idea. Lenny Stern."

"Lenny?"

"I owe him," I said. "He put me on to Sandoval and the students in the first place."

"Do you think he'd write a story?"

"Doesn't have to write one, exactly."

Sandy smiled. "But if a reporter roams around Bannister asking questions, people get nervous."

"Yes they do."

"And nervous people do stupid things."

"They do, indeed," I said.

"Certainly seems to be a lot of that on campus."

"Certainly does," I said. "Maybe, just maybe."

"Want me to call Lenny?"

31

"**W**hen are you headed back?" I said. When I reached Lenny Stern on the phone, he was in Sault Ste. Marie on business.

"Late afternoon," he said. "One more interview here, another in Mackinaw City. Thought I'd stop at Audie's for smelt since I'm there. Care to join me?"

We agreed to meet for dinner. That gave me enough time to read Sandy's report from court and write a response. "See you in the morning, boss," she said a little after five.

"Got plans for the evening?" I said.

She smiled. "Dinner, wine and a good book on the front porch."

"I should've guessed," I said.

"The rain's stopped," Sandy said. "Maybe I'll get a sunset, too."

"Hope the clouds go away," I said. "See you tomorrow."

I put my files in the top drawer of the desk and tapped my computer into sleep mode. My iPhone buzzed on the desk.

"Evening, Henri," I said. "Haven't talked in a long time."

"It'll be worth the wait," he said. "You running in the morning?"

"Planned on it, why?"

"I'll join you," he said. "I'm training for the Mackinac eight-mile. We'll talk."

"Okay," I said. "The parking lot at seven."

Henri clicked off and I slipped the phone into my pocket.

I grabbed my brief bag and rain jacket. I walked up Lake to Howard and turned left towards my building. A few holes of blue sky finally opened in the clouds that hung over the bay.

I beeped the door locks, put my bag and the jacket on the back seat and climbed in. Traffic was thick all over town, so I got in line at the light at Mitchell and waited to turn. Occasionally, I try to remember what it was like to live in a city that did not have peaks and valleys tied to the calendar. Resort towns explode with people in the summer. Everything takes longer, restaurants, Home Depot, turning at stoplights. But there's a rhythm to it I like. The rush of summer, the tranquility of winter. Not sure I'd like a year-round town anymore.

By the time I got to U.S. 31 north, I knew I'd be late. If this were winter, well, I'd drive faster, pass a car or two, all in the interest of arriving at my meeting on time. Honest, that's the only reason. But this is summer, and traffic on both sides of 31 is heavy enough to scratch that idea.

Almost sixty minutes later, I parked in front of the restaurant. Audie's has been around since the fifties, planted at the base of the Mackinac Bridge. Like Lenny Stern, AJ and I often stopped for breakfast or dinner on a trip to the Upper Peninsula. I went in the dining room side, to the bar next to the Chippewa Room.

"Russo." I looked through the divider near the door. Lenny Stern was at the bar, waving.

The room, called a lounge but I'm not sure why, is a rectangle with tables spread around the floor. The bar's on the left with comfortable, low chairs instead of stools. The walls are filled with a bevy of stuffed animals, large and small.

"How are you, Russo?" he said as we shook hands.

"Good, Lenny," I said and sat down in a low chair. "Thanks for meeting me."

"You drove up, Russo," he said. "I always stop here. Can't beat the smelt."

The bartender, a woman in her thirties, wearing a tight tank top and short skirt, stopped. "Hi, there," she said. "A friend of yours, Mr. Stern?"

"Guess so. My tab, Helen, whatever he wants."

"House Chardonnay, please."

She nodded. A moment later, she put a napkin and the wine in front me. "Enjoy."

I picked up my glass. Lenny grabbed his bottle of Heineken. "Thanks for the drink," I said. "What's the occasion?"

Lenny drank some beer and put the bottle down. "Since you called me, I assume you got information I want to hear."

"Suppose I don't?"

"Buy your own goddamn wine."

I laughed. "Deal," I said. "Don't think I'll need to."

Lenny moved his chair back, folded his arms over his chest. "Is that right?"

I nodded.

"Bannister College?"

I nodded.

"Lewis or Sandoval?"

I nodded.

"You gonna tell me, or just move your head again?"

I laughed. "Sorry. Just having some fun."

"Fun's over," he said. "Let's have it."

I moved my chair closer and leaned over. I told him about Lewis and Sandoval and the robbery.

"Jesus, Russo," he said. "I missed that. "How'd you find out he taught 3-D printing?"

"Henri found it. Bannister catalog of courses."

"Seriously?"

"Uh-huh."

Lenny loosened his tie and unbuttoned the collar. Never seen that before. He picked up the beer and drained the last of it. "Helen?" he said, and held the bottle in the air.

She put down a new beer and Lenny took a drink. He thought for a minute. "Murder and robbery have to be connected," he said.

I told him what Fleener and I knew and what we suspected. Lenny nodded again and again.

"Robbery came first," Lenny said. "Sandoval fucked up, got himself shot dead."

"Be my guess, too."

"It's not a guess, Russo. This is what I do. I've chased bigger fish than those twerps at Bannister. We need to find out what went haywire with the robbery."

"Or the ransom?"

"Or the ransom," he said. "It'll lead to Sandoval." He took another pull on the Heineken. "Good job, Russo. Have another glass of wine."

"There's more."

Lenny smiled. Seldom seen that either.

"Helen?" he said, and pointed at me. Helen got the wine bottle and filled my glass.

"The three Deans ..."

"Lewis, Sandoval and Reed."

I nodded. "The three own a condo at Bay Harbor."

He shook his head. I explained about the phony companies and the scholarship fund, Henri's tailing Lewis. All of it.

"So the rumors I heard about Sandoval and students are true?"

"Yes, I'm sad to say."

"I don't know, Russo. Can't figure how I missed two big pieces of this story. Two. Jesus, Russo."

"Don't be so hard on yourself, Lenny," I said. "Could happen to any-body. We got lucky, that's all."

"Lucky, my ass," he said. "You got lucky with smart work." Lenny looked up. "Do you think the woman, at Bannister ..."

"Margo Harris."

"Yeah, Harris. Think she'd talk to me? On the record?"

"Not sure," I said. "But she wants these guys in jail. I'll ask. See what she says."

"Think a student would talk to me?"

"That's a tougher one," I said. "After what Margo said, I wouldn't count on it."

"They got to be scared."

"Have to be," I said. "We don't even know who they are, Lenny.

"Could LaCroix describe them?"

"Probably. But what good's that going to do? We hang around campus 'till he spots one of them?"

"Could we contact a student who dropped out?"

"Officially? Probably not. Unofficially?" I shrugged.

"What about Harris?"

"Already thought of that," I said. "I'll ask her."

Lenny nodded. "Good. Do that," he said. "If we get one student on the record, we'll get more. If one cracks the fear, these things have a way of snowballing."

"We'll see what happens," I said.

Lenny leaned back in his chair. "Russo, you ought to be a reporter. You sure as hell dig like one. I owe you, my friend. Anything I can do, you let me know."

I smiled. "Glad you asked."

"I'm waiting."

"Go to Bannister," I said. "Be a reporter, be nosy, ask lots of questions."

"You want people out there to know I'm digging?"

"You bet I do," I said. "The more obvious, the better."

"Anybody in particular?"

"Leave that to you, Lenny. Do what you do."

"You want obvious?"

I nodded.

"How's about I start at the President's office?"

"You interview Evelyn Malcolm they'll all know it before you leave campus."

"You want to put the screws on."

"Exactly," I said. "I don't care if Malcolm talks to you or not. Who can't take the pressure, that's what I want."

I drank some wine and put the glass down. "Hell, Lenny, this is a good story. Let's see what pops."

"Speaking of my story, Russo. What about AJ?"

"Already asked her," I said. "Same deal as the Lake Street shooting."

"My print story, her digital go up at the same time?"

"Same time."

"That's good enough for me," Lenny said. We shook hands.

"Now," he said. "How about we order smelt?"

32

I sat on the couch in the living room, drank coffee and laced up my running shoes. It was six-fifty. I didn't feel much like scanning websites for news this morning. I was itchy to get into my run. Three days is a long time off for me.

Lenny Stern ought to shake things up. Especially with new leads for his story. I looked at my watch. Time to go. I went down the back stairs and looked for Henri. When he was in town, he stayed at the Perry Hotel on the other side of the parking lot.

The sun had a good start on the day. It was warm already, but the humidity did not return after yesterday's rain. Henri was stretching against a tree near my 335.

"Morning, Henri," I said. "I like your t-shirt." It read, "Mackinac Island 8 Mile, 2012."

"It's my inspiration," he said. "Bought the shirt last summer. It reminds me why I'm training."

"You carrying?" Henri often packed a small automatic under a loose t-shirt when he ran.

"No," he said. "Haven't been."

"How far this morning?"

"Five is good," he said. "Easy pace so we can talk."

"We'll take Rose to Arlington into Bay View. That okay?"

"Yeah," he said. "Let's go. Having breakfast with Brenda later."

We set our watches and took off. By the time we entered the Bay View summer colony, we'd warmed up. Tree lined streets filled with Victorian houses made the community a delightful place to run. It was early enough that traffic had not yet made the streets too congested for runners and walkers. Plenty of people were out doing both.

"How is life with Brenda these days?"

"Got to catch up on business first," Henri said. Which was his way of saying he didn't want to talk about it.

We dodged two moving vans parked in the middle of the street and resumed our pace. "Business it is," I said. "What's up?"

"Caleb Reed, for one."

"Let's hear it."

"Uneventful white, middle class life. Grew up in Willoughby, Ohio ..."

"That a burb of Cleveland?"

"Yep. East side. Went to Wright State. Ohio State for a Ph.D. in Education Administration."

My legs were loose and moving well in the warm air. Felt good. I glanced at my watch. Steady pace.

"He's single. Worked his way up. Jobs in small colleges around the Midwest led to Bannister."

"Hired as Dean of Education?"

"Yeah, 2014."

"Anything out of the ordinary?" I said. "Anything in his life make you suspicious?"

"Not until two days ago."

"What happened two days ago?"

"I caught him with a female student going into the condo."

"No shit?"

"Yep," he said. "Got a great photo of 'em, too. Sharp and clear."

I stumbled into a walk. "What did you say?"

"Come on, Russo," he said. "I'm training here. Get your ass moving."

I started up and fell in beside him.

"I said I got a good pic of Reed and a girl at Bay Harbor."

We kept moving while I digested what I'd just heard.

"You get photos of the students with Lewis?"

"Sure."

"Why the hell didn't you tell me?" I said.

"Planned to," he said. "Never got around to it, I guess."

"Good photos?"

"Of course, they're good," he said. Like I'd asked a foolish question.

"You got 'em with you?"

"My phone," he said. "At the hotel."

"Email them to me when you get back."

"Will do."

I tried to figure this out on the fly, so to speak. "I'll get Margo Harris. My office. I want you there. The pictures and your description might get us an ID on one of them."

We'd looped Bay View twice and headed back. We were on our time, but the streets were clogging up.

"Something else," he said. "You're not going to slow down again if I tell you?"

"Cut it out, Henri."

"Good source says the condo was bought with scholarship money."

I stayed with Henri, stride for stride.

"Your source say how they did it?"

"Great scheme," he said. "Grants and foundation money have a paper trail. They also solicited private contributions from the one-percenters. Harder to trace, easier to skim."

"All three Deans must be part of it then. They couldn't make it work any other way."

"Ready to slow up and walk," Henri said. "How 'bout you?"

"Your call."

After another quarter mile, Henri slowed to a walk. Still a lively pace, but walking. I clicked off my watch and fell in beside him. It was a good morning to run.

"Put a sharp forensic accountant on the scholarship fund," Henri said. "You'll find the money."

"Be my guess, too."

We slowed to an easy walk and took the back way to the parking lot.

I saw the big truck first. The black Tacoma blocked my BMW. Then I saw two men leaning against the driver's side of the truck.

Chief Wade Conroy and Deputy Floyd Jordan. In street clothes.

33

"The bigger guy," Henri said. "That Conroy?"

We walked slowly across the lot.

"Yeah. Other guy's a deputy. Jordan."

"Deputy's carrying," Henri said.

"A little obvious, don't you think?" The deputy wore a dark tan Carhartt jacket, zipped. On a warn July morning.

Henri and I separated a little as we got closer. They came off the truck and towards us.

"Hold it right there, Russo," Conroy said in that annoying drawl. We stopped. "I might be a good ole boy to you, but I know troublemakers when I see 'em."

Why did I remember "good ole boy?"

"We need to have us a talk, Russo, you and me," Conroy said.

Why did I remember that? "Good ole boy." I know. I called Conroy that the last time I saw Lewis.

Conroy looked at Henri. "Who might you be, boy?"

"Who's asking?"

"I am, asshole," Conroy said.

"That supposed to scare us?" Henri said. "Who are you?"

"Chief Wade Conroy," he said. "And Deputy Floyd Jordan."

"You don't look like peace officers to me," Henri said.

"Well," Conroy said, and grinned. "Just who do we look like?"

"Like a couple of overweight, overage assholes trying to roust us."

Jordan moved in two steps. "We got us a tough guy, Wade. Guy thinks he's tough. Got a smart mouth. How 'bout this guy?" The words came out rapid fire, like he was in a hurry.

"Jesus, Russo," Henri said, shaking his head. "This one sounds like Broderick Crawford."

"*Highway Patrol*," I said. "I love it."

"The fuck you talking about, boy?" Jordan said.

Henri laughed. "Old time TV. An overweight actor playing an overweight cop."

"Wade," Jordan said. "Think that's enough?"

"Hold on, Floyd," Conroy said. "Now, sir, I asked nice. Who are you?"

Henri wiped the sweat from his forehead and said, "You're dressed like tourists," he said. "This an official request?"

Conroy smiled. "Call it a friendly request."

Henri looked over at me. I nodded.

"Name's Henri LaCroix."

Conroy thought for a second. "Mackinac Island?"

Henri nodded. "Yeah."

"Heard about you, LaCroix," he said.

"Glad to hear it. I'm going for a shower. Nice to meet you." Henri turned away.

"Stop right there," Jordan said, pulling a short-barreled revolver from under his jacket. He pointed it at Henri. "We ain't done yet."

"Lower your weapon, Floyd," Conroy said.

"Asshole's disrespecting us, Wade."

"Listen to what the Chief's trying to tell you," I said. "You pulled a gun in the middle of town. In civilian clothes. The real cops might not like that."

"Put the gun away, Floyd," Conroy said. It took a minute for that to sink in, but Jordan lowered the handgun and slipped it under his jacket.

"Look, Russo, you're pissing folks off."

"You mean I pissed off Dean Lewis. That's why you're here, isn't? Lewis sent you."

"You're messing where you're not wanted. I'm giving you a chance. Take it."

"Tell the Dean I got a job to do. I'm telling you, too. One of these days, Conroy, the Sheriff's going to shut down Bannister Security and you with it."

"They can't touch us," Conroy said.

"Don't count on it," I said. "Guys like you give real cops a bad name."

"Consider yourself warned, Russo," Conroy said.

"Thanks a lot," I said. "Now why don't you move that truck of yours, or I'll call a real cop."

Conroy took in a lot of air and let it out slowly. "Let's go, Floyd." The two men moved a few steps backwards.

"Jordan." It was Henri.

Jordan stopped. Henri walked up to him, close.

"You ever pull a gun on me again, I'll kill you."

The Deputy didn't say anything, but the look on his face said it all.

"Floyd," Conroy said. But Jordan didn't hear him. "Floyd," he said again. "Let's go."

Jordan blinked like he'd just woken up. He glanced at Conroy, turned and went for the truck. They climbed in and drove out of the parking lot.

"Conroy heard you threaten to shoot Jordan."

"So what," he said. "Maybe I'll shoot Conroy, too."

"I heard you say it, Henri. You can't shoot me, I'm your lawyer."

"Besides, AJ'd be pissed," Henri said and smiled.

We walked over to the apartment building, near the back door. I turned on a hose and let the water run cold. I took a long drink and gave it to Henri.

"Why do you suppose Conroy showed up in broad daylight?" Henri said.

"It was Lewis," I said, and drank more water. "He was pissed when I upped the ante and told him I knew about the condo." I gave the hose back to Henri. "My guess, Lewis sent him."

"Why's Conroy take orders from Lewis?"

"Lewis pays him," I said. "Only reason that makes sense."

Henri looked at his watch. "Got to go, Michael."

"Right, breakfast with Brenda."

"I'll email the student photos soon as I'm out of the shower."

"Good. I'll get hold of Margo Harris."

"All right," Henri said. "Michael, that was your last 'get out of jail free' card from those guys, you know."

"Think a college Dean in a tweed jacket's going to order a beating?"

"You're not giving him much choice, Michael."

I took the back stairs to my apartment.

I made coffee and jumped in the shower. Henri's right. Lewis has fewer options if I keep pushing. He has to worry I'll find out about the girls, sooner or later.

I put on fresh plain-front khakis and a t-shirt that read "Petoskey" on the back. I added a lose fitting short-sleeve denim shirt. My hip holster's at the office. It's time to clip it on my belt.

34

"**D**espite what you and Henri think," Sandy said, "we're talking about college teachers here, administrators."

We sat in my office. Sandy sipped coffee from her usual chair on the wall. I had my feet on the desk and drank water.

"What's your point?" I asked.

"My god," she said. "They're professors and Deans, maybe even a President. We're talking about them like they were gangsters." Sandy put her mug on the desk. "Robbery, embezzlement, rape. Maybe murder. Almost makes Joey DeMio seem like a businessman."

"Not quite."

"Sure, sure," she said. "Do you think Wardcliff Griswold's part of the bunch, too?"

"Griswold's a pompous ass, Sandy, but that's a long way from robbery and blackmail."

"That's not what I mean, Michael," she said. "It's his attitude. You know what I think about Cherokee Point."

"Thoughtless, self-indulgent people who care only about themselves and protecting their turf. That about it?"

Sandy nodded. "Doesn't that sound like Bannister College? Deans embezzle scholarship money? Evelyn Malcolm protects her turf? Roger Thornhill Lewis abuses students?"

"I doubt Griswold'd condone abusing students."

"I certainly hope he wouldn't condone any of it," she said. "But he's a pro at protecting turf and fending off nosy investigators."

"Yes, he is."

Sandy looked at her empty mug. "You want coffee?"

"Maybe later," I said. "So where are we?"

"Petoskey, Michigan," Sandy said, and smiled. "'Up north' we call it."

"Sorry I asked."

"All right. Margo Harris will meet you and Henri, here, later this afternoon."

"Good."

"Dean Caleb Reed hasn't called back yet." Sandy folded her arms and got that curious look on her face. "You don't suppose he's dodging you?"

I shrugged. "Haven't got a clue."

"Maybe Lewis told him to stay away."

"Don't know," I said. "But it's possible."

"With this crew, anything's possible."

"You've made that quite clear," I said.

"I'm not being cynical, Michael."

"You sure?"

"Yeah, I'm sure. I'm not cynical, I'm disappointed. Bannister College is supposed to encourage intellectual growth and development. And what do we get? Bad people and ugly behavior. I'm angry, too, Michael. Because they might get away with it. I expect shit like that from Joey DeMio and his gang. But Bannister College?"

"Michigan State was never like this," I said. "That's for sure. Big campus? Lots of money for one thing or another?"

"You'd think it'd be easier to hide bad stuff in East Lansing," Sandy said.

"I'm not so sure, Sandy. It might be the other way around."

"Meaning?"

"Well, drop all those people and competing interests together, you don't have the same close relationships, the same overlapping responsibilities like you do at Bannister. People are much less tolerant of bad stuff in part because they don't know each other as well." I hesitated. "At least that's my theory."

"Yeah, Michael," Sandy said and shook her head, "But Bannister isn't supposed to be like this."

"No, it's not." There wasn't more worth saying.

Sandy stood. "Okay, boss. Enough for now. I've got two folders on my desk. You have to go through them before you meet Margo Harris."

35

"**M**ichael," Sandy said. "Dr. Harris is here."

I got up from my desk and went to the door.

"Margo. Good to see you."

"It's nice to see you, too, Michael," she said, and we shook hands. Margo wore a pale yellow man-tailored shirt over a white camisole and black jeans that fit very, very well.

"Come in," I said.

"Michael," Sandy said. "Henri'll be a few minutes late. Just got a text."

"Thanks."

Margo took a client chair and I sat down.

"Can I get you coffee or water, Dr. Harris?" Sandy said.

"Not yet, thanks. I just finished lunch. And call me Margo, please."

"I'll do that," Sandy said, and closed the door as she left.

"Thanks for coming over," I said.

"I admit I'm curious," she said. "Has something changed since we last talked?"

"As a matter of fact."

"This is about the Scholarship Committee, isn't it?"

I nodded.

"Looking at Lewis, Sandoval and Reed," I said.

"What about the books?"

"Haven't forgotten the Walloon Committee," I said. "But I'm focused on the Scholarship Committee right now."

I leaned forward with my elbows on the desk. "Because now we've got something to work with."

Margo almost smiled. "What happened?"

"First, I want you to know that Don Hendricks is on board."

"Seriously?"

"He remembered you," I said. "He admitted he didn't have enough to go on before. But if we give him something solid, he'll take it from there."

"Does he mean it?"

"You know who Martin Fleener is?"

Margo shook her head.

I told her about Fleener, the Collection and the murder.

"If I understand you," she said, "the Prosecutor and a State Police Captain think maybe it's all one case?"

"Exactly," I said. "And that's where you come in."

"Whatever I can do."

There was a soft knock at the door. It opened and Henri walked in. "Michael," he said. "Sandy told me to come in." He wore a black silk t-shirt over slate gray linen pants. A light jacket covered his shoulder holster and reminded me to dig mine out of the desk drawer.

Margo stood and reached out her hand. I introduced them and they shook hands.

"Can I interest anyone in coffee or water?" Sandy said from the door.

"Coffee, please," Margo said. "Black."

I went out to get water for Henri and me and Sandy brought coffee for Margo.

"Henri, Margo teaches at Bannister and she's the author of several successful novels."

Henri smiled. "Erotic romance," he said. "I know."

Margo turned towards Henri. "Really. You know about my writing?"

"Read the first four in the Victorian series," he said. "I liked *Memories of Love* best."

"That one didn't sell very well."

"It's a good story," he said. "Stronger characters, and you surprised me at the end."

"Did I. Well, that's interesting," she said, sipping coffee and looking over at Henri.

"Could we adjourn lit class long enough to talk about the bad guys?" I felt like I was interrupting.

Margo and Henri turned in my direction. That was nice of them.

"Margo, I wanted Henri here because he's the man I told you about. The one watching Lewis and Reed. Henri found the condo."

"How did you do that, Henri?" Margo said. "If you don't mind."

"Not at all," Henri said. "It's what I do. Pretty easy once you know how."

"Well," Margo said. "I am impressed."

Henri smiled. "Thank you," he said.

"Ah, can I jump in here?" I said.

"You bet, Russo," Henri said. "What do you need?"

"Margo," I said. "Had any luck identifying students who were black-mailed?"

"We know which ones dropped out, of course. You know about the one I talked to, and she won't file charges." Margo shook her head. "Sorry, that's the best I could do."

"I did better," Henri said. "I took photos."

"What do you mean, you took photos?" Margo said, clearly surprised.

"Three girls went into the condo," he said. "Two with Lewis, one with Reed."

"Seriously?"

"Yeah," Henri said. "Took photos of each girl. And separate photos of them at the building entrance."

"It's going to be hard for those guys to talk their way out of that," Margo said.

"That's the general idea," Henri said and smiled.

I pulled out my iPad and tapped the screen. "Here," I said, and stood the screen up so we could take a look.

"First three are close-ups," Henri said. "See if you recognize the girls."

Margo scrolled through the photos. "Don't know her," she said, pointing at the first image.

"Her I know. Name's Elizabeth Vanwall. She goes by Liz. She's in my writing class this semester."

I wrote down the name.

Margo moved to the last photo. "Sarah ... Sarah Kaufmann. Pretty sure it's Sarah Kaufmann."

"A student from last year?" Henri said.

Margo shrugged. "Probably two years ago." She looked up. "I'll double check and get back to you."

"Elizabeth Vanwall," I said. "At least we got one. You know her very well? Well enough to talk to?"

Margo sipped coffee and thought for a minute.

"Confront her," Margo said. "That's what you really mean, isn't it?"

"Yeah. Guess so."

Margo put down her mug and said, "It doesn't matter. I have to do it. But me first. Not you, not the cops. Agreed?"

"Yes," I said. "She's going to be embarrassed and scared."

"I'll figure it out," Margo said. "I'll talk to her."

"I don't want to sound harsh," I said, "but you need to do it as soon as you can. Those guys aren't going to stop."

"I know," she said. "Aren't the pictures good enough for the cops?"

"Maybe," I said. "A witness who'd file charges is much better."

Margo took a deep breath. "What do we do if this doesn't work? Can they get away with it?"

"If we have trouble," I said. "How would you feel about talking to a reporter? I know a guy, writes for the *Post-Dispatch*. He's good, knows his job."

Margo shook her head. "Not yet," she said. "If I have no other choice, I'll consider it. Those bastards have got to be stopped."

"They'll be stopped," Henri said. "One way or the other. Only a matter of how and when."

I knew what Henri meant. I doubt that Margo did. Probably just as well.

"All right," I said. "Margo, you'll get with Elizabeth Vanwell? And get back to me?"

"I will," she said.

"Henri, you'll stay on Lewis and Reed?"

"Yeah," he said. "It's easier now. They're predictable."

"Predictable?" Margo said. "I'm not sure I understand."

"Most people are very predictable," Henri said. "Follow somebody for a few days. Same route to work, same time, same restaurants, gas stations. That kind of thing."

"So if you followed me for a week," Margo said, "I'd be predictable?"

Henri nodded. "Be more fun than Lewis."

Margo took her mug from the desk, but put it back down without drinking any coffee.

"Henri," she said. "You said you read the Victorian series?"

"The first four."

"Would you offer a brief critique?"

"Lots of sex."

Margo smiled. "Erotic romance."

"Repetitive."

"Of course," Margo said. "That's why I sell so many books."

"A proven formula."

Margo nodded. "It worked for Howard Hawks and John Wayne."

"Rio Bravo."

"El Dorado," she said.

I think this is still my office. Sure looks like my office.

"Michael." It was Henri. "Are we done?"

"We are," I said. "Thank you."

"Which way are you headed?" Henri said to Margo.

"The parking lot out back. I'm on my way home."

"I'll walk with you."

"I'd like that," Margo said.

The three of us said our good-byes. Margo and Henri left together.

I got up and went out to Sandy's desk. I sat in a chair by the big windows.

"What?" Sandy said. "The look on your face. What is it?"

I smiled. "Henri and Margo Harris."

"What about them?"

"Our meeting? I think it was their first date."

Sandy laughed and clapped her hands. "No kidding? How cool is that?"

"If you say so."

"Come on, boss," she said. "This case is getting to you. Enjoy the moment. Romance is fun, remember?"

I raised my hands in the air in mock surrender. "Okay, okay."

"Here," Sandy said and picked up a slip of paper. "Dean Reed called back. He'll see you tomorrow. His office."

I took the note. "Same building as Lewis."

"AJ called, too."

"She called?" I said. "She never does that."

"She didn't want to interrupt you," Sandy said. "She'll meet you after work. Palette Bistro."

I looked at my watch. "Got time to run, if I get moving."

"Have fun, boss."

36

"**H**ow cool is that?" AJ said.

"Sandy said the same thing."

AJ smiled. "Smart women think alike."

We met at Palette Bistro on Bay Street, an easy walk across the parking lot from my office. The restaurant has a contemporary feel on its two floors. Tourists preferred tables near the tall windows overlooking Little Traverse Bay. That was fine with us. We usually chose the bar near the front door. We drank Chardonnay and shared a Mushroom Crostini at a tall table in the window.

"I almost felt like I was in the way," I said. "Good thing we got our work finished."

"Did Margo recognize any of the students?"

"One for sure," I said. "Maybe a second."

"Good job, there, Sam Spade," she said. "What else?"

I offered AJ a detailed rehash of my afternoon with Margo and Henri. Always a reporter at heart, a "detailed rehash" saves me answering a lot of questions.

"She'll be scared," AJ said. "The student."

"She ought to be scared," I said. "This is a big trouble."

"Can it be any worse than having to screw a sleaze bag?"

"But it'll all be public. Parents, friends, teachers." I ate a bite of Crostini. "Accuse prominent men at a respected institution of assault and blackmail? She'll be hit hard over and over again. How do you cope with that?"

AJ shook her head. "I don't know, Michael. Hell, I'd be scared doing the same thing and I got a lot of back-up."

"Like Henri and me," I said.

"You guys, sure. Maury'd give me whatever I needed, lawyers, time off. I have my professional standing in the community."

"But you'd still be scared?"

AJ nodded. "Women are socialized, Michael. You know that. Sit down, shut-up, don't make waves."

We sat quietly for a minute. AJ ate the last of the Crostini and we ordered another glass of wine. She put her hand on mine and squeezed gently.

"Are you frightened?" she said.

"Me? No, I don't think so. Angry, sure. More than scared."

"An awful lot of people will rush to defend Bannister," AJ said. "Lots of important alumni. Evelyn Malcolm has connections in Lansing and Detroit. Even that cop, Conroy, acts tough."

"I get that, AJ," I said. "After the charges are filed, we'll be in good shape. Once the sheriff and Don Hendricks are involved, I doubt there'll be anything to worry about."

"Then tell me why you put the gun on your belt?"

I'd almost forgotten that I took it out of the desk before I left the office.

"Henri thinks Conroy has upped the ante," I said. "That next time, he'll back it up."

"What do you think?"

"Hard to argue with Henri," I said. "But Conroy won't act on his own. We're sure he takes orders from Lewis."

"What's your point?"

"Lewis isn't Joey DeMio, and Conroy isn't Rosato or Cicci."

"It doesn't mean they can't hurt you, Michael," she said. "Look at the damage they've done already. They'd try to save themselves?"

"I know."

"They don't have to be the mob," AJ said. "Lewis just has to be desperate enough. When you and Henri're on the same page ..."

"There's no point arguing with us?"

"No point at all."

Bay Street was busy with visitors enjoying another warm July night. Lovers holding hands, parents laughing with their children, people staring at a map. None of them aware of the evil just below the surface of Petoskey's most trusted institution.

"Your appointment with Dean Reed is tomorrow?"

"Tomorrow morning, yeah."

"Are you still hungry, Michael?"

"Sort of. Why?"

"Let's go to my house," she said.

"I'm hungry for your sexy body," I said.

"I was thinking popcorn and a movie."

"What movie?"

"*All the King's Men.*"

"Willie Stark lives," I said.

"Nothing like a tale of political corruption on a nice summer evening."

"Darling," I said. "You're such a romantic."

"Pay the tab," she said. "Let's go home."

37

"Morning, boss," Sandy said. "Have a nice evening?"

I sat at my desk, feet up, drinking coffee. Hard at work reading the *New York Times*.

"When's the last time I got to the office before you did?"

"Who cares?" she said. "Did you and AJ have a nice time?"

"Popcorn and a movie at home."

"Sounds wonderful," she said, and smiled. "Especially if I was snuggled up with someone I love."

Sandy was right about that. Especially that.

After the movie, I'd walked home under a clear night sky. I cut around the Perry Hotel to get a better view of the bay. Lights in the houses across the water at Harbor Point twinkled like stars in the sky. Peaceful and calm.

"Michael," Sandy said from her desk. "Captain Fleener, on the land-line."

I picked up the phone. "Hey, Marty. What's up with the State Police this morning?"

"The lab finished with Sandoval's computer."

"That so."

"Guess what we found?"

I dropped my feet off the desk and sat up. He had my attention. "I'm waiting."

"A file for the Hemingway covers," he said.

"Is that right?"

"Yep. Took our tech guy a few minutes, he found it hidden behind three dummy files."

"Good work," I said.

"I matched the list of stolen titles against the 3-D covers in the file," Fleener said. "They're all there."

"Think Sandoval was that stupid, to keep the file?" I said. "Or did he get himself shot first?"

"Not sure it matters," Fleener said. "But it's another detail linking the murder and the robbery."

"By the way, Marty, did you get my email on Caleb Reed?"

"Uh-huh," he said. "That intel come from LaCroix?"

"Henri does good work, Marty."

"He's a trained killer, Russo."

"You can thank Army Ranger School for that," I said.

"Our tax dollars at work."

"Find anything about Reed interesting?" I said.

"Seemed like a boring academic life. First in the family to get a college degree. Any degree, let alone three of them."

"Usually academics come from a long line of academics," I said.

"Not this time," Fleener said. "Reed comes from a long line of Tennessee sharecroppers, 'till they moved to Ohio. Reed's father took a job at an old GM plant near Cleveland."

"Thanks for the heads up on the computer, Marty."

"I emailed you a copy of the file."

"Before I forget," I said. "Any follow-up on ransom demands?"

"Not a word."

"Odd, don't you think?"

"Yep. Take a look at the file, Russo," he said and hung up.

I moved over to my keyboard, tapped a few keys and brought up my inbox.

"Hey, Sandy," I said. "Come look at this."

Sandy walked in and went behind my desk. I scrolled though the file.

"Wow," she said. "*For Whom the Bell Tolls, A Movable Feast.* If I didn't know those could be real covers."

"That was the plan," I said.

"I've read them all. Some more than once."

"Me, too," I said. "But I always liked Fitzgerald better."

"Is that because the 'rich are different from you and me,' by any chance?"

"Very funny," I said. "You got a favorite?"

"Between Hemingway and Fitzgerald?"

I nodded.

"I like them both," she said. "For different reasons. I love Hemingway's adventure stories, but I get tired of the testosterone overload."

Sandy tapped my shoulder. "Michael, look at the time. You're going to be late for your meeting with Dean Reed. Get a move on."

I got out of my chair and grabbed my brief bag. "Speaking of testosterone. Next stop campus."

"Yeah," Sandy said. "I got an idea or two how to deal with that, you ever want to listen."

38

I walked quickly back to my building and got in the 335. I made it through the light at Howard and Mitchell on the first try. Bet that doesn't happen again 'till October. I went north out of town and ten minutes later, drove onto the Bannister campus. I followed Linton Road around the circle and pulled into my favorite parking lot behind Morrell Hall. I spend much more time here, I ought to qualify for a parking permit.

I climbed the stairs to the third floor. It was obvious the painters hadn't shown up since my last visit. Reed's office was at the other end of the hallway from Dean Lewis. The door was ajar, so I knocked and went in.

The decorators hadn't scheduled Reed's office either. It was a small room, about half the size of Lewis' office with one large window overlooking the parking lot. Floor to ceiling bookshelves lined two walls, but almost as many books, journals, and newspapers were stacked on the floor and on a small square table shoved into one corner. An old wooden desk, scratched, marked and stained by many a coffee mug sat back near the window.

Dean Reed stood. "Thank you for coming over," he said. Funny, I called him for this meeting.

We shook hands. "Have a seat," he said, pointing at a gray metal card table chair in front of the desk. He spared no expense.

Reed was sixty-one, five-eight, about one-forty-five. His hair, what there was of it, was brown and buzz cut. He dressed more casually than his colleagues in an open collar button down shirt, tiny red and white checks, blue jeans and blue Nike running shoes.

"Now, Mr. Russo," he said. "This is about the missing Walloon Collection, is it not?"

Reed didn't look at me. His eyes moved, here and there. Not sure what he looked at exactly. Nothing new in this room but me. He was uneasy, fidgety. Wonder why?

"Stolen, not missing," I said. "The books're being held for ransom, remember."

"Right, right," he said. "Ransom. Right." Be tough to take a class from this guy if he's always this nervous.

We spent the next fifteen minutes or so discussing details of the Walloon Collection I already knew. I tried to put Reed at ease before I hit him with tougher questions. It didn't work.

I decided it was time to move on when we heard a knock at the door. It opened, and Roger Thornhill Lewis came in.

"Gentlemen," Lewis said. "Don't let me interrupt."

You just did that, Rog.

"Caleb, I wanted to remind you of the steering committee meeting. One-thirty sharp. Ta-ta, gentlemen," Lewis said and backed out the door.

Reed seemed frozen in place. This guy couldn't have been more surprised if the cops had come through the door.

"Well," Reed said. Didn't know a one syllable word had so many syllables. "Where were we, Mr. Russo?"

"I was asking questions," I said.

"About the Collection."

"I want to know about the Scholarship Committee."

"What? Why? Why do you want to know about that?"

"Purely routine," I said. "It came up in the course of my investigation." I sounded like Lennie Briscoe.

"Okay, I guess," he said. "What do you want to know?"

"How does the committee work, you know, how do you select the students who receive scholarships?"

Reed described the committee's procedures in more detail than I asked for. He was laser focused on detail. That didn't help his nervousness.

"Do you ever threaten to pull a scholarship?"

"Well, threaten is not a word I'd use," he said, almost indignantly. "But, yes, we warn students if their scholarship is in jeopardy." Reed moved around in his chair. "Academic difficulties, trouble with the law, that kind of thing can lead to a reassessment of eligibility."

I tried without success to get comfortable in my card table chair.

"Is scholarship money ever used for any other purpose?"

"Well," Reed said. "Operating expenses are about two-percent. Is that what you mean?"

"I was thinking more along the lines of a condo at Bay Harbor."

Reed sat a little straighter, a little more indignantly. "I am aware that you know about ownership of our condominium."

I'd only guessed that Reed and Lewis had been talking. Nice of him to confirm it.

"I'm curious," I said. "Why'd you buy the condo? Is it a guy thing, you know, hang out with the boys, watch football, smoke cigars?"

"I don't see that's any of your business, Mr. Russo," he said.

"Costs a lot of money," I said. "Bay Harbor."

Reed leaned back in his chair and said, "Well, it can't do any harm. We bought it as an investment."

"Like a rental property?"

Reed smiled. I'd saved him having to think up another answer.

"Why, yes," he said.

"You know," I said. "I got this dumpy apartment downtown. It's time I moved up, you know? Man of my stature. How much a month?"

"Well, um, sir ..." The smile vanished.

"Is it a one-year lease? Two? How much is the security deposit?"

"I ... I'd have ..."

"Did you guys use money from the scholarship fund to buy the condo?"

That stopped him cold. "What are you implying, sir?"

"That you used Bannister money to buy your man cave."

Reed stood. "How dare you come here and accuse me of stealing.

I shook my head. "No, Reed," I said. "If I did that, I'd accuse you and Lewis of stealing the Walloon Collection first."

"What right do you have to pry into my private life?"

"Funny," I said. "Lewis wanted to know the same thing."

"It's time for you to leave," he said, coming around the desk and throwing open the door.

"How 'bout that. Lewis said that, too."

I climbed out of my less than comfy chair and met him at the door.

"I'll be back," I said.

I left and Reed slammed the door. I glanced down the hallway towards Lewis' office as I went for the stairs. The arrogance of these guys. I hope Margo Harris is wrong. I hope they don't get away with it.

39

"**H**ave you talked with Margo Harris?" Sandy said.

I sat near the window that overlooks Lake Street. The rain came down but with no wind. Predictably, tourists jammed the sidewalks. They wore colorful parkas with hoods pulled tight. Henri was in the chair next to me and Sandy sat at her desk, nibbling on a brownie.

I shook my head. "Didn't want to seem like I was pressing. She knows we have to move on this."

"We have to get the girls out," Sandy said.

"That's only the first step," I said.

"Maybe you should have told Reed you had pictures?"

"I didn't want him to know. Not yet. Same goes for Lewis. Want to run it by Fleener first," I said, and stopped. "Wasn't Marty supposed to be here?"

"He said he would be," Sandy said. "Want me to call?"

I shook my head. "Give him a few more minutes."

"We have to make sure the students are safe," Henri said. "So Lewis or Reed can't get to them."

"You think they're in danger, Henri?"

"Can't take that chance."

Sandy finished her brownie. "I hope Margo calls soon."

"About Margo," Henri said. "I need to be careful. I'd rather not mix business and pleasure ..."

"How is the budding romance?" Sandy said.

"Budding romance?" Henri said.

"That's what I said."

He glanced my way.

"Don't look at me. I'm staying out of this."

"All I want to say, all I'm comfortable saying, is that Margo talked with her student …"

"Vanwall?" I said.

Henri nodded. "Twice. She ID'd the other students."

"Both of them?" I said.

"Yes."

We heard footsteps on the stairs. We waited.

"Sorry I'm late," Martin Fleener said when he came through the door. He eased his way out of a wet trench coat and hung it on the hall-tree.

"Michael," he said. "LaCroix."

"Captain," Henri said.

"Okay if I get coffee, Sandy?"

"Of course."

Fleener filled a mug and pulled up the last client chair.

I paused for a second. "Henri, Marty, will you guys call a truce until we get these guys and the girls are safe?"

"As long as our ground rules still apply," Fleener said.

"Seems hardly fair I can't shoot anybody," Henri said.

"Can it, Henri," I said. "Now what do you say?"

Henri nodded and Fleener said, "Deal."

"All right," I said. "Before you came in, Marty, we were talking about making sure the students were safe."

I caught Fleener up. "Seems to me the pictures are evidence of crimes worse than robbery and embezzlement."

"I would think so," Fleener said. "From what we know."

"It's your call, Marty," I said. "You want to check with Don first?"

Fleener shook his head. "He said I can play it as I see it. But he wants to know if any of the students will come forward."

"Me, too," I said.

"Lewis and Reed'll circle the wagons no matter what we do next," Henri said.

"I bet they've already started," Sandy said.

Fleener got up, refilled his mug and walked to the window. It was still raining. He sat on the window ledge and said, "Here's what you're going to do, Michael."

"I'm going to do?" I said.

"Yes, you," Fleener said. "Let them circle the wagons. Throw a scare into them, see what happens.

Nothing specific about the girls or the pictures, but tell them you got enough for the cops."

"Be easier to shake Reed," I said.

"Why?" Fleener said.

"You talk with Reed lately?"

Fleener shook his head.

"Reed can be bluffed. Lewis thinks he's smarter than everyone else, but Reed can be bluffed."

"Then it's Reed," Fleener said. "The sooner the better."

"Okay," I said. "What about Conroy?"

Fleener shrugged. "I don't care about Conroy."

I glanced at Henri. He was stone-faced.

"What I do care about are those girls," Fleener said. "Have you called Margo Harris?"

"I didn't want to pressure her, Marty."

"Too late for that," he said.

Fleener put his mug next to the coffeemaker and got his trench coat. "Thanks for the coffee, Sandy."

"You're welcome," she said. "Anytime."

"We can't predict what those guys'll do, Russo. The train's left the station. Call her."

Fleener tugged on his coat and went out into the rain.

40

"**W**ant me to call Margo?" Sandy said.

Henri was still in his chair. Me, too.

"Yeah," I said. "Give her my cell if you don't get her."

"Where are you going?" Sandy said.

"See if I can find Reed."

"Think he's in his office?" Sandy said.

"Don't know where he is," I said.

"He's in class," Henri said as he flipped through pages in a pocket-sized notebook. "Teaching."

"Teaching?"

Henri nodded. "Knowledge Literacy Policy."

"What's that?" Sandy said.

Henri shook his head. "Beats me," he said. "Too many nouns. It's his only class. Three days a week."

"How'd you find that out?" Sandy said.

Henri stared at her for a moment.

"Never mind," she said.

"Where is he?" I asked.

"Olds Hall," Henri said. "Third building on the right when you turn onto campus."

I looked at my watch.

"He'll be there for awhile," Henri said. "Likes to talk with his students after class."

"How thoughtful."

"Uh-huh," Henri said and stood up. "See you later. I'll be around."

Sandy waved at me with the phone in her hand.

"What?"

"Harris on line one, boss."

I nodded and went to my office.

"Margo. How're you?"

"Okay, I guess" she said. "This is difficult, Michael."

"Yes, it is."

"I never imagined … they're just girls, kids. I don't know what I imagined actually," she said. "Don't misunderstand. I want to get those bastards. Whatever it takes. This caught me off guard, that's all."

"Things are moving on this end," I said. "I need to know where you are with your student."

"Liz Vanwall, yeah. I've talked with her a couple of times. She identified the other two in the pictures."

"Tell me their names." She did and I made a note for later.

"Can you get contact information for all the parents?"

"Unofficially, yes," Margo said.

"Good. Do it."

"She's scared, Michael. And I don't blame her."

"Me either," I said. "You told her we'd get her safe?"

"Sure, but I'm not certain she understands what that means. I'm not sure I do."

"Leave that to Henri and me," I said. "Think she'll meet with me or Don Hendricks?"

"You, a good chance. Hendricks or the cops, no. Not yet anyway."

"Think it'd be okay if Henri's there when we talk to her?"

"I'll tell her about Henri, let her decide. Is that okay?"

"Sure," I said.

"I should know more soon," Margo said.

I hung up and went to the outer office.

"What do you think?" I said to Sandy.

"About the girls?"

"Uh-huh. Will any of them press charges?"

"You're asking me to think like a twenty year-old?"

I shook my head. "Like a rape survivor."

Sandy straightened up in her chair. I've known Sandy Jefferies for more than a decade, but she only told me she was a survivor four years ago.

"It isn't the same, I know, but …"

"It's still forced sex," Sandy said. "No power, no control. Why doesn't matter."

"No, it doesn't."

Sandy leaned back and folded her arms. "She's scared. Scared she'll get beaten up, hurt by those guys."

"Henri and I won't let that happen."

"I know that, Michael, because I know you. But the kid doesn't know you."

"No, she doesn't."

"She's scared about the scholarship, too. Lose the money, school's gone."

"We should be able to help with that, too."

"But you can't do a damn thing about being scared when her parents find out."

"Her parents?"

"She'll be embarrassed," Sandy said. "How do we help her with that?"

I shook my head. "I don't know."

"That's what you have in mind, isn't it?" she said. "Have the parents take their daughters home, or someplace, until this is all over."

"Something like that, yeah."

"It has to be all three, you know, even if only one testifies. You can't leave even one of them out there. Not unless Lewis and Reed are in jail."

"I know." I sighed and ran my hands down my face. "I think I need to work through it again."

"As many times as you have to," she said. "Just get it right. Those girls don't deserve to be preyed on again."

"No, they don't."

"Margo's surrounded by college kids every day," Sandy said. "Run it by her, see what she says."

I nodded. "She must know them pretty well."

"What do you have to lose?"

Sandy sifted through some papers on her desk while I sat quietly and watched the rain pelt shoppers on Lake Street.

"Michael?" Sandy said.

I turned away from the window. "What?"

"Dean Caleb Reed, remember?"

41

Traffic on Mitchell moved quicker than I expected. I drove onto campus and watched for the third building on the right. Olds Hall was a four-story faded red brick rectangle with a center entrance and a parking lot in back. Wonder if the same architect designed all the old buildings around the circle road?

The lot was almost full, so I parked in a spot marked "faculty only." It was closer to the door. I got out, beeped the locks and dodged raindrops until I went in the large double-door rear entrance. Room 138 was four doors down the hall. Some enterprising student had carefully etched an additional "1" in the carved wood sign above the door, so it read, "1138." A George Lucas fan, no doubt.

The door was open. The room was square with tall, skinny windows on one wall, green chalkboards on two walls, and one-arm desks scattered around the tile floor. Several students, some sitting, some standing, chatted with Caleb Reed over by the windows. I sat in a desk near the door and waited.

Reed focused on his students. I waited almost ten minutes before he did a double-take after he caught sight of me. He stood up and said something to the students, who laughed as they looked over at me. I smiled and waved.

Reed came over as the students filed out. He was not smiling.

"Mr. Russo," he said. "To what do I owe this visit to my classroom?"

Seemed congenial enough. I doubt he thought it was a social occasion.

"Thinking about a career in teaching. Wanted your opinion."

"No, really," he said. "Why are you here?"

No point beating around the bush. Fleener said it was time to take the gloves off.

"We need to talk."

"This room's empty next hour."

"Sit down," I said and pointed to a desk.

"Are we going to be here that long?"

"Sit."

Reed moved a desk and slid into the open side.

"You're in big trouble, Dean Reed."

"That so?"

"Thought I'd give you a heads up. In case you want to talk to the Prosecutor before the cops come calling."

Reed got fidgety. The desk must have felt too tight. He tried to laugh. It didn't help.

"What would Chief Conroy want with me?"

I shook my head. "Not him, Caleb. Real cops. Michigan State Police."

"Now why would the State Police have any interest in me?"

"Let me lay it out for you, Caleb," I said. And make it up as I go along.

"Why don't you do that, Mr. Russo." He tried to sound confident. It didn't work any better than laughing.

"Here's what we know," I said. Or think we know and hope we can prove. "You, Roger Thornhill Lewis and the late Dean Tomas Sandoval stole the Walloon Collection and are holding it for ransom."

"We did no such thing." Indignant.

"Yeah, Caleb, you did. Sandoval made 3-D copies of the Hemingway books, put them on the shelves. Clever idea, if you ask me. You guys needed money, to cover the condo at Bay Harbor. Probably other things. Couldn't you steal more money from the Scholarship Fund, or did you all get greedy?

Reed was quiet.

"Or maybe Sandoval got greedy, so you killed him."

Reed stood up so fast the side arm of the desk caught his right hip. "That's it," he said. "Get out of here."

"Which is it?" I said. "Did you all get greedy or just Sandoval?"

"Get out," he said. "I'm not listening to any more of this."

"Tell that to the police when they come for you."

Reed picked up his umbrella and briefcase. He glared at me as he left the room.

It'd been a long time since I sat in a real classroom. This one felt more like undergraduate days at Michigan State than law school in Ann Arbor. It was a good feeling.

My phone buzzed. I pulled it from my pocket.

"Margo?"

"Hello, Michael," she said. "I have some news."

I waited. "Yes?"

"Liz Vanwall agreed to talk with you. But no cops. No guarantees either."

"What does that mean, 'no guarantees?'"

"It means Liz will talk with you first. Then decide about the police. I told her that would be all right."

"We need more than that, Margo."

"That's all you're going to get," she said. "At least right now."

"Then we'll start there."

"Something else," Margo said. "Liz will not meet anywhere on campus. No bars or restaurants either. Nothing public. Got a suggestion?"

"How about AJ's?" I told her about the house, the quiet neighborhood.

"I'll ask her, Michael. It sounds good to me, but she decides. Okay?"

"Okay," I said. "Vanwall's parents will have to know."

"I figured we'd get to that," she said. "That's how you're going to protect her, isn't it? To get her away from here?"

"Yes," I said. "At least for a while."

I explained what I had in mind for the girls and their parents.

"Let's protect Liz first," Margo said.

"You tell her that Henri's part of this?"

"Yes. She's okay with it."

"Good, 'cuz I busted Reed's chops a few minutes ago."

"Glad to hear it."

"Could be blowback."

"Yes."

"This is a lot to throw at a twenty year-old, Margo."

"Better than spreading your legs for Lewis."

"Yes, it is," I said. "I'm still angry about the whole thing."

"Now you know how I felt three years ago."

"Not really, Margo," I said. "I can't know how you feel."

"No, you can't. I'll get back to you, Michael," she said, and hung up.

I tapped AJ a note, "Food in or out?"

"Home by 6. We'll have sandwiches. Come when you can," she tapped back.

I put my phone away and realized students were entering the room and sitting down. Time to cut class. Just like old times.

The rain had stopped, but dark clouds hung low over campus.

Reed will tell Lewis I stopped by for a chat. Wonder how long before I hear from him?

42

parked the 335 behind my apartment building. I took the rain jacket, just in case, grabbed my brief bag and went upstairs. I called Sandy.

"You're done for the day, boss," she said. "First appointment's ten o'clock tomorrow. Colin Duckworth, about his trust."

"See you in the morning," I said and hung up.

I took my keys and went downstairs and out the front door. The rain stayed away but the heavy clouds were still there. I crossed the street and stood by the edge of the bluff. The sky was dark enough that I could see lights across the Bay in downtown Harbor Springs and the houses of Harbor Point.

If Fleener's right, Lewis and Reed are rattled and plotting their next move. Could be scared they're in over their heads. Academics believe they can think their way out of anything. Just like they thought themselves smart enough to devise a clever plot to steal the Walloon Collection. It never occurred to them anything would go wrong. But when a dead Dean turned up, it had gone very wrong, very fast.

Amateurs are unpredictable. If Joey DeMio was running this game, more people would be dead, but his next move, each move, would be easy to figure out. But Lewis is an amateur. So is Reed.

A light breeze came off the bay. The wet tarmac glistened in the street-lights. I went back upstairs and took a shower. I put on an old, well worn pair of denim shorts, a white long sleeve T that said "Taste of Mackinac" across the front and a beat-up pair of Brooks Addiction running shoes.

I went down the back stairs and walked towards the Perry. I ducked through the skinny tree line that separates the two parking lots.

I caught movement first. Out of the corner of my eye. They came from the left, from behind a big Cadillac Escalade. Jordan just ahead of Conroy. I tightened up for Jordan. Mistake. Conroy shoved me, hard, into the front of a sedan next to the SUV. It bent me backwards on the hood. As I tried to straighten up, Jordan swung fast and slugged me right below the ribcage. It took the air out of me and I slid to the tarmac.

"Get up, motherfucker," Conroy said.

Easy for him to say. I didn't move fast enough and Conroy grabbed me under the arms and yanked me to my feet. He slammed me against the Escalade.

"You don't listen, boy," he said, and Jordan put a heavy right into my left side.

"Time to pay attention." Conroy hit me in the stomach. Jordan kept me from dropping to the pavement.

"Stay away from my campus. You understand, boy?" Conroy took my shoulders, pulled me forward and slammed me against the side of the SUV. Jordan hit me in the midsection again and I dropped to the ground. Jordan kicked my left side just above the waist.

I grabbed my ribs, trying to hold back the pain. It didn't help. Conroy was yelling … something … don't know what.

Sharp lights came from somewhere. I heard another voice and looked up. Two deputies in dress blues had moved between me and my pals from Bannister College. Headlights lit up our corner of the Perry Hotel parking lot. The LEDs on the patrol car flashed like a Christmas tree out of control.

One of the officers bent down. He was in his twenties, lean and tall.

"Mister?" he said. "Stay put. Catch your breath."

The other officer, older, shorter and thicker through the middle, stood, hands on hips, facing Conroy and Jordan. His name tag read "D. Hulme."

Conroy spoke first. "I'm Wade Conroy, Chief of Bannister Security."

"That so," the officer said. "Got any ID?"

Conroy slowly reached for a wallet, took out a card and gave it over.

"You, too," he said to Jordan.

Hulme looked at both IDs. He handed them to the younger officer. "Check 'em, Larry."

Officer Larry went to the patrol car.

"You got a reason for the beat down?" Hulme said, gesturing at me.

"This man's a stalker. He's harassing professors on campus," Conroy said.

"That so."

"We were gonna arrest him when you pulled up."

Officer Larry returned, handed the IDs back to Officer Hulme.

"They check out?"

Officer Larry shook his head.

"Can you stand up?" the officer said.

"Yeah," I said. The younger cop helped me to my feet. I leaned against the SUV.

"You have anything to say?" Hulme said to me.

I shrugged.

"We're gonna take him back to campus," Conroy said.

"You're not taking me anywhere, Conroy," I said. "You can't arrest a dog for pissing on the sidewalk."

"We'll see about that," Conroy said and started to move, but a long, beefy arm came out and stopped him.

"Hold on there," Officer Hulme said. "Just wait a minute."

The officer looked closer at me, at my face. "I've seen you before," he said. "At the station. You're a lawyer, right?"

"Michael Russo. Yeah."

"I'll ask again. You have anything to say?"

"I'm out for a walk and these guys," I pointed at Conroy and Jordan, caught my breath. "These guys wanted to have a talk."

"Uh-huh. You bothering professors?"

"I hope so," I said. The younger cop tried to hide a laugh.

"It ain't funny," Conroy said.

"What's funny is you playing cop," I said. "You, both of you, are employees of Bannister College. You're not police officers." I looked at Officer Larry. "Civilians, right?"

Officer Larry nodded.

"He's causing trouble on my campus," Conroy said.

"Everybody relax," Officer Hulme said. "Mr. Russo. You want to file a complaint?"

"No," I said, staring at Conroy.

Hulme shrugged. "This isn't campus," he said to Conroy and handed over their IDs. "Go back to Bannister. You, too," he said to Jordan.

Conroy glared at the officer like he'd been insulted. Couldn't happen to a nicer guy.

"Come on, Floyd," he said. "Let's get out of here." The two men walked down out of the parking lot towards Howard Street.

"You ought to get looked at," Officer Hulme said.

I shook my head. "I'll be all right."

"Suit yourself," he said. He nodded at Officer Larry. The two men returned to the patrol car, switched off the flashing lights and drove away.

I stood there, in the parking lot, like nothing had happened. But I was very sore.

43

"What the hell happened to you?" AJ said at the door. "Your clothes are wet, Michael. Are you all right?"

It didn't seem worth the effort to go back home, so I walked to AJ's.

"I got sort of sidetracked on the way here."

"What did you do, sit in a puddle?"

"Something like that," I said. "Can I come in?"

AJ laughed. "Of course," she said. "But straight to the laundry room and get out of those clothes. I'll get your sweats."

I kept basic clothes in the spare bedroom closet. Running clothes, a couple of sweaters, khakis. Walking on a flat surface didn't hurt much, but the stairs down to the laundry room were another matter. My ribs didn't like it.

"My god, Michael," she said, looking at my midsection. "You're all bruised." She reached out, but thought better of it.

"Go take a shower," she said. She handed me boxers, a long-sleeve T and black cotton sweatpants. "Put these on when you're done."

"You want a drink?" AJ said when I got to the living room. Once I sat down, I didn't hurt as much.

"Just ice water right now."

AJ went to the kitchen and came back with a large tumbler of water for me and a glass of white wine for her.

"Okay. Let's hear it."

I gave AJ the full version since it was only slightly longer than the condensed version.

"Why didn't you file assault charges?" she said. "The cops asked you."
I shrugged. "Well …"

"Never mind," she said. "I ought to know better than ask a dumb question like that." She drank some wine. "You want them yourself, don't you?"

"The first couple of times, I was annoyed. I took Conroy for what he was. A pest, a bully." I sipped water. Maybe scotch in a few minutes. "But this pissed me off. It's time someone knocked that clown off his pedestal."

"And you're just the person to do that, I suppose?"

I smiled and raised my glass in the air. "Yes," I said. "If not me, who?"

AJ shook her head. "Men."

"Could I have a scotch and some ice?"

"You must be feeling better," AJ said.

"Not really, but it sounds good now."

AJ got up and returned with a small glass and handed it to me.

"Thanks," I said and sipped some scotch. It tasted warm going down.

"Are you hungry?" she asked.

"Yes and no," I said. "Let's sit for a minute."

We sat and held hands as we often did. AJ updated me on the latest from the *Post Dispatch* offices. I updated her about getting a new sports sedan. She wasn't the least bit interested, but she loved me and pretended to listen. It was no surprise that our talk soon returned to Bannister College.

"It seems that Margo Harris is the best bet to crack this open," she said.

"Unless Lewis does something stupid," I said.

We were in the kitchen putting together shaved turkey sandwiches. Sourdough bread, sliced tomatoes, leaf lettuce. Chips.

"Think he will?"

I shrugged and popped a chip in my mouth. "I have no idea."

"But it'd be easier to nail his ass if he did," AJ said, and took a bite of sandwich.

"Him or Reed. Or Conroy, for that matter."

"Are you sure about Conroy?"

"I have no doubt," I said. "Think it's a coincidence Conroy and the deputy rousted me so soon after I threatened Reed with the cops?"

"That would be a stretch," she said. "Looks like Marty Fleener was right. Throw a scare into Reed and Conroy comes on like an attack dog."

I bit off a chunk of sandwich.

"At least we have some control on Margo's end," I said. "If her student cooperates, we can make all of them safe. That's got to be our priority. Then we go after Lewis."

I sipped some scotch. "But if Lewis realizes he screwed up ..."

"There's no telling what he'd do," AJ said. "He might threaten the girls."

"Or use them to bargain somehow."

"That'd never work, Michael. Lewis would have to know that."

"Don't be so sure," I said. "Lewis is too cocky for his own good. Those guys don't think they're capable of mistakes."

"Well, if Joey DeMio's right, their first mistake was trying to ransom the Walloon Collection."

"Amateurs."

"How's the sandwich taste?"

I smiled. "Really good. Getting beaten up made me hungry."

"Don't make a habit of it."

I nodded. "Count on it."

"Next time you run into those guys," AJ said, "be ready."

"Count on that, too."

"Are you staying with me tonight? Otherwise I'm driving you home."

"But ..."

"Don't you dare argue," she said. "I don't care if it is only four blocks. It's my car or my bed. Take your pick."

"All right, all right," I said, raising my hands in surrender. "I'll stay here."

"Good. That was easier than I thought it'd be."

"It's just, in the middle of the night, if you cuddle up like you do ..."

"Yeah?"

"Please don't wrap your arm around my waist too tight."

AJ laughed. "I won't, Michael. Promise."

44

"Hey, there, sleepy head," AJ said.

I pulled the quilt off my face and looked up. AJ smiled. She wore her fluffy white terrycloth robe and held a mug of coffee.

"What time is it?" I said.

"Seven-thirty."

"Didn't hear you. How long you been up?"

"An hour or so," she said. "You were out cold, my man. I didn't need to be quiet. I walked back and forth, took a shower. You never moved."

"Not sure I want to move now."

"I could tease you, see if that would help." She put her mug down and pulled the tie on her robe. It opened.

"That's not fair," I said.

"Is this better?" she said, and slipped the robe almost off her shoulders. She wore a green and white striped bra and bikini panties. And filled them out nicely.

"No," I said. "And don't make me laugh. My ribs hurt too much."

"You're no fun," she said and closed the robe. "Does coffee sound better?"

I nodded.

"Want me to get you some?"

I shook my head. "I'll meet you in the kitchen." I put the covers back and sat on the side of the bed. Our chubby rent-a-cops threw a meaner punch than I thought they could. I eased myself up, put on the sweatpants and shirt from last night.

"You don't look any the worse for wear," AJ said as she put a mug of hot coffee on the small table in the kitchen. "But I can't see your ribs."

"You don't want to see them," I said. "Trust me on this."

I sat down and sipped coffee. "Tastes good. Thanks."

"You're welcome," she said, and poured more coffee into her mug.

"Are you going to the office this morning?"

"Got a ten o'clock."

"Think you're up to it?"

"Yeah. I can sit quietly and talk," I said.

"Then what?"

I held the mug in two hands and looked over it at AJ. "Is the real question, am I going after Conroy?"

"Was it that obvious?"

"I know you too well, darling," I said. "But I need to get hold of Margo Harris first. Henri, too. Conroy can wait."

AJ put her hand on mine. "Okay," she said. "I just get scared sometimes."

"I know that," I said. "But I'll be all right."

"You probably said that last night, look where it got you."

I shook my head. "That won't happen again," I said. "I underrated those guys."

"Yes, you did," she said. "I don't want to debate this, Michael. I'll drop you at home on my way to the office and you're going to stay here tonight."

"I'll be fine, AJ."

She nodded. "Sure you will. But I'll worry less if you're here. Just a night or two. Okay?"

"You don't have to worry," I said.

"I get to worry because I love you."

I smiled. "Okay. A night or two."

AJ stood and said, "We leave in five minutes."

She dropped me at home. I took a fast shower and dressed in something more presentable that cotton sweats. I added a navy blazer to my usual khaki pants and blue button down. To impress my ten o'clock.

I went out the front door, up Howard Street to Lake. I watched traffic and glanced at parked cars. I didn't think Conroy would try anything so soon. At least not until I made another move. I went upstairs to the office.

Sandy was at her desk and Henri sat in one of the window chairs.

"Good morning, Sandy," I said.

Henri smiled. "Just finished an Almond Danish. Mighty good, wouldn't you say, Sandy?"

"I would, indeed," she said.

"Any left? Only had a banana this morning."

Sandy pointed to a bag on the coffeemaker table. "One left."

I put the Danish in a napkin, poured coffee and joined Henri at the window. I told them about my unfortunate encounter with Bannister's version of the Keystone Cops.

"Geez, boss," Sandy said. "I'm with AJ on this. You have to be more careful. Maybe Henri ought to tag along for awhile."

"Might be a good idea," Henri said. "Could have me some fun."

"No, it's not a good idea," I said. "You got better things to do. How are things, anyway?"

"Things are fine," he said. "I'm running up to Mackinac for the day."

"Renters giving you trouble?" Henri owned a small apartment building in the village, Harrisonville, on the island.

He shook his head. "Got a meeting. Be back tonight. I'm having dinner with Margo."

"How are the lovebirds?" Sandy said.

"You're the only person could get away with saying that, you know."

Sandy smiled. "That's why I'm asking."

Henri stood up and took his mug to the table. "Got to go," he said. "Can't be late for my meeting."

"Pluck, pluck, pluck," Sandy said as Henri went down the stairs. We heard him laughing.

I shook my head. "You got nerve, Jefferies."

"What's he going to do, shoot me?"

I started to say something when my cell buzzed. I looked at the screen. "It's Fleener," I said and went into my office. "Morning, Marty."

"Uh-huh," he said. "I'm looking at a stiff."

"Feel compelled to tell me who, exactly?"

"Caleb Reed."

"No shit?"

"That's what I said."

"How?"

"One bullet, base of the skull."

"Just like Sandoval."

"Uh-huh," Fleener said. "Just like Sandoval."

"Where?"

"His house."

"State Street? By the Catholic Church?"

"Want the address?"

"Nah," I said. "It'll be the one surrounded by cars with flashing lights."

"Then get over here. Might as well ruin your day, too."

I put the cell back in my pocket.

"What?" Sandy said from the doorway.

I told her what Fleener told me.

"I'll cancel your ten o'clock," she said. "What's a big fee anyway."

"I'll remind you of that on payday."

I downed a large gulp of coffee and went to get my car.

45

"That Bannister College sure is a rough place to work," Fleener said. "Dead professors, ransom money, campus cops beating up lawyers."

We stood in the kitchen of Caleb Reed's small two-story. The clapboard house felt tired, like it hadn't been updated in sixty years. Reed was face down on the yellowed linoleum, a small pool of blood off his left shoulder.

"You heard about Conroy?"

"City cops to the rescue."

I nodded. "Yeah."

"You didn't press charges."

"Nope."

"Heard they beat on you pretty good," Fleener said. He looked up from the body. "You wouldn't be thinking payback, would you, Russo?"

I shrugged.

"Leave it alone," he said, pointing at Reed's body. "We got enough trouble at Bannister as it is."

"Any idea who shot him?"

"No. Yes. Hell, I don't know. We'll test the bullet when they dig it out of his neck."

"Think it'll match Sandoval?"

"Wouldn't be surprised," Fleener said.

"Me, either."

Two men unrolled a dark bag and put it on the floor next to Reed.

"Let's walk outside," Fleener said.

The small living room was full of men and a few women. Cops, medical people, crime scene investigators. A path cleared as Fleener made his way to the front door. I followed him out and down to the sidewalk.

It was a pleasant neighborhood with small, neatly kept houses like Reed's built mostly in the 1930s and 40s. The spire of St. Francis Xavier Church stood above the rooftops a few doors away. The corner of Lake and Howard was an easy walk from Reed's front door.

Fleener put his hands in his pockets and looked up and down State Street.

"Nasty bunch," he said.

"Bannister?"

Fleener nodded.

"You don't think this is a coincidence?"

"Do you?"

"No," I said. "What if ballistics says two guns?"

"Two guns ups the odds on two gunmen," Fleener said.

"You think this case's got two shooters?"

"No," Fleener said.

"Me either."

"I'll tell you what's coming next," he said.

"After Hendricks blows his cork, you mean?"

"Uh-huh. The city fathers'll scream bloody hell at Hendricks. Cops, too. What are we getting paid for if we can't do our jobs. They'll run to the *Post-Dispatch*. Scream all the way to Lansing, for all I know. The killing has to stop, they'll say. This isn't Dodge City, they'll say."

"All they want to do is make this go away. Do you think they care how?"

"They'll want us to find the killer," Fleener said. "Arrest the killer, put him on trial, put him in prison."

"So it all lands with a thud at your feet."

"Yes, it does," he said. "Got to shift gears. It's time to push harder, see what happens."

"You told me that before I talked to Reed. Somebody got rattled. I got beaten up for my trouble."

Fleener stared at me. "Reed's dead. What're you complaining about?"

"Whose buttons do we push next?"

Fleener thought for a minute. "It always circles back to the same two Bannister committees."

"Walloon and Scholarship," I said.

Fleener laughed. "Of course, the way they're killing each other, we better hurry."

"Roger Thornhill Lewis?"

"Him. Sure," Fleener said. "And Conroy. That tin badge's gone to his head. Thinks he can wander downtown and …"

"I plan to see him myself," I said.

"No, Russo."

"I'm only going to talk to him."

"The hell you are," he said. "I know you better than that."

"Would I lie to you, Marty?"

"Stay away from Conroy," Fleener said. "Keep Rambo away from him, too. Understand?"

"I don't tell Henri what to do, Marty."

"LaCroix's a menace. Both of you stay away. Let us do our job."

"What about Evelyn Malcolm?"

Fleener shook his head. "Madam President is Don's problem," he said. "Board of Regents, too. I don't play that ballpark unless Hendricks gives me a green light."

"That means Don's got Wardcliff Griswold, too?"

"Wardcliff," Fleener said, and shook his head. "I almost feel sorry for Don."

"Griswold's a bit player in this," I said. "He only cares about Bannister's public image."

"More than he cares about dead Deans?"

"Man's got to have priorities," I said.

"Crazy world we live in, Russo."

Two men rolled a stretcher down the front walk to an ambulance waiting at the curb.

"So who's first, Lewis or Conroy?"

"Lewis," he said. "Hard to imagine Lewis taking orders from Conroy."

"Hard to imagine Lewis taking orders from anybody," I said. "Man's a case of arrogance off the rails."

"Conroy didn't go after you on his own," Fleener said. "Reed's dead, so it's got to be Lewis giving the orders."

"How 'bout the deputies? Jordan and the other guy."

"Ribble," Fleener said. "John Ribble."

"I haven't seen him since that first time on campus."

"That kid might be the only real cop over there."

"Think he's part of this?"

"They're all part of it, far as I'm concerned," Fleener said. "The whole bunch. They're guilty until I say otherwise."

"Not sure a judge would like that."

Fleener shook his head. "No judge I know likes dead bodies either."

"Good point."

A few city people came out of Reed's house and went to their cars. Most of their work was done. Fleener noticed things were wrapping up.

"Have to get back inside," he said, pointing at the house.

"Call me on the ballistics?"

"Soon as I hear," he said, and walked back inside.

46

"What do you think?" I said to Sandy.

I was at my desk, feet up on the window ledge, with a bottle of water. Sandy sat in her usual spot on the sidewall. She'd managed to reschedule my ten o'clock for late in the day and the man had just walked out.

"About our nice fat fee?" she said, waving a small white envelope.

I rolled my eyes and drank some water.

"Okay, okay," she said. "Here's what I think. Same gun, two guns. So what? One guy shot 'em both."

"Really?"

"Yes."

"Got a candidate?"

"Wade Conroy," she said without hesitation.

"Conroy? Seriously?"

"He got the drop on you, didn't he? Twice. Packed a hard punch, you said."

"Why not Lewis?"

"Lewis is a wimp. He gave the order, but he didn't shoot anybody."

"Takes balls to order a killing," I said.

"That's not the same as putting a gun to a guy's head and pulling the trigger. You kill a guy that way, you get blood all over your clothes."

"You seem pretty sure."

"It's the only thing that makes sense, boss," she said, and leaned foreword in her chair. "They stole the Walloon books for money. They concocted a scheme to get sex. Then something went wrong."

"Such as?"

She hesitated, so I said, "Go ahead, Sandy, you're on a roll."

"Money's my first guess, boss." Sandy's eyes roamed around my office like she was looking for something. "I don't know," she said. "Maybe, maybe Conroy wanted a bigger cut of the ransom. I don't know."

"Conroy's still alive."

Sandy and I looked at each other.

"But Reed's not," she said. "Or Sandoval."

"Do you think Reed or Sandoval got greedy?"

Sandy shrugged.

"This is your scenario," I said. "Have at it."

"I guess it makes sense, one of 'em got too greedy and was killed for it."

"But two greedy dead guys?"

We heard someone on the stairs. A moment later AJ appeared at the door.

"Hi, there, you two," she said, and sat down in a client chair in front of the desk. "What's up?"

Sandy and I looked at each other. AJ caught it.

"What?" she said. "What'd I miss?"

"Reed's dead," I said.

AJ's mouth actually opened. Just for a second.

"When?" she said. "Where was he?" Once a reporter, always the next question.

"Fleener called ..." I said.

Sandy got up. "I've heard this part," she said. "Back in a minute."

I finished bringing AJ up to date when Sandy sat down with a mug of coffee.

"Well?" Sandy said to AJ.

AJ shook her head. "Well, hell," she said. "Bannister College has this reputation, you know? A wonderful part of our community. A lot of eggheads in tweed jackets, sure. But a lot of smart people teaching kids, doing research. Then one morning, the ivy covered walls break apart. It's pretty sad. That's all."

"I've never thought much about Bannister," Sandy said. "It's always been there. Like the County Building or the park."

We sat quietly for a minute. Sandy sipped some coffee.

"I forgot to ask," I said to AJ. "Why'd you stop by?"

"I came to pick you up," she said. "You agreed to stay with me tonight. Remember?"

"Yeah, I remember. But I don't think …"

"Michael," AJ said. "No arguments. Remember that part, too?"

"Boy," Sandy said. "You guys got a pretty strange relationship." Her sarcasm was not subtle. "You're going to argue about spending the night with a beautiful woman?" she said, looking at me.

"He agreed because he got the shit beat out of him, that's why," AJ said. "By the way, Michael, how are your ribs?"

I shrugged. "Not as sore."

"Glad to hear it," AJ said. "You're still coming with me. Besides, I stopped at Julienne Tomatoes and got two spinach pies …"

"Spanakopita," Sandy said. "Opa."

"Don't encourage her," I said.

"Carry on, sister," Sandy said.

"Thank you," AJ said. "Got a fresh baguette and wine, too."

"Enough," I said. "Let's go home."

"You're way too easy, boss," Sandy said. "I'll pack up the office and be out the door in a few minutes."

"Anything in the morning?" I said.

"Nothing 'till eleven," she said. "Take your time."

"How 'bout that," I said. "A peaceful evening and a slow morning."

47

"Is that you?" AJ said.

We were all tangled up in sheets and legs and arms. It was dark.

"Is that your phone?"

I must have mumbled an answer.

I felt AJ's hand in the middle of my back. "Yours," she said.

"Careful of my ribs," I said. "I'll get it."

I untangled my arm and felt for the bedside table, then the phone. Didn't recognize the number. It's either a drunk teen with nothing better to do in the middle of the night, or …

"Hello?"

"Russo."

"Henri?"

"Put your lawyer hat on," he said. "I'm in jail."

"The hell you doing in jail?"

AJ sat bolt upright. She pulled the sheet across her chest.

"You know about Reed?"

"Yeah. You shoot him?"

"Fleener hopes so," he said. "Get over here."

The line clicked off. He'd called from the jail phone.

"What?" AJ said.

I threw back the sheet, got out of bed and put my boxers on.

"Henri's in jail for Reed." I tugged a t-shirt over my head.

"Henri didn't shoot him," she said. "Did he?"

"He said Fleener thinks so."

"Are you going over to the jail?"

"Soon as I get dressed," I said, and went to the spare bedroom. I put on khakis and pulled a red cotton crewneck sweater over my head. AJ met me at the door with my running shoes.

"Want some coffee?"

"I'll get some at the station."

"How're your ribs?" she said.

"Sore." I tied my shoes. "Not as sore as yesterday."

"Want to take my car?"

I shook my head. "I'll walk. The fresh air'll feel good."

"Be careful, Michael," she said. "Watch out for Conroy. You don't need another beating."

"I'll be careful."

"Let me know about Henri."

"Soon as I can," I said. "Love you."

"I love you, too," she said.

I left by the kitchen door. I could see a small bit of light above the rooftops. It was warm and sticky but there'd be no rain today. I went straight down Bay Street. I watched everything that moved. Couldn't help it. I didn't expect to see Conroy, but that's how he caught me before. I walked at a good clip and went through the front door of the Bodzick building.

Two professors dead. Valuable books ransomed. Students forced into sex. Can't wait for the next time someone tells me college was the "good old days."

48

"Caleb Reed," Henri said, shaking his head. "I'd have knee-capped him first, been me. Then I'd have shot him."

We sat in a small interview room off the main hallway at the jail. Two pale green metal chairs and a table filled most of the space. Henri and I sat on opposite sides of the table. There was no two-way mirror, but I was sure the room was miked.

"Say nothing or say it quietly," I said. "Understand? This is your lawyer talking."

Henri nodded.

"Tell me what happened."

"Not much to tell," he said. "Had a beer with friends ..."

"When did you get back from the island?"

"Seven-thirty," he said.

"Come straight to Petoskey?"

He nodded.

"I thought you were meeting Margo?"

"That was later," he said. "Friends for a beer first."

"Where?"

"City Park Grill," he said. "Left to go to Margo's. Two sheriff's deputies were waiting at the car. Said to come with them."

Henri shifted in his chair. Like it would be more comfortable if he did.

"I asked if I was under arrest."

"What did they say?"

"Not unless I didn't go voluntarily."

"Heard that one before," I said.

"I get here, Fleener's waiting. Says he likes me for Reed. I say what about Reed. Fleener says he got shot. I was surprised, Russo, Fleener saw that."

"He knew you'd call me."

Henri nodded.

I sat back. The metal chair was uncomfortable and so was I. My ribs hurt more now than last night.

"When I got here," Henri said.

"Yeah?"

"They put me in here. Not a holding cell. Just this room, all night. Wouldn't let me call 'till a few minutes ago."

"They're fucking with you."

Henri nodded. "Uh-huh."

"All right," I said. "Sit tight. Let me find Marty, see what's going on."

I went out and closed the door behind me. I looked down the hall towards the main desk. Fleener stood next to a window leaning against the wall, his arms folded. His suit was sharp, his shoes shined and his tie sat just so at the collar. He held a cup of coffee. I walked over and leaned against the wall.

"You want to tell me what's going on?"

Fleener scratched the side of his face and ran his fingers through his hair. But he didn't say a word.

"Why you rousting Henri?"

"He threatened to shoot people," Fleener said.

"Says who?"

"Conroy," he said. "And the deputy, Jordan."

I came off the wall and turned towards Fleener.

"I'm Henri's lawyer now, Marty. So let's be clear. Conroy and Jordan told you Henri threatened to kill Caleb Reed?"

"Not in so many words, no."

"No? What did they say then?"

"They told me Henri threatened to shoot Jordan."

"What's that got to do with Reed?"

"We got reason to think they're in this together," he said.

"We all think that, Marty. Why'd you bust Henri?"

"Because I told him to. That's why."

It was Don Hendricks, walking our way at a good clip. He carried two plastic cups of coffee. He gave one to me and kept one for himself. I took a drink. Lousy coffee, but the only coffee I'd had this morning.

"Doesn't answer my question, Don."

"Yeah, it does," Hendricks said. "LaCroix's dangerous. Trouble follows him. He's a pain in the ass. I told you that."

"Can't arrest a guy for being a pain in the ass. You'd have to jail half of Emmet County, you do that. What's the real reason?

"Because I can," Hendricks said. "Because I can. Deal with it."

"Bad thing to tell a guy's lawyer."

"I don't give a shit, Russo," Hendricks said. "I don't like LaCroix. I don't like that he's in my county. I don't like that you got him in this case. I want him to know I can bust him. Want you to know it, too. I will bust him anytime I get the chance."

"You arrested my client because you don't like him." I said. "Have I got that right?"

"LaCroix's not under arrest," Hendricks said. "Marty brought him in for questioning."

"For questioning?"

Hendricks nodded. "He's free to go. When you leave."

I drank some coffee. It was worse than I thought. I looked down the hallway. Just the three of us. I put my coffee on the window ledge.

"I'm late for a meeting," Hendricks said.

Fleener nodded and Hendricks left us.

"That was all bullshit, Marty," I said.

Fleener looked out the window. People were coming into the building to start the work day.

"You been up all night?" I said.

"More or less."

"Anything new?"

"No."

"What about the bullet?"

"Ballistics'll have it sometime today."

"Bet it matches Sandoval," I said and finished my coffee.

"Uh-huh," he said.

"Reed your case, too?"

Fleener nodded.

"Police officer to the Deans," I said. "Lucky you."

"Fuck me," he said and walked away.

49

"Let me get this straight," Henri said. "I spent the night in that stupid room because the Prosecutor doesn't like me?"

We walked down Bay Street. The sun was up and it would be a warm summer day in northern Michigan. Another perfect tourist day.

"I was supposed to spend the night at Margo's," he said. "Hendricks doesn't like me. What kind of bullshit is that?"

"Fleener doesn't like you either," I said. "Hope that makes you feel better."

"You're a big help."

"I'll make coffee at the office," I said.

"I'm starved," Henri said. "Haven't eaten since lunch yesterday."

"All this excitement, forgot you missed dinner with Margo."

"Let's go to Roast & Toast," he said. "A Denver Wrap sounds good."

We cut through the Lake Street parking lot and took the stairs to the back door of the coffee shop. We ordered food, got coffee and sat at a small two-top in the front window. Roast & Toast was a rectangle of a room with tables on the floor and a few booths on the wall. It had a very urban feel, with high tin ceilings and neon. It was a busy place in the morning.

"A lot of coincidences," Henri said. "Now Reed."

"One coincidence is bad enough," I said. "Sure as hell don't like a string of them on one case."

Henri went to the counter to pick up our food. He'd took a bite out of his wrap almost before he sat down. Henri finished half the wrap and followed it with coffee. "That's better," he said.

I tried to catch up, but the good coffee held my attention.

"We got ourselves two dead Deans, same college, same committees, same condo." Henri shook his head. "It'll be the same gun killed 'em both."

"Sandy said the same thing."

"Smart woman," he said and went to refill our mugs.

"How are your broken ribs?"

"Don't think they're broken," I said. "I've been roughed up before. I'll get checked if they don't feel better in a day or two."

"I should have killed those guys when I had the chance," he said. "Now I'll have to wait for the right opportunity."

"No, Henri, you won't kill them. Last night's what you got for being a pain in the ass. Think what you'll get if you really do kill Conroy or Jordan."

Henri waved his arm, dismissing the whole argument. I finished my wrap and drank some coffee.

"Good morning, guys," Sandy said. "You two are up bright and early."

"That's one way to look at it," Henri said.

"Grab a chair and sit down," I said.

"I have work to do upstairs, boss."

I shook my head. "Work's here right now. Get a chair and coffee."

Sandy got both and sat down with us.

"Where you going, boss?" she said. "When you leave here."

"To the office, why?"

"I want an update."

"Henri's on the update desk this morning," I said.

Sandy listened while Henri recounted his evening without Margo Harris.

"It'll be a cold day in hell before Fleener gets another donut from me," Sandy said.

"Hendricks put him up to it, Sandy."

She shrugged. "If they screw with us, I screw with them. I got your back, Henri."

"Thank you," Henri said. "I'll return the favor some day."

"That's enough, you two," I said.

"Anything new on Reed?" Sandy said.

"Not much," Henri said. "Reed was single. Had no woman friend in his life. At least none I could find. Sex seemed limited to his students."

"Don't remind me," Sandy said.

"Sorry."

"Actually, I've been thinking about Reed," she said.

"Just what has Stephanie Plum been thinking," I said.

"We agree that Conroy killed Sandoval and Reed."

"We do?" Henri said.

"For purposes of my theory," she said.

Henri nodded. "Okay."

"I assumed it was money," she said. "The two Deans got greedy and Lewis had Conroy kill them."

"You changing your theory?" I said.

"Sort of."

"Not money?" Henri said.

Sandy sat back in her chair and smiled. "Well," she said. "The 'Stephanie Plum Handbook' tells me Reed panicked. Michael, you told him the cops were about to break down his door. You scared him. He's an amateur. You said it yourself. He was in over his head. Maybe he wanted to save his ass and go to the cops."

"Good reason to kill the man," Henri said. "Or have Conroy kill him. Following your theory, of course."

"Yeah," I said.

"I wonder if the same thing occurred to Fleener?" Sandy said. "Why don't you ask him."

I shook my head. "Not today."

"This isn't the best day to call Fleener or Hendricks about anything," Henri said. "Not with another dead body in town."

"I forgot," Sandy said. "Sorry."

"Still, Michael," Henri said. "We need to talk to Fleener sooner or later."

"We?"

Henri nodded. "Listen, if I can, ah, overlook last night, so can you."

Henri started to say something more, but I put up my hand, palm out and said, "Just give me a day."

"Michael, if by chance Conroy's the shooter, well, Fleener's the one who can arrest him."

"I know," I said. "Tomorrow. I'll call Marty tomorrow."

"Got another idea," Henri said and smiled.

Sandy and I looked at Henri. She got it out first: "Well?"

"We ought to, what was the phrase? 'Bring him in for questioning,' I think it was. That's what Hendricks said, 'for questioning.'"

"Seriously?" I said.

Henri smiled. "How 'bout it?"

"Do I think it's a good idea? No. It's a bad idea. Doesn't mean I won't do it."

"You guys are a real pain, you know that?" Sandy said.

"Thank you," Henri said, smiling.

"Then why roust Conroy? Why rough him up? That's what you're going to do, isn't it? Rough him up."

"Because, Sandy," I said. "Every once in awhile it's fun to throw a baseball at a hornet's nest. See what happens."

50

"**I**t's tonight," Margo said. "After she gets out of work."

It had been a slow morning. No appointments, no bad buys trying to crack my ribs, no Johan's because Sandy ran errands and came in late. Then Margo called.

"What time?"

"Liz gets out of work at five," Margo said. "Probably five-thirty."

"Where does she work?"

"At the Gold Mine Shop on north 31," Margo said. "Will AJ be okay with tonight?"

"Yes," I said. "I let her know. She'll be out of the house in plenty of time."

"I told Henri already. It'll be the three of us and Liz."

"Okay," I said. "See you later."

I tapped my iPhone and put it down. Sandy was at her desk and I sat in one of the window chairs.

"That was Margo," I said. "Liz'll talk to us tonight."

"Girl's got guts," she said. "More than I would have had at her age."

"It seems to me you did all right at that age."

Sandy nodded slowly. "I know, I know," she said. "I just feel scared for Liz right now. Considering all she's been through. And I don't even know her."

"Life's going to get better now."

"I hope she understands that," Sandy said.

"She will sooner or later."

"That can be a long time when you're scared."

We heard someone on the stairs. It was Martin Fleener. He came through the door and over to Sandy's desk. He put down a box.

"Johan's," he said.

"I don't believe it," Sandy said. "Come in here like nothing's happened. You put Henri LaCroix in jail? You got nerve, I'll say that for you."

"It was an interview room, Sandy."

"I doubt Henri appreciated the distinction."

Fleener came over and sat next to me. "Good morning," he said.

"Don't try to butter him up," Sandy said. "I'm the one's who's mad."

I raised my arms up high. "Truce. The man brought a peace offering."

"You going to let him off the hook that easy?" Sandy said.

"Yes," I said. "And so are you." I looked at Fleener. "That was a stunt you pulled, Marty, plain and simple." I looked back at Sandy and said, "Truth is he can do it again today, to any of us. He's got a badge. We don't. So let it go."

"Brought along something besides the cookies," Fleener said. He reached inside his suit coat and pulled out an envelope. "Ballistics report."

"Do tell."

"Same gun killed Sandoval and Reed. Perfect match. Want to read it?"

I shook my head and Fleener put the envelope away.

"Any idea who pulled the trigger?" I said.

"Other than Henri LaCroix," Sandy said.

"Sandy," I said.

Fleener ignored her. "We believe Conroy killed both men."

"I told you," Sandy said. "Want me to tell him my theory about Caleb Reed?"

"What about him?" Fleener said.

Sandy explained her theory about greed and panic.

"We ran that idea around, too," Fleener said. "In the end, it probably doesn't matter."

"Until you have to prove it?" I said.

"Until we have to prove it," he said. "It's all circumstantial at this point."

"Do you have enough to bring Conroy in for questioning?" Sandy said. She looked at me when she said "for questioning." I looked at the wood floor.

Fleener shook his head. "Not yet, if he doesn't want to come."

"If one of the female students went on the record?" I said. "Would that be enough?"

"Of course." Fleener said, and paused. "Has something changed?"

"I'm meeting one of them tonight," I said. "She seems ready."

"Will she make a formal statement?"

"Don't know for sure," I said. "My guess, not yet."

"It'd make a big difference."

"Let me talk to her first."

Fleener got up. "Okay," he said. "You'll let me know?"

"Yeah," I said. "Soon as I know one way or the other."

Fleener moved to Sandy's desk and tapped on the Johan's box. "Chocolate chip and the last three sugar cookies."

"Thank you," she said.

"You're welcome," he said, and left the office.

After a moment I said to Sandy, "You didn't have to yell at him."

"Yeah, Michael," she said. "I did. I don't care if he's got a badge. That was small town bullshit, what they did to Henri."

"This is a small town, Sandy. Heaven knows we have more than our share of bullshit."

Sandy sat back in her chair. "All right, Michael," she said. "It's just, I just get pissed off at stunts like that."

"Me, too," I said. "But it's over."

We sat quietly. Sandy rubbed her eyes like they stung after a sleepless night. I was about to get up when Sandy slammed her fist down so hard that the coffee mug holding pencils and pens slid off the desk and smashed on the floor.

"Goddamn it, Michael. Are you going to nail those guys? Are you? Is the Vanwall girl going to help out or not?"

"Guess we'll find out soon enough."

51

"**A**re you sure she'll come?" I said.

I sat with Margo and Henri at the table in AJ's kitchen. It was almost six.

"Yes, Michael," Margo said. "It took her awhile to make up her mind. But once she did? She'll be here."

"She know the way?"

Margo gave me a funny look. "Yes, Michael. She knows the way. She's a smart college kid with AJ's address and GPS."

I nodded. "Sorry," I said. "This is our chance."

"I know that," Margo said. "So does Liz. She'll be here."

"I would've felt better if you or Henri were with her."

"We talked about that," she said. "But Liz was clear. We do this her way or not at all. She wanted to finish her shift at the store like always and leave alone."

"You think Lewis or Conroy suspect anything?"

"Been watching 'em pretty close," Henri said. "Especially Lewis. Nothing odd going on. They haven't gone to the apartment either."

"That's something to be thankful for."

We heard a car in the driveway. Henri got up and went to the window. He eased his .45 out of the shoulder holster and held it close to his leg.

"It's Liz," he said, and put the big gun away.

"I told her to pull up and come in the back door," Margo said, opening the kitchen door.

"Hey, Liz," Margo said. "Come in."

Henri closed the door and threw the deadbolt.

Elizabeth Vanwall was five-two, maybe 115 pounds, with shoulder length brown hair pulled back. She had a round face and soft features. She wore jeans, a brick red t-shirt and carried a canvas backpack on her left shoulder.

"Liz," Margo said. "You know Henri. This is Michael Russo, the man I told you about."

"Hello," she said. Her voice was soft but steady.

"Hello, Liz," I said. "Thank you for coming."

She glanced around kitchen, leaned back to see in the living room. "Is it us?"

"Yes," Margo said.

"AJ Lester knows why we're here," I said. "She won't come home until I say it's okay."

"Let's go in the living room," Margo said. "It's easier in there."

"Can I get you something," I said. "Water. If you're hungry, I could fix something."

"No," Liz said. "I'm not hungry." Still soft but steady.

Margo led the way and sat on the couch. Liz sat next to her with her hands in her lap. I took the side chair next to the cold fireplace and Henri stood near the window where he had a good view of Bay Street.

"Michael's going to ask you some questions," Margo said. "You know, like we talked about. This is what he does. He knows how to ask the right questions and make it easier for you."

"Okay."

I leaned forward in the chair. "Liz, what can you tell me about Roger Thornhill Lewis, Tomas Sandoval and Caleb Reed? Start anywhere you like."

Liz looked up at me, at Henri and at Margo.

"I had sex with all of them."

Her words hung in the air. Nobody moved. I didn't expect that answer that soon.

Liz looked at us again. "That's why we're here, isn't it? You don't really care about school stuff. Right?"

"Not unless it helps," I said. "When did it start?"

"Last fall," she said. "Right after I got to campus. Just before classes started."

"This is your first year at Bannister?"

She nodded. "I went to Bay Mills CC last year."

"In Brimley?"

She nodded. "I lived at home so it was cheaper. I worked after school for two years to get the money for tuition and books. My dad's a pit boss at the casino. Mom waits tables. We don't have a lot of things. I only had money for one year at Bay Mills, so I applied for a scholarship here. I got an interview that summer and won a scholarship for last fall."

"Who interviewed you for the scholarship?"

"Dean Lewis," she said, and looked down.

"When did you first learn you had to have sex if you wanted to keep the scholarship?"

"What I said. Last fall when I got to campus."

"Who told you about having sex?"

"Dean Lewis."

"Where was this?"

"In his office."

"Were the two of you alone?"

She nodded. "At first."

"At first?"

She nodded. "Lewis told me what the deal was."

I noticed that she didn't call him "Dean." She glanced at Margo and refolded her hands.

"He called in Dean Reed and Dean Sandoval. He introduced them, and then they left."

"Did Lewis tell you that you'd have to have sex with them, too?"

She shook her head. "He didn't have to," she said. "It was obvious. He told me they were all part of a team. That's what Lewis called it, a team. The team made scholarship decisions, he told me."

"I want to understand, and it's important that we be precise," I said. "What was the 'deal,' as you called it?"

"If I wanted to keep my money, I had to have sex with them."

"Lewis explained it in those words?"

"Oh, he was very clear."

"You agreed to the deal?" That seemed like stating the obvious, but I had to ask.

Liz started to cry. It was soft. Tears came down her cheeks.

"I'm the only one to go to college," she said. "In my family. My cousins, aunts, whatever. Not them. Me." She took a tissue out of her jeans pocket and blew her nose. "I wanted to stay in school. I wanted to … do something more. I don't know, different. My dad, he kept saying, you know, how important college was. I had to stay."

She wiped her eyes. Margo reached over and took her hand.

Liz said, "I'm okay."

"Do you want to break for a minute?"

Liz nodded. I waited a minute.

"When did you first have sex with one of them?" I asked when she'd stopped crying. "After that meeting, I mean."

She shrugged. "I don't know. Two, three days I think."

"Who was it?"

"Lewis."

"How did it happen? I mean, did he call you? How did you know it was time?"

"I'd get a text," she said. "It was the same day usually. Daytime. Only a few times at night."

"What happened if you had a class or worked?"

"They had my class schedule and my work schedule. I had to give the College my work schedule because of the scholarship." Liz put her hand out and touched Margo's arm. "Can I use the bathroom?"

"Next to the kitchen door," I said. "Where you came in."

Liz got up and left the room.

"I don't know what to say," Margo said. "I tried to imagine what it would be like to be her. I mean, it's so matter-of-fact."

"Thought out and well-planned," Henri said.

Liz came back and sat down.

"Liz, did you ever say no or that you couldn't go?"

"Once," she said. "The schedules got messed up at work. Somebody was sick."

"What happened?"

"I had to meet Lewis in his office. Reed was there, too. I was supposed to be with Reed. At the apartment."

"What did they say?"

"I thought I'd get yelled at, you know, they'd take my money. Or say they would. Lewis tried to make me feel bad, you know?"

"No," I said. "I don't understand."

"He told me how disappointed he was we didn't go to the apartment. So sad it made him that I let him down. That kind of stuff. They wanted to make me feel guilty."

We talked on for awhile. Liz was thoughtful, clear and courageous. She added more detail, but the story remained the same.

"Liz," I said. "Are you ready for the police? We have a friend from the State Police who's investigating the murder of Sandoval and Reed. I've known him a long time. I could set up a time for you to talk with him."

"We'd be there with you," Margo said. "All of us, or just me ..."

"Can I talk to him now?"

I looked at Margo, who nodded immediately.

"I'll call him," I said. "If he can come over, we'll have to call your parents, Liz. I know Margo explained that to you."

Liz looked at Margo, then me. "I already called them. In my car, at work. That's why I was late. My mom, she put dad on. He was home. He works nights." Tears started down her cheeks.

"Did you tell them what was going on? Why you were calling?"

"Enough to get them here," she said. "I gave them this address. Was that okay?"

"Yes, Liz," I said.

"I mean, I knew what would happen. Why I was here. I knew if I talked to the cops, I had to tell them."

"I'll be right back," I said, and I went into AJ's study to call Martin Fleener.

When I returned to the living room, I said, "Liz, Captain Fleener's on his way. It'll only be a few minutes."

Liz nodded. "Okay."

52

"**F**leener's here," Henri said. "Just pulled up."

We waited quietly. I'd put out some cheese and crackers, some unsalted almonds. Liz nibbled on the cheese.

"Marty," I said. "This is Elizabeth Vanwall."

Fleener went over to Liz and reached out. "Ms. Vanwall," he said. "Thank you for talking to me."

Liz shook his hand and said, "Liz is okay. Call me Liz."

Fleener nodded and sat down.

For a time, we talked, Liz and Fleener and me. I gave the general outline of the nasty tale. Liz offered a comment from time to time, and Fleener asked some questions. She added some detail, but it was the same ugly tale.

"Truck's slowing down out front," Henri said.

"A black F-150 with red pin-stripping?" Liz said.

"Uh-huh."

"That's my dad's truck. I should go to the door," she said.

"Let me go," Margo said. "It'll be all right."

Margo went out the front door and down the walk. The Vanwalls got out of the truck and the three of them talked for a minute.

The Vanwalls came into AJ's with caution and uncertainty. Margo introduced them to us. Ernie Vanwall, like his wife, was in his late forties or early fifties. He was five-nine, maybe 180, with thinning black hair brushed forward. He wore black jeans and gray short-sleeve shirt. Joan was tiny, five-one, maybe 105. She looked very much like a 1950s house-wife.

Joan went straight for her daughter. Liz got up. "Mama," she said and grabbed her mother. They both cried.

Ernie stared at them like he didn't know what to do next.

"My daughter didn't tell us much," Ernie said. "Only that she was in trouble but okay. So we came down." He looked at all of us. "Will one of you tell me what's going on?"

I got two chairs from the kitchen so there'd be enough places to sit. Except for Henri, who stayed at the window. Joan sat with Liz and Margo on the coach.

"Liz," I said. "If it's all right with you, I'll fill your parents in."

Liz nodded and held her mother's hand. Tight.

For the next few minutes, I told them the story, using only enough detail to make sure they understood the gravity of the situation. By the time I finished, Ernie was clearly agitated. He did not expect to hear that kind of story. Joan had her arm around Liz and held her. They both cried.

"Which one of you is police again?" Ernie said.

"Me, sir. I'm Captain Martin Fleener of the State Police."

"What he says, is it true? These men … used my daughter?"

"And the other girls. Yes, sir."

"Are they in jail?"

"Not yet, no, sir."

"Why the hell not? You all know what they did?"

Fleener explained the importance of Liz to building a case.

"Okay," Ernie said. "My daughter told you what those bastards did. Do they get arrested now?" He was angry and annoyed.

Fleener dodged a direct answer. "As soon as we get the other two girls with their parents and safe."

"You'll guarantee my daughter's safety? Is that what you're telling me?"

"Yes, sir," Fleener said.

"You'll fix it with the school, her just up and leaving?"

"Yes, sir."

"Her grades, tuition, like that?" he said. "The scholarship?"

"Yes, sir," Fleener said. "We'll take care of it."

"That's some big promises you're making there, mister," Ernie said.

"Mr. Vanwall." It was Henri. We all looked at him. "The Captain's good for his word. He says your daughter'll be safe, she'll be safe."

Fleener did a subtle double-take but kept quiet.

"Russo and me, we're not going anywhere either. We're here until those men are gone away for a long time."

"I'm here, too, Mr. Vanwall," Margo said.

Ernie looked at his wife and shrugged. "Joanie?" She nodded.

"All right," Ernie said. "Now what?"

"Now you leave," Fleener said. "As soon as Liz finishes her statement, go home to Brimley. Live your lives as you always do. Liz, you'll stay close to home for awhile, okay?"

"Sure."

"I could send someone to your dorm room, but I'd rather not. You okay with that?"

"It's just clothes and stuff," Liz said. "I got some important things in my backpack."

"Did you know you weren't going back to school?" Joan said.

"It wasn't hard to figure out, mama," she said. "Once I decided to do this."

"All right then," Fleener said. "You should go home now."

Joan looked at Ernie. They seemed frozen until Liz stood up. A few minutes later, the Vanwalls were on their way to Brimley.

53

"That kid's got a lot of guts," Margo said. We were still in the living room, Margo, Fleener and me. Henri finally left the window and sat down.

Fleener stared at Henri.

"Don't let it go to your head, Captain," Henri said.

"Don't worry," Fleener said.

"It was the best thing for Ernie Vanwall to hear," I said. "That's all that mattered."

"We need to get the other girls out of Bannister," Fleener said. "You have the contact information?" he said to Margo.

She nodded. "Girls and parents."

"We'll get the girls first," Fleener said. "Make sure they're safe, then call the parents."

Margo reached down beside the couch and took some papers out of the briefcase. "Class schedules," she said, handing a sheet to Fleener. "Neither one has a night class. I've got cell numbers, dorm rooms, too."

"Margo," Fleener said. "If I get a policewoman in plain clothes, would you go with her to get the girls?"

"Tonight, you mean?"

"The sooner the better."

"Want to take Henri along?" I said.

"No," Margo said. "Two older woman might pass as mothers, but Henri?" She shook her head. "Not a good idea."

"I'll be right back," Fleener said, and went to the kitchen to call.

"I'm nervous," Margo said. "Scared, I guess."

"About picking up the girls?" Henri said. "If that's what you're worried about …"

"No," Margo said. "That's not it. It makes me nervous, sure, but …"

"What then?" I said.

"I can't believe we're actually here," she said. "Doing this. I guess I should feel sorry two men are dead, but I don't. Not those men. I mean, I'm sorry it got that far. I'd have been happy to see them rot in prison."

"I'd be happy to make that happen for the others," Fleener said when he came back from the kitchen. He handed a note to Margo. "Phone number for Officer Bonita Sanchez. She'll go with you to find the girls. She expects your call. Set it up."

"Thanks," Margo said. "Do you really think Bannister will make good on classes and tuition for the girls? They're not very generous when you drop out in the middle of a semester."

"I'll take care of that, Margo," I said. "That place is so invested in covering its ass, it'll do whatever we want. If they balk for a moment, I've got two press people who'd love to write it up. I can see the headlines now," I said, pretending to hold a newspaper. "Can you imagine how wealthy benefactors will react to their money being used for lavish living and sex with minors?"

"Meaning you'd blackmail them?" Margo said.

"Meaning I'd encourage Bannister to do the right thing and help their students in a time of need."

"And if that doesn't do the job," Fleener said, "I'll drop by the President's office and talk vaguely about a criminal conspiracy on campus. I don't care if it makes headlines or not, the girls will be covered."

"Don't forget the Board of Regents," I said. "Ward Griswold …"

"All right, all right," she said. "I get the idea. Do what you have to, but get it done. I don't want those girls victimized again."

"The first step's yours, Margo. Find the other girls," Fleener said. "You think that'll take long?"

Margo shook her head. "It's a week night. Kids are studying, maybe working. They could be at the beach or the park. It is summer semester, after all. But it won't be that hard to find them."

"Good. Officer Sanchez will take care of them after that."

"Who will you arrest first," Margo said. "Lewis?"

Fleener shook his head. "All of 'em. Lewis and Conroy, the deputies, Jordan and Ribble. We don't want anybody leaving town or plotting a cover-up."

"I'd like to be on the other side of the glass," I said. "When you question Lewis."

"See what I can do," Fleener said. "We did some good work today. Especially getting Liz Vanwall to give a statement. You'd make a good cop, Margo."

"I'm flattered you think so," she said. "I don't have the stomach for it."

Fleener smiled. "I know what you mean." He looked around the living room like he'd forgotten something. "Time to go," he said. "I suspect Hendricks is waiting."

After Fleener left, I pulled out my phone. "Two calls to make," I said.

"Tell AJ she can come home now?" Henri said.

I laughed. "Yep."

"Who else?" he asked.

"Lenny Stern."

"The reporter?" Margo said.

"One and the same."

"You da man," Henri said and laughed.

"I thought you wanted to see if Malcolm or the Provost would help out first?" Margo said.

I shrugged. "By the time I talk with her or Fleener does, she'll be eager to help."

"Because she'll know her cooperation determines how rough the story will be," Margo said. "Am I right?"

I shrugged again. "More or less," I said. "Yeah."

Margo looked at Henri. "You think that's a good idea, too, don't you?"

"Russo'll be a lot nicer than I'd be," he said.

Margo shook her head.

"Margo," I said. "Bannister needs a little incentive to help those girls. They'd like it just fine if the kids never came back to school. Out of sight, out of the headlines. I want to give them an incentive."

"I don't know," she said. "It seems so, I don't know, so nasty."

"Margo," Henri said. "You know Bannister as well as anyone. You think they'll jump at the chance to support the girls who've just put a high profile member of the community in jail?"

"No," she said. "As much as I hate to admit it, no. They'd more likely run away from it. But you guys, I just don't know."

"A little leverage," Henri said. "That's all."

"Margo," I said. "This is what we do. Once an institution like Bannister College gets a cover-up rolling, well, we need to see that doesn't happen."

"You do it very well, I'm afraid," she said.

54

"That's one helluva story, Russo," Lenny Stern said on the phone.

I sat at the kitchen table with a mug of coffee and a sliced banana. AJ stood at the stove, scrambling eggs in a frying pan. She dished up two small plates and put one of them down for me. I took a bite.

"Any word about the other girls?" Stern said.

"They're okay," I said. "Margo called last night about the first one. There was a text on my phone when I got up this morning about the other."

"Heard from Fleener?"

"Not yet," I said. "But he'll move fast now."

"I've heard a rumor floating out there about cop activity. No details."

"Could be we'll hear soon."

"So how do you want to play this?" Stern said.

"I'm at AJ's," I said. "She's here and you're on speaker."

"Hey, Lenny," AJ said.

"Morning, AJ."

"First," I said. "You two already agreed the story gets to print and electronic at the same time. I don't want this to be an issue. Not now."

"It's okay with me," Stern said. "As long as AJ's still on board."

"I'm good with that, Lenny," she said. "But I have to tell you, Michael, I've never liked restrictions on reporters or editors, setting guidelines on what to write."

"I ain't crazy about it either," Stern said.

"Hey guys," I said. "I'm not telling you what to write, Lenny. What to put in, what to cut."

"It feels that way," AJ said.

"Lenny, write the story. Don't leave anything out. Not one damn detail. Make it clear to Malcolm or Griswold, whoever you talk to, you're going to write the whole story. But make it clear you can play it up big time or ease up on a trusted local institution. That's all."

"What's your take, Lenny?" AJ said.

"Well, I never thought the story'd turn out this ugly. I want to write it, all of it. It's an important story, AJ. I can live with using my work to get Russo some leverage with the powers that be. This time, anyway."

"Then do your job, Lenny," AJ said.

I switched off the phone and ate some more scrambled eggs. They were getting cold.

"Thanks, AJ," I said. "For supporting me."

She put down her fork. "I didn't do it for you, Michael," she said. "What you asked was out of line. You took advantage of our relationship. You took advantage of Lenny, too. Don't do it again."

"Why'd you say okay, then?"

AJ sat for a minute. She dabbed the corner of her eyes with a napkin. "I didn't do it for you. Or the cops. Ever since this started, I tried to imagine what it must be like to be eighteen or twenty, standing on the edge of a cliff. I couldn't do it. Hard as I tried, I couldn't do it."

AJ dropped the napkin on the table but her eyes were still wet.

"I can't know what that felt like. Spread your legs for those bastards, keep the promise of a future. Stand up for yourself, bury your future in a series of dead-end jobs. How do you make a choice like that? At eighteen? Tell me, Michael, how do you make that choice?"

I shook my head. "I don't know, AJ."

"I didn't do it for you, Michael," she said, and stood up. "I have to take a shower. I'm late for work."

I put the dishes in the dishwasher and wiped off the table. I sat down with my iPad and fresh coffee. I was reading through the *Free Press* when my phone buzzed.

"Good morning, Marty."

"We picked up Lewis a few minutes ago," Fleener said. "Took him right out of a meeting. Word'll spread fast."

"He there now?"

"On the way," he said.

"What about Conroy?"

"He's here already. Jordan, too."

"Good to hear."

"Ribble's out of town. Due back late today, so Jordan says. We'll pick him up."

"What now?"

"Hendricks wants me to talk to Lewis first," Fleener said. "Want to be here?"

"On my way."

55

"The Captain left a message," the Officer behind the desk said. "He wants you to go to Mr. Hendricks' office."

"Thanks," I said. "I know the way." I went down the hallway and through the double doors.

"I figured you'd show up," Sherry Merkel said, looking up from her screen. "Sooner or later."

"How are you this nice summer morning, Sherry?"

"Fine. They're waiting for you," she said, nodding at the door behind her.

"Morning, gentlemen," I said. "Thanks for waiting for me."

Don Hendricks, ever rumpled no matter the time of day, sat behind his desk wedged in between a computer screen and a ragged stack of files. Marty Fleener sat at the side of the desk, coffee in hand.

"Nothing to wait for, Russo," Hendricks said, and pointed at the chair in front of his desk. I sat down.

I looked over at Fleener. "Something happen?"

He nodded. "Our esteemed visitor, Dean Roger Thornhill Lewis of Bannister College, won't talk to us without his lawyer."

"You sound like you're surprised," I said and looked back at Hendricks. "Every rerun of *Law & Order* has some character demanding a lawyer."

"We hoped the arrogant Dean Lewis might chat without an attorney present," Hendricks said. "But no such luck."

"I'm missing something," I said. "Jagger-Stovall represents Bannister, has for years. Their office's next to the bank building."

"Right firm, Russo," Hendricks said. "Wrong office. We were notified by Jagger-Stovall that," Hendricks picked up a sheet of paper, "Lucille Hagen from their home office in Denver will be the attorney of record."

"Denver?"

"Seems Ms. Hagen's specialty is criminal law."

"No kidding," I said. "I wonder who decided so quickly that Lewis needed a criminal defense?"

"The College, the law firm," Hendricks said. "What's the difference who decided? We wait either way."

"You talk to Conroy?"

"He clammed up, too," Fleener said.

"Will Jagger-Stovall represent him?" I said. "Or the other two?"

"Conroy for sure," Hendricks said. "Probably because he's the Chief. Deputies Jordan and Ribble are on their own. I assume that means a Public Defender."

"That'll add a few days," I said.

Hendricks nodded.

"You pick up Ribble yet?" I said to Fleener.

"As soon as we can. We're watching his apartment."

"So that's why we're waiting," Hendricks said.

I nodded. "All right," I said, and got up.

"Marty'll call, something changes."

"A good day, gentlemen," I said and left.

I cut through the building and went out the Lake Street exit. The morning was clear, sunny and warm. One of these days, I have to take some time, grab AJ, and play tourist. We used to get some cheese, maybe wine, at Toski Sands and find a spot to sit at the State Park after work. Just the two of us. Be nice to do something like that before the sun of summer becomes rain in the fall. I stopped by McLean & Eakin and picked up my *New York Times*.

"Good morning, boss," Sandy said when I got to the office. Henri sat by the window. I tossed him the paper, put my brief bag on my desk and poured a mug of coffee.

"Thought Fleener'd take longer than that to interview Lewis," Henri said.

I sat down and told them about my trip to jail.

"Boy," Sandy said. "It sounds like those guys were prepared for jail."

"My money's on Bannister," Henri said. "Sending a criminal attorney."

"Don't know who made the decision," I said. "But Sandy's right. They were prepared. Maybe it's standard procedure for Bannister in cases like this."

"In cases like this?" Sandy said. "Bannister College has a procedure for murder, robbery and sex with minors? That sucks."

"Uh-huh."

"She's got a point," Henri said. "Makes you wonder how often they need a criminal lawyer at that place."

"Procedure or not," I said. "The lawyer's coming all the way from Colorado, so she must be damn good."

"And expensive," Henri said.

"So they got 'em all but the one deputy?" Sandy said.

I nodded. "They don't know where Ribble is, but they'll get him."

"I know where Ribble is," Henri said. "At least, where he was the last two days, where I think he is now."

Sandy threw her hands in the air in mock exasperation. "I won't ask how," she said. "Not this time."

"Traverse City. Park Place Hotel 'till this morning."

"Well, if you won't, I will. How the hell'd you find that out?"

"Henri LaCroix," Sandy said. "You have more contacts in more places than anyone I know."

"True," Henri said. "I do. But in the interest of full disclosure." Henri got this sheepish grin and looked right at Sandy.

"What?" she said.

"*Facebook*," Henri said. "I found him on *Facebook*."

Sandy burst out laughing so hard tears ran down her cheeks. She had trouble catching her breath.

I shook my head. "You better explain yourself, before our friend over here," I pointed at Sandy, "keels over."

"It's no big deal," he said. "Really. People put up all sorts of stuff. A birthday, when family comes to town. Or when a man and a woman take a couple days off to have fun in Traverse City."

"Ribble put that on *Facebook*?"

Henri shook his head. "His girlfriend. Picture of them and another woman at the Beacon Lounge. Top of the Park Place."

"Seen the place," I said. "Never got inside. Always too crowded."

"They were there two nights," Henri said. "Checked out early this morning. I bet she had to be back at work. Reid Furniture, in the office."

"Where's Ribble, then? Cops are watching his apartment."

"Probably at her place," Henri said. "House on Quinlan, just off Jennings."

"Did you get that off *Facebook*?" Sandy said.

Henri shook his head. "Phonebook," he said. "She's still got a landline. As for him being there … woman posts all the time, so her friends know Ribble spends a few nights at her place every week."

"Henri?" I said.

"No cops," Henri said. "Let's have a chat with the man first. You never know what we might find out, no cops around. Plenty of time to call Fleener later."

"Then let's go," I said.

56

"It'll be the third house on the right," Henri said. "Brick ranch."

Henri drove his SUV up Howard, left on Jennings to Quinlan. "You been here before?"

"No," Henri said. "But she posted a photo."

We moved slowly down the street.

"You think that's him?" I said. "Cutting the grass?"

"That's the house," Henri said.

We parked at the curb and walked up the driveway. John Ribble, a tall, lean black man in his late twenties, wearing shorts, a faded blue t-shirt and sweating heavily in the hot sun, saw us and turned off the mower. He pulled a small rag from a pocket and wiped his face while he watched us carefully.

"Russo?" he said.

"Hey, John."

Ribble looked at Henri. "You Henri LaCroix?"

Henri nodded. "Cops are looking for you."

"Me?" Ribble said. "What cops?"

"State Police," I said. "Conroy's in jail. Jordan, too. You're next."

The man didn't seem particularly surprised that the staff at Bannister Security was in jail.

"We need to talk," Henri said.

Ribble gestured at the house. "Inside."

We followed him through the front door. It opened into the middle of the living room, a small rectangle with a long couch, two stuffed chairs and a rocking chair, all of which faced a huge TV over the fireplace.

Ribble went through an arched doorway at the rear of the room into a galley kitchen. He took a beer from the refrigerator and twisted off the cap.

"Get you one?" he said, and took a long pull.

Henri shook his head. "You didn't know your boss was arrested?"

He shook his head. "Just now. What's the charge?"

"Haven't heard the specifics," I said. "But murder's on the table, blackmail, rape."

"Jesus," Ribble said, and drank more beer. He was nervous now.

"Don't forget stealing the Walloon books," Henri said.

"Murder?" Ribble said. "You think Conroy killed Sandoval or Reed?"

"You were in it, too," Henri said. "That little police force of yours."

"Not mine," Ribble said. "It's not my police force. I don't know what you're talking about."

"Bannister Security is a private club," I said. "The four of you."

"More like a street gang," Henri said. "Raping teenagers."

"I never heard anything about that," Ribble said.

"That right?" Henri said. "You blackmailed students for sex."

"Don't know about that," Ribble said, shaking his head.

"So you have heard about it," Henri said.

"No. No," Ribble said, shaking his head harder.

Henri moved fast, two steps, grabbed Ribble with both hands and slammed him against the refrigerator.

"Bullshit."

Henri's face was inches away from Ribble's. "You're a fucking liar, Ribble. You know that?"

Henri pushed the palm of his hand hard under Ribble's chin. Ribble tried to move out of it, but Henri only pushed harder. Then, just as quickly, Henri let go and Ribble staggered forward a step. Henri slammed him against the refrigerator again. In one movement so fast I almost missed it, Henri pulled out his big gun and laid the barrel alongside Ribble's head.

"Tell us what you know," Henri said. "Then we tell the cops. We're going to nail you for murder and rape."

Henri slowly moved his gun and stuck the barrel under Ribble's chin. "Cut yourself a deal or I'll make damn sure the fathers of those girls get you in a locked room."

"Henri," I said.

"I'm just getting started, Russo."

"Henri. Give the man a chance to answer."

Henri eased the gun away from Ribble's chin, but he did not put it away.

"Mr. Ribble," I said. "Do yourself a favor."

Ribble didn't answer, but he didn't try to move either.

"Mr. Ribble?" I said.

"Off the record," he said. "Get the cops to agree. I'll talk …"

Henri pushed the gun under Ribble's chin again.

Ribble tried to talk, but the gun barrel was pressed tight. He tried again and Henri dropped the gun an inch.

"I can give you Conroy," he said.

Henri put the gun down.

Ribble cleared his throat. "I can give the cops enough to start," he said. "I had no part in it. None of it."

"We should believe that bullshit?" Henri said.

"They kept me on the outside," Ribble said. "Believe it or not."

"Give us something," I said. "Convince us, I call the cops. If not." I shrugged.

"I know where the Walloon Collection is."

"Where?" Henri said.

Ribble shook his head. "I deal with the cops."

Henri looked at me. "Call Fleener."

57

"You want to tell me how you found him before we did?"
Fleener arrived at Ribble's house in quick order. We were on the front steps.

"Later," I said. "Ribble wants to deal."

"Goody for him."

"Says he knows where the Walloon Collection is."

"Does he now," Fleener said. "Well, let's go inside and have a chat."

We went in the house. Henri and John Ribble were still in the kitchen. Ribble sat at a small table near the back door. Henri leaned against the counter so he had a clear view of the driveway and the living room.

Fleener nodded at Henri.

"Captain," Henri said.

Fleener went to the table.

"Captain Martin Fleener," I said. "This is John Ribble, Bannister Security."

"Captain," Ribble said.

Fleener nodded. He moved over to Henri and stopped. He glanced at the back door and into the living room. He looked in both directions again and said, "Always careful, aren't you, Henri. Always cover the angles."

"Iraq'll do that to you," Henri said.

Fleener nodded, then turned his attention to Ribble.

"Russo tells me you know where the Walloon Collection is. That true?"

"Yes."

"Know who stole it?"

"Yes."

Fleener nodded. "Know where it is right now?"

"Yes."

"Where?"

Ribble shook his head. "Are we on or off the record?"

"Depends," Fleener said. "You want a deal, we're on the record. Off the record, well, let's say it goddamn well better be worth my time or I'll leave you with these guys. You got ten seconds."

"On the record," Ribble said, taking no time at all. "I want a deal."

Fleener took a chair from the table, moved it near a wall and sat down. He tipped the chair back.

"Where's the Collection?"

"What's my deal?"

"Your deal is you tell me what you know."

"I had nothing to do with the bad stuff," Ribble said. "Didn't even know much about it. They kept me on the outside."

"I'm waiting," Fleener said. "But not for much longer."

"I helped steal the books," Ribble said. "Helped get them off campus."

"Where are they?"

"Conroy's house," Ribble said. "A dumpy little place on North Fletcher, just outside of town."

"Didn't you just say they kept you out of it?" I said.

"I didn't realize what these guys were into when I took the job," he said. I didn't want any part of the robbery, but Conroy put me in the truck with the books. Jordan drove." Ribble shook his head. "They made me do it so I was guilty of the crime. So I wouldn't turn against them."

"Who planned the robbery?" Fleener said.

"Dean Lewis dreamed it up. He planned it with Sandoval and Reed."

"What about Conroy and Jordan?"

"Conroy does whatever Lewis tells him to. Jordan's too dumb to do anything but tag along."

"Conroy get money from Lewis?" I said.

"Yeah," Ribble said. "Jordan, too."

"Why'd they steal the books?" Fleener said.

"Isn't it obvious?"

"Enlighten me," Fleener said.

"They wanted money. A lot of money."

"Who killed Sandoval?"

"I wasn't a part of that," Ribble said. "Told you that already."

"How about Reed?" Fleener said.

"I was way outside by that time. Nothing on that."

"Wait a minute," I said. "What do you mean on the outside? It's a small office, Bannister has two lousy cop cars. How'd they keep you out? They didn't trust you?"

"Of course they didn't trust me," Ribble said. "Isn't it obvious?"

Henri left his spot and went over to Ribble.

"La Croix," Fleener said. "Get back where you were. I don't want to tell you twice."

Henri stiffened and turned around. He looked at me. I nodded and Henri moved to the other side of the kitchen.

"It's not obvious to me," Fleener said.

Ribble shook his head. "You don't get it, do you?"

"Nope," Fleener said.

"I'm the house nigger, goddamn it. Get it now? They're good ole boys, Conroy and Jordan. They hated me before I ever showed up for work. They didn't hire me. Bannister College hired me, a black cop. I'm an Affirmative Action hire."

"There're lots of African-Americans on campus," I said.

"They're faculty, administrators, Russo. There are some black faces, but Bannister is a caste system. Some colleges hire experienced police officers with distinguished careers because law enforcement on campus is important. You think Conroy and Jordan were hired to make Bannister Security a professional police force?"

"Why'd you take the job?"

"I needed a job," Ribble said. "Graduated Michigan State, Criminal Justice. Near the top of my class. Bannister's reputation is well known. I thought I had a plum job to start my career. You know what Conroy called me? 'Afro.' They both did. 'Afro,' get the mail. 'Afro,' pick up the pizza. I'll be lucky to be a cop when this is over."

"Mr. Ribble," Fleener said. "Do you know who killed Tomas Sandoval?"

"Not for sure, no," he said. "Conroy, probably, but I can't prove it."

"Why?"

Ribble gave a small laugh. "Greed. He wanted a bigger share of the ransom."

"Did Lewis give the order?"

Ribble shrugged. "Probably. Maybe him and Reed together. I don't know."

"What about Reed?"

"No idea," he said. "He just ended up dead one day."

"You know about the girls? The apartment at Bay Harbor?"

Ribble shook his head. "Not really. They didn't talk about that in front of me. I heard things, small things. Made me wonder."

It went on like that for awhile longer. Fleener asked most of the questions. I asked a few. We compared details to Liz Vanwall's statement against Lewis, Conroy and Jordan. When we were done, Fleener called for a car to take Ribble to the station.

The officers handcuffed Ribble in the living room.

"Got anything else you want to tell me?" Fleener said.

"Jordan," Ribble said. "Conroy's a hard-ass. Start with Jordan. He'll give you Conroy."

The officers took Ribble to the car and drove away. Fleener, Henri and I went out front. The sun was high in the sky and very warm, the air humid and the grass only half cut. The dingy red lawnmower sat in the front yard, half way down a cut row.

"Either of you got a reaction to Ribble?"

"Decent man in the wrong place at the wrong time," Henri said.

Fleener turned and looked at Henri. He nodded. "Russo?"

"Hard to argue with Henri."

"Yeah," Fleener said, and headed for his car.

58

"I know the books are safe," AJ said. "But where are they?"

I sat with Margo, Henri and AJ at Douglas Lake Bar. We had a four-top near the big fieldstone fireplace. The embers were cold tonight. DLB, as it's called, is an old-fashioned northern Michigan roadhouse. In the best sense of that phrase. A lot of wood on the floors and walls, and a patio that looked over the lake. A long bar sat near the door.

"In police custody," I said. "They're still evidence."

"We made sure they were put in a controlled room," Margo said. "The right temperature and humidity."

"We?" AJ said.

Margo nodded. "Kelsey Sheridan. The police wanted us to look the books over."

"I take it they were all right?"

"Yeah. Fine," Margo said. "We wanted them in a good place until they could be returned to the library."

"What kind of room did you find?"

"A safe deposit vault."

AJ laughed. "Guess that's safe enough."

Henri drank a beer and the three of us had glasses of Chardonnay.

"Any news from the jail?" Margo said.

I shrugged. "We're still on hold. Conroy's talking to his Public Defender, but nobody else."

"At least they got him cold on the robbery," Henri said. "Hard to talk your way out of stolen books in your house."

"What about the other deputy?" AJ said.

"Ribble," I said. "What about him?"

"He's not in the same cell as Conroy?"

I shook my head. "He's away from Conroy and Jordan."

"Does he know more than he told you?" Margo said.

Henri shrugged. "Maybe bits and pieces."

Our waitress arrived at the table. "Have we decided on dinner?" she said. "Or would you like more time?"

"I'm ready," AJ said

"Me, too," Margo said.

"You start, Margo," Henri said.

AJ and Margo ordered salmon, Henri got the sixteen-once ribeye and I ordered the Parmesan encrusted Walleye.

"So that leaves us with Roger Thornhill Lewis, doesn't it?" Margo said.

"Top of the list," I said. "Of course, Sandoval and Reed are dead."

"At least he's off the streets," AJ said. "He won't damage any more students."

"I worry he'll get off," Margo said. "I can't believe Bannister's paying for a criminal lawyer."

"CYA," Henri said. "Bannister's worried about its reputation. I'm sure Evelyn Malcolm and Wardcliff Griswold would be thrilled if Lewis disappeared."

"I doubt they care about Lewis at all," I said. "They don't care if he's in jail or a shack in Peru. Just so he's out of sight."

Margo shook her head. "I don't know. After everything that's happened, I'd like to think the administration would want to do the right thing. Embarrassed or not."

"I'd like to see that, too, Margo," AJ said.

"What if Hendricks doesn't put him away?" Margo said. "Lewis could get a job someplace else and put the same scheme together."

"It wouldn't happen in Michigan," I said. "Too much publicity. Lewis is too well known."

"On behalf of Lenny Stern and myself," AJ said, trying to sound pompous, "the Fourth Estate says, 'you're welcome.'"

The food arrived hot and appealing. I took a bite of Walleye. We spent the next few hungry minutes enjoying our dinners.

"The other deputy, Jordan," Margo said. "He's got a Public Defender, too?"

"Yeah," I said. "The PD was young and inexperienced. Kid knew he was overmatched with Fleener asking the questions. Marty's pretty sure Jordan will implicate Conroy in the murders, he gets the right deal."

"Both murders?" Margo said.

"Yes," I said. "Most likely. That'll give Marty enough leverage. He'll get Conroy to roll on Lewis."

"Can't happen too fast for me," Margo said.

My phone buzzed. I pulled it out of my pocket. "Fleener wants me to call," I said. I got up and went to the parking lot in front of the restaurant. By the time I got back to the table, the waitress had replaced our dishes with small dessert menus.

"Anything wrong?" Margo said, with caution in her voice.

"Our high-priced lawyer from Denver arrived," I said. "She spent time with her client late this afternoon."

"Is that good news or bad news?" Margo said.

"Doesn't matter," I said. "We knew she was coming. Better to keep things moving."

I looked at the dessert menu. "Anybody?" No takers, so we asked for the check.

"Hendricks offered Jordan a deal if he implicates Conroy in the murders."

"Think he'll take it?" Henri said.

"Be a damn fool not to," I said.

"If Conroy talks," Henri said. "Lewis is in serious trouble."

"Couldn't happen to a nicer guy," Margo said with more than a touch of sarcasm.

"One more thing," I said. "Fleener'll have a shot at Lewis in the room."

"With the Denver lawyer, I assume," Margo said.

"With counsel, yes."

"Ought to be interesting," Henri said. "Be fun to watch Fleener at work."

"I got me a front row seat," I said. "Fleener asked if I wanted to sit on the other side of the mirror."

"When?"

"Tomorrow afternoon."

59

"**G**ood morning, darling," AJ said. "Just wanted to check in. Tell you I love you."

I sat on the couch with my iPad and coffee. It was just as well I went home after dinner last night.

"That's very sweet," I said. "I love you, too."

"I missed you last night."

"I would have kept you awake," I said. "Too restless."

"Sorry to hear that. You're not worried about today, are you?"

"I shouldn't be."

"Martin Fleener's a pro in the room, Michael. You've said so yourself. Didn't you tell me other cops line up to watch him work?"

"Yeah," I said. "His reputation borders on legend."

"Do you think the Denver lawyer won't know about his reputation?"

"Won't know or won't care."

"Is that why you're worried?" she said.

"I can't shake this case, AJ. You know that. It's in my head and it won't go away."

"It's ugly, Michael. That's all there is to it."

"Even if I leave the two murders aside. We got three Deans and a cop..."

"All men, I might add."

"All men, yeah," I said. "Men entrusted with the lives of young people. They were responsible for helping them grow, learn, whatever. And they betrayed them. They're just kids and they screwed them over, AJ."

"Yeah."

"Guess I'm worried something'll go wrong. They'll get off."

"You sound like Margo," AJ said. "Worry if you want to, Michael, but Hendricks and Fleener aren't going to let that happen."

"It's just that ..."

"Come on, Michael. Snap out of it. They'll do their job."

"I know."

"I have to go, darling," she said. "Call me later."

I put the phone down and took my mug to the kitchen. I should have run this morning, might have cut the tension. Too late now.

I put on the usual detective-causal outfit of khakis, a blue button down shirt and loafers and left for the office.

"Morning, boss," Sandy said when I got in.

"Still only one appointment?"

"Yep," she said. "At ten-thirty. That's it until you go to jail after lunch."

The morning dragged on. I finished my appointment, a rather routine affair fortunately. I picked up sandwiches for Sandy and me at Roast & Toast and we sat in my office. My iPhone buzzed and I picked it up.

"Hey, Henri."

"Thought you might like to know," he said. "Cops are searching Conroy's house again."

"Are you there?"

"Down the street."

"Know what they're looking for?"

"My source said the warrant's for a gun."

"Your source say what gun?"

"No," Henri said. "Only one gun cops are interested in."

"The gun that killed Sandoval and Reed?"

"That'd be my first guess."

"Pieces keep dropping into place," I said. "Let's hope they find it."

"And that it's a ballistics match."

"If they find a gun," I said, "it'll be the murder weapon. It'll match. You going to stick around and see?"

"I'm out of here," he said. "They sure as hell won't stop to tell me."

"No," I said. "Call me later, you hear anything."

I rolled up my sandwich papers. "I'm going for a walk," I said. "Need some air before I meet Hendricks."

60

"**T**his started with books and a murder," Hendricks said. "Then worse."

I met Don Hendricks in his office. He sat behind his cluttered desk with a legal size yellow pad in front of him.

"A lot worse," I said. "You talked to Evelyn Malcolm lately?"

"Not since the *Post-Dispatch* splattered Lewis all over the front page. She was beside herself with embarrassment."

"For herself or Bannister?"

"It was hard to tell," he said. "Some of that embarrassment belongs to the Regents."

"Especially Wardcliff Griswold," I said.

"Especially him," Hendricks said. "I still can't believe Malcolm, the Provost, one of the Regents, somebody on the business side of the College, didn't spot money moving in and out of the Scholarship fund. Especially after Sandoval was killed."

"I suppose that's better than thinking someone knew and covered it up."

"Marginally, better."

We heard a knock at the door and Martin Fleener came in.

"Afternoon, Don," he said. "Russo."

We returned the greeting. Fleener put a small leather attache case on the floor and took the side chair underneath the large map of Emmet County.

"Mighty fine suit you got there, Captain," I said. It was a black, single-breasted suit over a white, spread collar shirt with a red and black striped tie. Simple, elegant, professional.

Hendricks laughed. "It's Marty looking his best Michael Corleone. Sharp, smart, and ruthless. It'll be two against one in that room in a few minutes."

Fleener nodded. "Always dress for the part you're about to play."

"You know about the Denver lawyer?" I said.

"Her name's Lucille Hagen," Hendricks said. He took the top file from the ragged stack and opened it. "Lucy, for short. Born Schenectady, New York in 1964. That'd make her about fifty-three. Went to Providence. She played basketball, her team made the Final Four that year. Yale Law School. A couple jobs out of law school before starting at Jagger-Stovall. Worked her way up to partner."

"Criminal law always her specialty?" I said.

"As far as I can tell," Hendricks said. "I checked her out. A friend of mine in the Mayor's office out there used to be a prosecutor. He said Hagen can be a hard-ass. Knows her stuff, always prepared, tough as nails when she has to be."

Fleener smiled. "That sounds about right."

"Right up your alley, Marty," Hendricks said.

"Any news from Conroy's house?" I said. "They find the gun?"

Fleener looked at Hendricks, who looked at me.

"How'd you know about that?" he said.

I shrugged.

"LaCroix's out there, isn't he?" Fleener said.

I shrugged again. Hendricks shook his head slowly, but to his credit, he didn't say a word.

"No gun yet," Fleener said. "They just learned Conroy's got a storage unit north of town. They'll check it out."

"Did they get a warrant?" Hendricks said.

"On its way."

"Good," Hendricks said. "No screw ups on this. If they find the gun, I want it legal."

The desk phone lit up and Hendricks picked up the receiver. "Yes?" He listened. "Thanks," he said, and hung up. "They're ready."

Hendricks took his yellow pad, Fleener picked up his attache case. I didn't have anything to carry. We went down the corridor and stopped at a room with an officer by the door. Hendricks nodded and we went in.

The room was square and small enough to be claustrophobic. Three faded green metal chairs lined the back wall. A table, with a chair on each side, was next to the large window. Hendricks put his pad on the table and sat down. I took the other chair at the window. Fleener stood, hands in his pockets, waiting.

On the other side of the two-way mirror was an equally small room with a metal table and four chairs.

The door to the other room opened and in walked Roger Thornhill Lewis and Lucille Hagen. Lewis wore a herringbone jacket and dressy slacks. Hagen was tall, five-ten, trim with black hair that curled at the collar of her very tailored navy suit. She had a small red silk scarf tied around her neck. It matched her four-inch heels.

"Geez," I said. "Look at those heels. A basketball player doesn't need those shoes."

Hendricks laughed. "You need to get out more, Russo."

Fleener laughed, too.

"What am I missing?"

"The red heels?" Hendricks said. "She's making a statement."

"Yeah."

"Those are don't-fuck-with-me shoes."

"Seriously?"

Hendricks laughed again. "You got to love it," he said.

"Class and brass," Fleener said.

"You ready, Marty?" Hendricks said.

"Sure," he said. "I'll stop in the men's room. Get some coffee on the way back. I'm in no hurry. Let Lewis sit awhile."

"Don't you think Hagen's told him what to expect?" I said.

"If she's as good as Don's said, she did. Still, let him wait. Back in a few minutes."

"Lewis doesn't look particularly uncomfortable," I said.

"Looks are deceiving in the room," Hendricks said. "A real bad guy ..."

"Like Joey DeMio?"

Hendricks nodded. "Like him, exactly. A bad guy's comfortable. He's been through it before. But an amateur," Hendricks said, and pointed at the window. "Even an arrogant prick like Lewis is an amateur. Thinks he knows the score, he doesn't know shit."

"You think Lewis'll fold?"

Hendricks shrugged. "You've seen Marty work."

"Uh-huh."

Fleener opened the door carrying a plastic cup. "All set, Don?"

Hendricks nodded. "Good luck."

Fleener took a manila folder from his case and the coffee. A moment later, he entered the other room and put the file and coffee on the table.

61

"Hello, Ms. Hagan," Fleener said, and reached out his hand. "I'm Captain Martin Fleener."

Hendricks adjusted the volume.

Lucille Hagan stood and they shook hands. "Captain," she said, and sat down.

Fleener took off his suit jacket and carefully put it on the back of the empty chair. He pulled out his chair, sat down, and moved his coffee to the side. He slid the file over and took out a pencil.

"The master at work," Hendricks said. "I've watched this first scene so many times."

Fleener opened the file, pretended to read for a moment then said, "For the record ..."

For the next several minutes, Fleener covered the necessary preliminaries.

"Mr. Lewis," Fleener said.

"Dean Lewis."

"Beg pardon?" Fleener said.

"I prefer to be addressed as Dean Lewis."

"Sorry," Fleener said.

"Sorry, my ass," Hendricks said. "I thought he'd give the poor guy a few more minutes."

"Dean Lewis, I'd like to move on to a few specific questions."

"Only a few?"

"Is Lewis getting cranky already?" Hendricks said.

"He's always like that with me," I said.

Fleener smiled. "Shouldn't take long, Dean."

"Good," Lewis said.

"How long have you been a Dean?"

"Captain," Hagan said.

"Ms. Hagan?"

"Is this territory we need to cover again?"

"Seems like a pretty basic question to me."

"A basic question?" Hagan said. "You're going to waste the Dean's time on basics?"

"Wouldn't think of it," Fleener said.

"We agree that Dean Lewis is a highly regarded professional, that his accomplishments …"

"It's going to be a long day, she keeps that up," I said.

"Yep," Hendricks said.

"… The Dean's career is an open book."

Fleener nodded. "Dean Lewis, you know that the stolen Hemingway books have been found?"

Lewis smiled. "I am aware of that, Captain," he said. "Scholars across the country will breath easier, I assure you."

"Are you eager to resume your duties as chair of the Walloon Committee?"

"Most certainly."

"You also chair the Scholarship Committee. Is that right?"

"Yes."

"That's the committee responsible for thousands of dollars designated for worthy students."

"Yes, indeed."

"The money comes from private donations, foundations, grants, like that?"

"For the most part, yes."

"And you control what happens to the money, is that correct?"

"Captain," Hagan said. "Assets in the Scholarship Fund are controlled by committee, as you are well aware."

"But the other two guys are dead, Ms. Hagan."

"Don't you just love it?" Hendricks said.

"Your point, Captain?" Hagan said.

"My point, Ms. Hagan, is this. The other guys are dead. If your client gets out of jail, he'll control all assets of the fund."

"If I get out of jail?" Lewis said. "What's that supposed to mean?"

"Roger," Hagan said, and put a hand on his arm. "Move on, Captain."

"How long have you been divorced?"

"You have no right," Lewis said, and pushed his chair back like he was going to leave. He didn't.

"I ask you again, Captain," Hagan said. "The point?"

Fleener ignored her. "Where'd you get the money for the condo at Bay Harbor?"

"Don't answer that, Roger," Hagan said. "Tell me where this is going or we're done here."

"Maybe they're both annoyed," I said.

"Hope so," Hendricks said.

"Ms. Hagan," Fleener said. "Your client lived a decent, but not lavish, life until his divorce in 2010. His wife got cash, the house in Harbor Springs, even the cottage in Cedarville. The Dean here got a dumpy two-bedroom on the Charlevoix Road."

"The details of the divorce are well known."

"Dean Lewis, where'd you get the money to buy a lavish apartment in Bay Harbor?"

"You don't have to answer that, Roger," she said.

"I came into some money," Lewis said anyway. "Family money."

"Our forensic accountants are going over the books," Fleener said. "They'll trace every penny."

It went on like that. Fleener danced around the edges of ransom and embezzlement. Hagan deflected the questions. Lewis floated back and forth between arrogant and petty.

"When did you first come up with the idea of blackmailing students for sex?"

"Roger, wait," Hagan said. "Captain, we understand the charges, but my client was at the mercy of others."

"And cows jump over the moon," Hendricks said.

"Maybe in Denver," I said. "It's the thin air."

"But the others aren't here," Fleener said. "They're the same dead guys. You see my problem, Ms. Hagan? Your client's the only one left."

"So you're going to place all the blame on my client," Hagan said. "Because he's, how did you put it, the 'only one left?'"

Fleener shuffled papers in the file and pulled out two photos. He put one of them in front of Lewis. "Recognize the young woman?"

"That photograph is a violation of my client's privacy," Hagan said. "We have no way of verifying its authenticity."

"For Pete's sake, Ms. Hagan, if I put it up on *Facebook* would you accept it as authentic?"

"Good job, Marty," Hendricks said.

Fleener moved the photo closer to Hagan.

"That's your client," Fleener said as his right index finger came down hard on the photo. "That's Elizabeth Vanwall." He put down another photo. "And that's the apartment building at Bay Harbor."

"She consented," Lewis said.

"Ms. Vanwall's an adult, Captain, as you are quite aware," Hagan said. "We plan to challenge her statement."

Fleener put down the other photo. "What about her? She consent, too?"

"Yes."

"How'd you pay for the condo?"

"Move on, Captain," Hagan said. "We've covered that."

"What happened to Sandoval?"

"I'm afraid I don't understand," Lewis said. "He's dead."

"Did Sandoval get greedy? Did he want a bigger share of the ransom? Is that why he was killed?"

"Don't answer that, Roger," Hagan said. "Enough about stolen books, the ransom or the unfortunate deaths of Dean Lewis's colleagues. Stick to the charges."

The door opened behind Hendricks and an officer handed him a note. He read it and tapped on the window.

"Excuse me," Fleener said, and left the room.

Hendricks gave Fleener the note when he came in.

"Where is it now?"

"On the way to the lab probably."

"They find the gun?" I said.

"At Conroy's locker," Hendricks said. "In a shoe box."

"Think it's the same gun?"

"Of course it's the gun," Hendricks said. "Ballistics'll prove it."

"Get it here, Don," Fleener said. "It can go to the lab later."

"What've you got in mind?"

Fleener looked at the window. "I'll tell Lewis we found the gun."

Hendricks shook his head. "Hagan'll jump all over that, Marty."

"Let her. I'll tell them Conroy rolled. Told us the whole story. Told us who killed Sandoval, who killed Reed and why."

"Conroy doesn't even know we found the gun."

Fleener pointed at the window. "They don't know that."

Hendricks turned and looked at Lewis and Hagan. "Officer?"

"Sir?"

"Tell our guests in the next room to take a break. Fifteen, twenty minutes."

Fleener sat down.

"How do you want to play this, Marty?"

Fleener shrugged. "I'll make it up as I go along."

I went and got coffee for Hendricks and me. I wanted to ask Fleener about his ad-hoc plan, but I didn't. We sat quietly and waited.

The door opened and the officer handed Hendricks a small canvas tote bag. Hendricks took out a sealed plastic bag with a handgun in it. He put it on the table.

"Do you still think you can bluff Hagan?"

"I'm not worried about her, Don. I want to catch Lewis off guard."

"Hagan'll stop you."

"She'll try," Fleener said. "Maybe we'll get lucky, who knows." Fleener shrugged. "What's the worst that can happen? I'm a son-of-a-bitch 'cuz I pulled a fast one?

"It's your call, Marty."

Fleener never hesitated. He put the plastic bag back into the canvas tote and left the room. We turned our attention to Lewis and Hagan, who had returned to their seats. Fleener went in, put the tote on the chair next to his and sat down.

"Dean Lewis," Fleener said when they were ready.

"Yes, Captain. What is it now?"

"I think we're boring him," I said.

"Not for long," Hendricks said.

"Tell me about Deans Sandoval and Reed."

"If I must," Lewis said. "What do you want to know?"

"Why did you shoot them?"

"No," Hagan said as her hand clamped down on Lewis's arm. "Say nothing. That was not appropriate, Captain."

Fleener ignored her. "Did you order someone to kill them?"

"I didn't ..."

"Not a word, Roger," Hagan said. "Captain. This line of questioning ends now."

Fleener reached for the bag and put the gun on the table, between the two of them.

"We got the gun, Lewis. We got Conroy down the hall. You're a smart guy, Lewis. You want to add it up or have me explain it to you?"

Lewis froze. Not a move, not a word.

"When he's done talking we're going to get you, because you planned it."

"Roger," Hagan said, her hand still on his arm. "Not a word."

"Tomas Sandoval?" Fleener said.

Lewis slowly pulled his arm away from Hagan.

"Tomas ..."

"Roger," Hagan said, and put her hand out again.

Lewis quite deliberately removed her hand. He reached out and touched the gun.

"Tomas got greedy," he said, and shook his head.

"Roger," Hagan said. "Do you hear me?"

Lewis looked at Hagan. He took his hand and patted her arm. "It's all right," he said. "It will be all right. I'll make them understand, you'll see."

"Caleb Reed," Fleener said. "Was he greedy, too?"

"Caleb," Lewis said with disgust in his voice. "Caleb got scared. That detective. Russo?" Lewis shook his head. "He let that ignorant detective scare him."

"Got to hand it to you, Russo," Hendricks said.

"You're welcome."

"I want to reiterate, Roger," Hagan said. "This is not good. I'm here to protect your rights."

"Ms. Hagan. That's quite enough. You don't have to protect me from him," Lewis said and pointed an index finger at Fleener.

"Bingo," Hendricks said. "Big mistake number two."

"Two?" I said. "What was number one?"

"Thinking he was smart enough to be a criminal."

"Don't you see?" Lewis said. "Don't you see? It wasn't me. Tomas wanted more."

"More money?" Fleener said. "A bigger share of the ransom?"

"Of course, the ransom," Lewis said. "Tomas was selfish. He wanted a sports car, an apartment in New York." Lewis took his fist and repeatedly thumped the table, gently not hard. "That money wasn't for us. It was never for us. But Tomas had to have a sports car. What kind of man wants a sports car?"

"Shut up, Don," I said as Hendricks chuckled on the other side of the table.

"The money was never for us," Lewis said. "I thought Tomas under-stood that."

"Who was it for?" Fleener said.

"The girls," Lewis said. "It was always for the girls."

"Jesus," I said.

"Yeah," Hendricks said.

"We did it for the girls. Everything was for them," Lewis said. "This was never about us. We never sought personal aggrandizement."

Lucille Hagan took a sudden interest in the top of the table and rubbed her forehead.

"They didn't come to Bannister merely for an education," Lewis said. "They were there for life itself. Bannister was only a foundation. We shaped them. We enriched their lives. Where would they have been without us?"

"He's serious," Hendricks said.

"Sure sounds like it," I said.

"We planned a series of independent study courses," Lewis said. "Two in London, one each in Paris and Rome. The museums, my god, have you been to the Louvre? The British Museum? That would have required substantial funding. The girls needed our tutorage to grow, to develop their intellectual curiosity."

Lewis shook his head and put his palms up. "Tomas wanted a sports car."

"Why didn't you simply raid the Scholarship Fund again? That's how you paid for the condo, wasn't it?"

"Sure," Lewis said.

Hagan started to say something, thought better of it, and looked straight into the mirror.

"Think she can see you smiling, Don?"

"Sure hope so, Russo," Hendricks said. "Sure hope so."

"The condo didn't cost that much money," Lewis said. "But we had to be careful. The hotels, the restaurants. Those European cities are expen-sive for nine people, let me tell you."

"Nine people?"

Lewis nodded. "Tomas, Caleb and me."

"That's three."

"We were in the process of selecting six girls. Only the most deserving girls, who in our estimation would benefit most from our largesse."

"I don't believe this," I said.

"He makes it sound rational."

"So you'd put the girls up in expensive European hotels, correct?"

"Only the finest suites in the finest hotels," Lewis said. "Especially Paris. The Georges V. We offered the girls a luxurious vista on the culture of Europe. The kind of experience they would have with no one else."

"What was the arrangement you had with the girls?

"What do mean?" Lewis said.

"Was it like at Bay Harbor?" Fleener said. "You'd take one of the girls to a hotel room?"

"Here we go," Hendricks said.

"Certainly not," Lewis said. "We had three beautiful suites reserved. Two girls in each suite."

"Let me see if I got this," Fleener said. "Each of you would stay in a suite with two girls?"

"That's correct," Lewis said. "That way they could absorb the cultural richness only we could impart."

"How often did you expect sex?"

"Sex is a natural part of life, Captain," Lewis said. "It's as necessary as good food and good wine."

"Really?"

"Of course," Lewis said. "Only through regular and frequent physical contact would the girls learn to appreciate what a full life means. We owed them that much."

"I've never heard anything like this," I said.

"Me, either," Hendricks said. "And I've done this a lot longer than you."

"Why did you become a teacher?" Fleener said.

"To do good," Lewis said, in a tone that suggested it was a stupid question. "To help young people grow and develop." Lewis wagged his finger at Fleener. "Oh, I know what you're thinking. But life can't really be lived without physical relationships, Captain. We prepared our girls for the best life has to offer."

Hagan hadn't moved. She leaned on the table. She held her hand, curled into a small fist, tight against her mouth.

"Didn't Sandoval appreciate all the good you were doing?"

"Outrageous, that man," Lewis said. "We created the perfect learning environment and he wanted a sports car."

"Why didn't you just buy him one? A nice Corvette, perhaps?"

"No, you fool," Lewis said. "I told that idiot Conroy to kill him and be done with it."

Hagan was on her feet. "Roger Lewis. Stop. Shut up." She put a strong arm on his shoulder. She looked at the mirror. "We're done," she said. "No more. Captain Fleener, leave the room. I want time with my client. Now."

Fleener tossed his empty cup in the wastebasket. He took his coat, the file, the gun and walked out.

Fleener came in and put the gun on the table.

"Good work, Marty."

"You're welcome," Fleener said, and shook his head. "How many years I been doing this?"

"Yeah," Hendricks said.

"That's a special kind of evil," Fleener said.

62

"Sandy got it right," Henri said. "She had all the pieces."

I sat with AJ, Margo, and Henri at a patio table at Mary's Bistro. The sky was sunny and warm. We watched passengers board the Star Line ferry after a long summer day on Mackinac Island.

"She was at her desk that day," I said. "And rattled off her version of the whole messy business."

Henri drank a beer. AJ, Margo and I had glasses of Newton Chardonnay.

"You know," AJ said. "The Lewis interview? It's so hard to believe."

"No, it's not," Margo said. "I worked with those guys every day. Especially Lewis."

"Will you be ordering food?" our waiter said when he stopped by the table.

"No, thanks," I said. "We're fine with drinks."

"Are you sure you guys don't want to stay for dinner?" AJ said.

"No," Margo said. "Henri and I leave for Traverse City tonight."

"Margo's going to explain the finer points of erotic romance writing," Henri said.

Margo laughed. "Decimal points," she said. "Decimal points and dollar signs."

We all laughed at that one.

"We've got reservations for a late dinner at Red Ginger," Henri said. "You both staying here?"

"AJ says I never take a vacation, so I reserved a room at the Windermere for the week."

"Good for you," Henri said.

"Margo," AJ said. "Did you ever imagine it was such an elaborate plan? What Lewis did."

"No," Margo said. "I thought they used their power to force sex. That was ugly enough."

AJ shook her head. "The whole scheme, the trips to Europe, the bizarre rationale that it was good for the girls. It was a monstrous plot."

"It was," Margo said. "But in the end, it was about sex. An elaborate charade to get sex from an endless supply of young girls." She sat back. "It cost those girls so much."

"And two lives," Henri said.

"I assume Lewis will spend the rest of his life in prison," Margo said. "What about the others?"

"Conroy and Jordan couldn't blame Lewis fast enough," I said.

"Did they say Lewis ordered the murders?" Margo said.

I nodded. "Sandoval got greedy, like Lewis said. Reed panicked and was about to run to the cops when Conroy shot him."

"A plot point that Sandy also nailed, I might add," Henri said.

"That she did," I said. "Conroy and Jordan will go away for a long time, too."

"That leaves the other deputy," Margo said.

"Ribble got caught up in the cesspool he hired into," I said. "Hendricks seems open to cutting him a deal."

"Liz Vanwall's coming back to school next semester," Margo said. "I got an email from her yesterday."

"That's nice," AJ said. "What about the other girls?"

"The ones who left school when Liz did?"

AJ nodded.

"I haven't heard one way or the other," Margo said. "Bannister gave Liz a full scholarship. It covers everything. If she decides on graduate school, that's paid for as well."

"I'm happy to hear that," I said.

"It was the least the administration could have done," Margo said. "Of course, it's trying to rebuild a reputation."

"It needs all the help it can get," AJ said.

"Do you think the folks at Bannister learned anything, Margo?" I said.

Margo shrugged. "I don't know. They straightened out the finances, that's for sure. They track every penny now. Is that what you're talking about, Michael?"

"Part of it," I said. "But Bannister is still a very small world. The administration and faculty feed off Bannister's reputation. Not always in good ways."

"The same thing happens in East Lansing or Ann Arbor, Michael," AJ said.

"I don't know about that, AJ. Both schools are big, public universities. When something bad happens, they have plans in place to deal with it. They have to be ready because they're under constant scrutiny."

"You don't mean to tell me big schools never play it close to the vest?"

"Sure they do," I said. "But it's tougher to get away with. Bannister's like a family. It's so small it turns inward when something goes wrong. Even tragedy is treated like a private matter."

"Until it comes crashing down around them," AJ said.

"They'll limit the damage," I said. "Sweep it under the rug as much as possible. We may never know if it really touched them."

63

"**H**ave fun," AJ said, waving at Margo and Henri. They waved back from the top deck of the *Miss Margy*.

The captain blew the horn signaling the ferry's departure for Mackinaw City.

"Maybe we ought to spend a few days in Traverse City," AJ said. I put my arm around her shoulder. We stood and watched five ferries all leave the harbor at the same time.

AJ turned to me. "It'd be fun," she said. "We could stay downtown. I'd love to go up the Leelanau Peninsula. Northport, Sutton's Bay."

"I haven't driven M-22 in years," I said. "How about after Labor Day?"

AJ nodded. "It'll be a lot quieter."

Interesting road, M-22. Lots of curves for a good sports sedan.

"I know what you're thinking, Michael," AJ said.

"What do you mean, darling?"

"Don't 'darling' me," she said. "Driving that BMW of yours on a twisty road. That's what you're thinking. I know you too well."

"Yes, you do," I said, laughing. "But right now we're on vacation. A whole week on the island. Come on, let's go."

I took AJ's hand and we walked, slowly, up the dock to Main Street.

"Which way?" I said.

AJ hooked her arm around my waist. "Let me think." She looked one way, then the other like she wanted to cross the street.

"Michael," she said. "I know what we haven't done in years. Not since our first few visits here."

"And that is?"

"Watch the sun go down over the bridge," she said.

"From the end of the boardwalk?" I said.

AJ nodded.

"Like the sound of that," I said.

I took AJ's hand and we maneuvered our way down the busy sidewalk. Windermere Point was full of visitors, laughing, playing Frisbie, or sitting at picnic tables at the Doghouse food stand.

"Look at the seagulls," AJ said. At least a dozen gulls flew in large circles, thirty feet off the ground. "You think they're looking for food?"

"Chips, buns, maybe a hotdog or two," I said. A couple of children swung their arms and screamed with delight when two gulls dove towards the ground.

We strolled along the boardwalk that heads west out of downtown. Just beyond the school, we found an empty few feet of boardwalk and sat down.

"It's crowded already," AJ said.

"It'll be a pretty spectacular sunset," I said. "There's haze in the air and a few clouds."

We held hands and looked out, over the Straits, at the Mackinac Bridge.

"They're all spectacular, Russo," AJ said. "Especially when we watch them together."

ACKNOWLEDGEMENTS

Like the first two Michael Russo mysteries, I made everything up. All of it. Readers have told me that this character or that character must be modeled after this real person or that real person. Not so, but I'm delighted that readers think so because my characters must feel genuine and sincere. I had particular fun this time tossing a curveball at Henri LaCroix and playing with the relationship between AJ and Russo. Several people helped make this mystery more believable and realistic. They include Frances Barger, Marietta Hamady, Bill Fullerton, Aaron Stander, Wesley Maurer, Jr., Marta Olson, Mallory Getz, Jill Beauchamp, and the writers around the table at the Mystery Writing Workshop at the Interlochen Center for the Arts. Three of the four scenes written and critiqued at the workshop made it into this novel. How about that?

Heather Shaw and Scott Couturier edited the manuscript. Their critique was so helpful, so incisive that I couldn't find much to argue about even though I tried. *Devils Are Here* is better written and more interesting because of their skilled work and their interest in my writing. One of Scott's suggestions was particularly helpful because it encouraged me to rethink descriptive details for next time.

PETER MARABELL

Peter Marabell grew up in metro Detroit, spending as much time as he could street racing on Woodward Avenue in the 1950s and visiting the Straits of Mackinac. With a Ph.D. in History and Politics, Peter spent most of his professional career on the faculty at Michigan State University. He is the author of the historic monograph, *Frederick Libby and the American Peace Movement*. His first novel, *More Than a Body*, was published in 2013. The first two Michael Russo mysteries, *Murder at Cherokee Point* and *Murder on Lake Street*, were published in 2014 and 2015, respectively. As a freelance writer, he worked in several professional fields including healthcare, politics, and the arts. In 2002, Peter moved permanently to northern Michigan with his spouse and business partner, Frances Barger, to live, write and work at their Mackinac Island business. All things considered, he would rather obsess about American politics, or Spartan basketball, after a good five-mile run on the hills of Mackinac Island.

OTHER BOOKS BY PETER MARABELL

More than a Body

Murder at Cherokee Point

Murder on Lake Street

also

Frederick Libby and the American Peace Movement

57922760R00173

Made in the USA
Charleston, SC
28 June 2016